Water and Flame

Witches of the Elements
Series Book 1

ALEJANDRA VEGA

&

P.E. PADILLA

Crimson Cat Publishing

Cover Art by Damonza (https://damonza.com/)

Published by Crimson Cat Publishing

ISBN-13: 978-1-943531-04-2

DEDICATIONS

from AV

To Danielle,

You are my greatest motivation and the most important
reason for everything I do. I am so proud of you and the
woman you are becoming. *Te amo mija.*

from PEP

To Ale,

It was a privilege and a pleasure working on this project
with you. Good luck with your storytelling. I wish you all
the best.

.

CONTENTS

1

The world ended in a wash of white hot light as flame consumed all within sight.

Abigail Henderson jerked upright from where she had been slouching in her chair, her heart pounding so hard she thought someone in the next room could hear it. Footsteps sounded in the hall, urgent, coming quickly to her door. The pounding of a fist preceded her father's face peering around the door.

"Abbie, what is it? I heard you scream. Are you all right?" Landon Henderson scanned the room with wide eyes as he walked toward her. He took her hand. "What's wrong?"

"Mama," she said, still trying to slow her galloping heart. "She's…I…I had a vision."

Her father cradled her head to his chest, stroking her hair. "Shhhh. Calm down. It was a dream. Your mother is out performing the Spring Rain ritual. She's fine."

"But it was so real, Papa. I saw everything, felt everything. It's like I was there, connected to her. No,

1

like I *was* her." She sounded to herself like a child, even though she was nineteen years old. It was so real, though.

"Do you want to tell me about it?"

"Yes. Maybe it would help."

"Fine, then," he said, tilting down to kiss her forehead. He took a seat in the wooden ladderback chair he pulled from the corner. "Take a few breaths and then describe it all to me."

Abigail took two deep breaths and let them out slowly. "It was like I was her, as if I was experiencing everything myself through her body." She settled into the seat and sat up straighter. Then she began to tell him in detail what she had experienced.

Olivia Henderson drew out the little figurine from her pocket and rubbed it absently with her thumb. It wasn't a detailed carving, but it was recognizably an angel, wings folded and arms crossed in front of its chest. Her daughter Abigail had carved it from aquamarine. It was Olivia's most cherished possession. She felt the familiar curves as her thumb traced the rounded edges, worn smoother from the countless times her fingers had passed over it.

A small smile played across Olivia's doll-like face as she looked upon the pale blue—almost green—stone, tracing the swirls within it with her eyes. At only five foot two inches tall, everything about her looked feminine and fragile, though appearances did not tell truly. The skin of her cheeks stretched as her smile widened at the thought of her daughter and the little figurine she had carved using only water magic almost ten years before.

The smile faded with the memory as Olivia put the

angel back in its resting place in her pocket. She had work to do yet. It was no time to get lost in thoughts of other things.

The Spring Rain ritual was important to practicers of water magic, maybe the most important celebration of the year. It was two days before the ancient festival of the world tree, Yggdrasil, and different in many ways.

Most rituals were communal efforts, even to the point of being social events for elemental witches. The rite of Spring Rain was not. It was a solemn event consisting of each member of a coven reflecting in their own way about the beginning of life and the continuity of the great cycle. Two or three privileged witches performed the motions signifying their profound reverence for the great water cycle on behalf of the entire coven. Olivia was one of these, of course, as befitted her office of High Water Caster, the leader of the Guiding Council for her coven.

Olivia's partner for this year's ritual arranged the necessary items: a simple abstract carving consisting of sweeps and turns representing the water cycle and two incense urns on a ceremonial woven rug draped across a flat rock. Emma Williams was a short, round woman who resembled a Mrs. Claus doll. Her fleshy cheeks were always one shade of red or another and most often crinkled in a smile. She was like everyone's grandmother, kind and happy and always wanting to do things for others. Olivia adored Emma and was happy to share this day's work with her.

Olivia looked over the smooth surface of Lake Tranquility. It was sacred to her coven of water witches. Power generated in its deep water, and energy accumulated over the decades, even centuries.

It was one of the reasons her ancestors had settled in the area.

The lightening sky cast shadows over the edges of the lake, mirror images of the surrounding trees appearing on the water. Sunrise would come soon.

"It looks like we're just about ready, Emma," Olivia said, taking up her place.

"Yes. All set and ready to go." The older woman looked around as if she had forgotten something. "It feels like the energies are out of balance. It may take more doing than normal to align everything for the ritual."

Olivia had felt something a little off, too, but her memories had distracted her. She looked around, a foreboding seeping into her. The trees and the thick underbrush surrounding the lake and its meadow could hide just about anything. Shaking her head to dispel the feeling, she began her incantations. She didn't have time for flights of fancy.

The incantations and motions for this festival were particularly tricky. In fact, she'd only trust a handful of witches to do it effectively. Emma was gifted—and powerful—and it was a joy to meld her own flows with the older witch. Olivia got caught up in the euphoric feeling of the magical energies as they swirled about, pulling power from the water of the lake and flowing through the two women.

Olivia sensed the danger just before projectiles began flying. A group of non-magical humans had surrounded Olivia and Emma, all of them apparently carrying guns. Olivia had picked up on the intent, on the feelings of the enemies' auras. She immediately stopped her spell and threw up a hardened water shield around her. It was a hasty thing, so it didn't cover Emma completely but did completely surround Olivia herself.

Emma was a little slower to get her shield up. She grunted as a bullet, or maybe more than one, struck her. Judging by how Emma continued to cast her magic to complete her shield, it did not seem as if it struck her in a vital location. She could still bleed to death, of course, the same as any non-magical human—or "only" as the witches sometimes called them—but Olivia didn't think they would have time to bleed to death. She sensed other users of magic nearby moving along with the onlies, held in reserve to avoid detection. It seemed to be a well-orchestrated attack.

Olivia was a powerful witch, but even powerful users of elemental magic rarely had the ability to sense other witches. They must have known she possessed that talent—or at least suspected—so they used the onlies first. She felt at least a half dozen magic users nearby, coming closer, though she could not be sure to which element they were attuned or whether they were witches or warlocks. She did know that if she and Emma didn't escape before all their foes were arrayed against them, they would not survive.

"Emma!" she called. "Are you okay? Where were you shot? How many times?"

"I think,"—the older woman gasped in pain—"I was only hit twice, both in my left arm. I can still fight, though I might have to improvise with some of the hand and arm forms."

"We need to get out of here," Olivia said. "There are at least six magic users surrounding us. If they are allowed to get in place, we're finished."

"You go, Olivia. I am too old and fat to run fast,

but you can get away. I'll keep them at bay for as long as I can."

"No."

"It is better if one of us survives," Emma said. "Now go. Don't waste your life. I've lived a long time already. You are more important. You must be the one they came for. Go."

Olivia silently strengthened her shield and searched the surroundings. She saw movement off to her left and made a motion with her hand. A dozen missiles of hardened water rocketed toward where she aimed them. A scream of pain told her that she had hit at least one of the onlies. She grabbed Emma's arm and started dragging her toward the hole she had just made in the line of her foes.

Olivia was thankful Emma did not choose this time to be stubborn. She moved along while casting magics ahead of them to help clear the way. If they could just move faster, they might escape.

Flame leapt up in front of the pair, a wall of fire ten feet high and twenty feet wide. Peculiarly, it was floating several inches off the grass in the meadow. Why not let it go all the way to the ground?

Their magic-using enemies had entered the fray.

Olivia and Emma stopped, the former trying to decide if they should make their stand where they were or try to push through the obstacle in front of them.

"If we stop now, we're dead," Emma said, now pulling on Olivia's arm to drag her toward the fire. "They're trying to stall us so they can surround us completely."

Of course, she was right. The High Water Caster had delayed for a few seconds already. She must get moving or it could prove to be fatal.

Putting all her focus into the shield, expanding it to surrounding Emma as well, Olivia plunged into the fire wall. It was not thick, only a few feet, but the heat was intense. She could feel the air within her bubble heating up, becoming more uncomfortable and causing her to fear that the shield would not be up to the task of protecting her.

And then they were through into blessedly cool air, and a clear path opened to the forest ahead. Oak, elm, and linden trees intermingled and provided an ideal place to hide. If they could just get into the cover of those trees, her foes would not be able to surround them as easily.

Emma went down.

It wasn't a bullet—though those were flying around them and bouncing off their shields—but something simpler. The older witch had struck her foot on an exposed root and tripped, losing her grip on Olivia's hand. She hit the ground hard, her focus on her spells shattering. Her shield winked out.

Olivia watched in horror as Emma burst into flames. Her scream echoed in the morning air and silenced when several bullets struck her.

So quickly.

Olivia pushed the last of her strength into her shield and ran for all she was worth. She might still make her escape. If her shield held, she might yet get away.

She made it another ten steps.

Out of the trees in front of her, four figures stepped into her path. One was an older woman, brown hair with a few streaks of gray and eyes ablaze with the mystic energies she held. Olivia knew this would be her last stand. She shifted her shield so it was stronger in front of her and prepared to make a desperate gamble.

The water witch reached into her pocket and held the angel figurine tightly, drawing strength from its presence, thinking of her daughter. She took a deep breath and attacked.

Water swirled around her, pulled from the misty morning air as well as the lake a few dozen yards away. It took on the hardness of steel and formed a maelstrom of hurricane force, spinning, whirling, obscuring the view of her. With a sharp exhalation, she threw her power out, expanding the circle like an explosion. The results were devastating. But were they enough?

Her magically propelled projectiles tore through the onlies around her, shredding their bodies beyond recognition. The fire witches and warlocks fared a little better, but not by much. The weaker had their own shields—thrown up hastily when they realized she was attacking—torn and defeated, hardened water missiles punching through not only the armor but their bodies as well. Only three of her foes survived the onslaught.

Three too many. She slumped, her energy waning. That attack had taken all her strength.

One of the three, a tall, muscular woman, burst into living flame. Olivia blinked, not believing her eyes. The flame came toward her, movements a mixture between a person and a flickering fire. Olivia poured what little strength she had left into a shield and rebuffed her foe, pushing her back toward her companions. The fire thing dug her feet in and started toward Olivia again. This time the water witch would not be able to hold it back.

At a motion from a dark-haired woman, the flame backed up and stood silently at the other's side.

"It was a valiant effort," the woman—obviously their leader—said. "You nearly made it. But not quite." She made a series of complex gestures with her hands, and Olivia felt as if a great weight pressed down on her. She lost her hold on the magic, too exhausted to fight any longer.

Olivia looked into the woman's dark eyes, fixing the face of her murderer firmly in her mind.

"Why?"

"Because it's time to clean out the useless, to make way for those with the power to control this world," the woman said calmly. "We can't have weak spirits like you cooperating with other elements and undermining our plans. You will be a problem no longer."

As the woman and the other of her two companions prepared their final, fatal spells, Olivia concentrated the last of her energies not on breaking the bonds holding her, but on casting her mind out to her children. Encapsulating the visions of her harrowing battle into a pocket of magical energy, she sent it out to them, hoping they were sensitive enough, powerful enough, to receive it. It was the best she could do. A small smile played across her face as she thought of them. She clutched the angel figurine.

An intense flash of flame and heat washed over Olivia Henderson, and the water witch was no more.

2

~~~

*L*andon Henderson stared at his daughter as she wept. He shook his head and blinked, snapping out of his daze. "It's fine, Abbie. It's a nightmare, nothing more. We'll all laugh about this when your mother gets home." The details of the vision disturbed him more than he could let her know. *Please, Olivia*, he thought, *please be safe*.

Abbie nodded as she wept into his chest.

A few hours later, Abbie and her father were sitting in the dining room, talking over tea when Sophia Hill came in. She was one of the witches on the Guiding Council for the coven, an old friend of the family who spent more time at the Henderson estate, Aqua Terra, than at her own home thirty miles away.

Her blue eyes were rimmed with red and her hair was windblown, not at all in character for the woman. "There has been...an accident."

"An accident?" Landon said. "What do you mean an accident?"

"Olivia…and Emma…" Sophia broke down in tears. "They are gone. Dead. They were attacked."

"Was it fire witches?" Abbie asked before her father could speak.

Sophia looked at Abbie, the surprise evident on her face. "How did you know?"

"Call the Council," Landon said. "We have something to tell them."

"They are already called. I came to get you straightaway, but I sent Isabella to find the others."

As Landon got up, he motioned for Abbie to join him. "You will need to tell them what you saw and felt." She nodded and followed him. "Why? Why would they start a war after so long?" He mused aloud. "I just don't understand it."

He and Abbie went to meet with the Council, and she recounted the entire episode again. He was proud of the way she got through it without breaking down. Even listening to it again made it difficult for him to sit there calmly. He wanted to scream.

After her account, Abigail was dismissed. She told her father she would find her brother and sister and tell them what had happened. Landon looked to Charlotte Whinson and she jerked her head toward the door, indicating that he should go to his family. She was acting leader when Olivia was not present.

"Thank you," he said as he got up and left the room right behind Abigail.

Two weeks later, he was sitting in the Council meeting room again, trying his hardest to pay attention as images of Olivia flashed through his mind. He blinked to dispel the moisture threatening to pool in his eyes.

"It is clear," Charlotte Whinson said, "that hostilities are flaring up between elemental magic users as they have not in centuries. Some of the old ways need to be brought back."

"But, Charlotte," Landon Henderson countered, "if we give in to the paranoia, there may be all out war."

"Is it paranoia that there have been deaths? Landon, they killed Olivia and Emma. Will it stop with them? Why were they even targeted? You may call it paranoia, but I call it good sense. We must know what is going on to prepare, to prevent these things from happening again."

"What is it that you propose?" Sophia Hill asked.

"Only that we begin gathering information," Charlotte said. She had been elected High Water Caster of the water coven after Olivia's death, a logical choice since she was already the acting leader. "We can send out witches or warlocks to spy on the other covens. Then, at least, we will not be surprised as easily.

"Listen, I know as well as all of you that though it appeared to have been onlies—excuse me, non-magical humans—who killed Olivia and Emma, we know it wasn't. The vision sent to Abigail and the sole remaining item from the attack, the little soot-covered stone angel carving, make it clear that fire witches attacked them. Someone went through a great deal of trouble to make it look like they were attacked by others. All I'm saying is that we need to know what is happening to prevent future surprises."

Landon wasn't sure he agreed. It sounded as if things could easily get out of hand and devolve into open hostility. "Olivia believed in working with the other elemental witches, cooperating with them. She was having good luck in the negotiations with the air and earth covens. She had almost achieved the unheard of: open communication and joint efforts between elements."

Charlotte nodded her head, the tight bun of her pale yellow hair bobbing with the motion. Her voice was soft, sympathetic. "I know, Landon. She was doing great work, and I think that work may have caused her to be targeted. We don't want anyone else attacked. The loss of Olivia and Emma was too great. We can't have that happen again."

"I guess you're right. I wish you weren't, but we do need information. As long as it's gathered tactfully, secretly. It won't do to allow the other covens to know we're spying on them."

"Yes," Charlotte said, "though if my guess is correct, the earths and the airs have witches out there right now doing the same thing. We're not the only ones who have a history of conflicts with the fires. The other two elements know full well how aggressive those who manipulate fire magic are."

"It is done then?" Julian Hill, Sophia's husband, said. "The decision has been made and we will start sending out operatives to gather information?"

"Yes," the High Water Caster said. "It is decided. Let us hope we gather information that will help us prevent any other attacks that could lead to a war of elements."

*****

An hour after the meeting, Abigail Henderson

knocked on the door of the room that had been set aside as the office of the High Water Caster.

"Come in," Charlotte's muffled voice said through the door.

Abigail walked in and stood in front of the desk. The room was familiar, the same one used as her mother's office when she held the position. The room, its furnishings, in fact the entire estate was familiar. She grew up here. It belonged to her family but was also used as the headquarters for her coven of water witches and warlocks.

"High Water Caster?" she said.

"Abbie, you can call me Charlotte. This isn't a Council meeting or a formal occasion." She smiled a sad smile at her. "Sit down and tell me what I can do for you. How are you doing?"

It had only been two weeks since her mother's death, and she still felt as if her skin had been peeled off and her raw body was being pelted by hail. Her eyes started to tear up, but she clamped down on her emotions and took a seat.

"I'm doing about as well as can be expected, given the circumstances." She rubbed the little angel figurine in her hand furiously with her thumb. It calmed her. A little.

"Yes. I suppose so."

"Charlotte," Abbie said, "I'm not sure what the Council has been talking about in all these meetings lately, but I'm sure some of it has to do with trying to find out what happened with mother and trying to find those responsible. I want to help. Whatever it is that I can do, I want to do it. Please, give me a purpose, something that is important. I need something to believe in right now."

"I don't know if that would be a good idea, Abbie. The type of work we need requires emotional distancing, steadiness, for success. Give it some time and maybe you can help later."

Abbie's heart sank. "I understand. Please keep me in mind. If there's anything I can do, I'll do it. I'm sure you can find something."

"I will discuss it with the Council and let you know. Thank you for offering, Abigail. You remind me so much of your mother. I know you will be a great help to the coven, but for now, mourn. There is time enough for work later."

Charlotte allowed her a few months, but then Abbie was asked to participate, along with several other witches and warlocks, in "missions" to gather information about the activities of other covens. Abbie was smart and powerful, and applied herself fully. Soon she was one of the top operatives.

It made her feel good to help prevent other attacks, but she never received an assignment involving her mother's murder. The facts of that particular crime were still unclear to the coven Guiding Council. Of course, it was very clear to Abigail what happened. All she needed was the identity of the killer she saw in the vision.

3

~~~

*B*enjamin Mason brought the fork to his mouth as his azure eyes met those of the woman sitting across the table from him. He was wearing a navy suit with a red and yellow tie, his short, light brown—close to dirty blond—hair styled in a wave.

"Ben," she said, "this place is fantastic. The food, the atmosphere, and especially the company."

He swallowed and smiled at her. "It is nice. Thank you for having dinner with me, Susan. We don't get to spend enough time together."

Her eyes sparkled in the light from the candles on the table. "I know. That's something we'll have to remedy, isn't it?"

"Definitely."

The two hadn't been seeing each other very long. Only a few dates, but Ben felt comfortable with Susan French, more comfortable than with any of the young socialites his mother wanted him to associate with. He looked over at his date and smiled. She was definitely more pleasant than most of those young rich kids.

Her blonde hair was long enough that she sometimes played with it, tying it in knots idly as they talked. Her blue eyes, almost matching the color of his, were bright, full of life, and glittered when she laughed. He liked it when she laughed, a good, wholesome sound that was so hard to find among the wealthy people that his mother wanted him to be friends with. Their fake laughter made him cringe.

He watched her as she ate, the movement of her lips making him lick his own.

"What are you thinking?" she asked, tilting her head slightly as she took a sip of wine.

"I was just thinking that you look fantastic, much better than any of the food here. Positively delicious."

Her fair cheeks flushed slightly. It was one of the things he liked most about her. There were a few beautiful women among those his mother paraded in front of him. They were all from wealthy families, of course, and one thing Ben had found to be true was that when they were complimented, they took it as a given. Not so with Susan. She acted surprised every time someone called her beautiful.

"Oh, you are a sweet-talker, Ben. But that's not what you were thinking of. I saw your eyebrows draw down as if something unpleasant came into your mind. Tell me."

Ben made a show of sighing loudly. "Oh, I can't hide anything from you. I was just thinking about how my mother would not like me seeing you. Not because you're not perfect or anything. Just because your family is not on the cover of *Fortune Magazine*."

"Does that bother you? That I'm not rich?"

"No," he said, shaking his head. "Not at all."

"Well, then, don't worry about it. I'll win her over. You'll see."

"Maybe. If anyone can, it would be you."

They finished dinner and left the restaurant. Spring had finally taken hold, and it wasn't as chilly as it had been the week before, so they walked arm-in-arm around the lake near the eatery. It was a pleasant stroll and they chatted and laughed. Ben felt comfortable with Susan and was excited to see how the relationship would progress.

After he drove her home and kissed her goodnight, he was in good spirits. Things were going to be good in the coming days. He had a feeling about it. Driving home to the Huntsman Estate, he couldn't help but sing along with the music on the radio. It was a fine night. Yes it was.

*****

A week later, Margaret Huntsman sat in her stuffed leather chair as if it was a throne. In a sense, it was. She was the most powerful woman in two hundred miles. No, the most powerful *person* in two hundred miles. She knew it, and those with any sense knew it as well. But not everyone had sense. Standing in front of her was a case in point.

Her handlers led the girl into the study where Margaret would hold court. The conversation would be just between her and the young woman being escorted in, though. Other than the two shadowy figures keeping control of the girl, no one needed to know of this meeting.

This study was one of the smaller rooms, tucked

away in a corner of the estate that most visitors never saw. Margaret sat behind a large mahogany desk, shined to a mirror sheen. It was spotless, with only a cup of her favorite tea and a saucer beneath it resting on the surface. Bookshelves lined the walls, containing tomes and little bits of art: a bust of some composer, glass sculptures, Fabergé eggs. The two huge windows had their curtains drawn against the night. A massive fireplace dominated one wall, big enough for two people to walk into at the same time while standing almost erect. There was a fire burning there, as always. Margaret insisted on keeping all the fireplaces in the house burning at all times—other than during cleaning—even if there was no chance she would visit a room. More than one servant had been *fired* for not following that simple command. She chuckled inwardly at the pun.

The girl was really very pretty. Her pale hair was parted in the middle and long enough to fall over her right shoulder. She held it in her hand as if it was a talisman against this most awkward of meetings. Her oval face was the type some men would find alluring, Margaret thought, with dazzling blue eyes large enough to capture and hold any man they latched onto. She did not wear the confidence of a woman who knew she was beautiful, though. Margaret had done her research and found that the girl was what people would call "down to earth." Margaret saw why her son would be attracted to her.

"What is the meaning of this?" the young woman asked in a voice that was strong but smooth. Yes, Margaret could definitely see why her son would be enamored of this one. Even in anger, her voice seemed soothing, almost pleasant. "Why have your goons brought me here? Where is Ben?"

"Benjamin is none of your concern, now or ever." Margaret sipped her tea, not bothering to ask the woman to sit. She looked the younger woman over as if inspecting her for purchase. Silence and a piercing gaze caused most people to crack, to become more pliable.

"We have talked twice before, you and I," Margaret finally said. "Yet you persist. I don't understand this."

Susan French, bit her lower lip and then seemed to realize what she was doing and straightened, firming her mouth into a thin line. "You don't scare me, Margaret."

Margaret took another sip of tea and as she put it down, smiled a wicked smile. "Oh, but I do, Susan. I do. But perhaps I don't scare you enough."

"You can't keep Ben and me apart. He cares for me and I share the feeling. He's an adult and can do what he wants."

"Again, you are mistaken, Susan. He is my son and under my roof. I will decide what does and does not happen in his life. If you think differently, then I am afraid we have a serious disagreement."

Susan bit her bottom lip again. The girl was strong-willed, but she displayed her feelings too readily. She would never make it in business. She was too transparent. Well, it was to be expected of lower-class trash.

"What does it matter to you?" Susan asked, trying another approach. "Surely you want to see your son happy. Why can't you give it a chance? I know we could be happy together."

Margaret tsked. "Oh, Susan, you are so droll. I

don't care about Benjamin's happiness. I care only about how he will increase the family and how he will make alliances with others who are worthwhile. You know—your betters. People completely unlike you and your lower-class, trash-grubbing family. I will make sure he does what is best for himself and for the family. Being with you is not it."

She had never put it in such blunt terms with the woman, not when there was a chance of her repeating it to Benjamin. Susan's pretty rosebud mouth opened wide in shock. It took her a moment, but she lifted her chin, looked Margaret in the eyes—she gained a few points for that—and spoke.

"You can't do anything about it. We will continue to see each other and find out if we are meant to be together. You and your plans can go to hell."

Another sip of tea as she allowed the woman in front of her to stew in the silence, and then Margaret decided she'd wasted enough time. She put her cup down again and sighed.

"Yes, I may go to hell, if there is such a place. But I think I'll be at home there. You, on the other hand, will not know one way or the other. I'm afraid you are too stupid to be allowed to continue your existence."

Susan French's pretty face wore a mask of confusion. It was understandable. People rarely thought horrible things were possible, especially in their own lives. Well, Susan would learn different, though she would only have moments for the lesson to sink in.

"What—?" she started, but Margaret used her magic to bind the woman tightly in place, including her mouth.

The two men who had brought the young woman

stepped back toward the door. They knew the signs of someone bound with Margaret's power and knew the woman wouldn't escape. They also knew, no doubt, that it could be dangerous and messy to be too near her.

Margaret moved her hand as if controlling something in front of her. Susan, eyes wide in fear but her mouth stopped up with some power she did not understand, floated across the room toward the giant fireplace.

"You, my dear, were given several chances to cut off all ties with my son. You stupidly refused. This is what comes of your decision. If there is a hell, maybe I'll see you there. Don't wait up."

Margaret clenched her fist and the young woman in front of her burst into flames and moved further into the fireplace, levitating inches above the floor. Even if Margaret's power had not held her mouth immobile, Susan would not have screamed. The conflagration was so rapid that she went from soft human flesh to ash in a matter of seconds. The two men lifted their hands to shield their faces from the heat and light.

A few moments later, everything was as before. The small fire in the fireplace burned merrily and the three people remaining were exactly where they were when the fourth was disposed of.

The faint, sweet smell of burning flesh hung in the air, but the combustion was so rapid even that odor would fade quickly. Still, Margaret gestured toward the mantel above the fireplace and several scented candles came alight.

"You are sure no one saw you abduct the girl?" Margaret asked them as she took another sip of tea.

"No one saw," one of the men said.

"And what of her vehicle or other evidence?" Margaret asked. "We don't want any clues left lying about."

"We picked her up on a running trail. Pete took her car to the demolisher, the one that chews the cars up and shreds them so they can't be traced. There were no witnesses."

"Good. You may go."

They turned without a word and left the room. Margaret looked to the fireplace and grimaced. She would have to let the fire die down so that all the extra ash could be cleaned out. Well, it was no matter. She wouldn't use this study again for a time. She really only used it for these "conversations" with troublesome people and she didn't foresee any more of these anytime soon.

She had other work to do. Finishing her tea, she set down the cup, rose from her chair, and exited the room.

The fire continued to burn in the fireplace despite the extra ash.

4

~~~~

"One of our operatives has been killed," Charlotte Whinson told the four witches and two warlocks sitting at the large table.

From the lack of her presence, Abbie knew who it must be. A lump formed in her throat.

"Elizabeth Green had been working near the air coven, trying to keep track of their activities. Her apartment burned down and she was trapped inside."

"That's impossible," Jackson Evans said. "There's no way a water witch of her ability would be trapped in a fire. She could have pulled water from the air and put it out, or at least blown the side of the building off and escaped with a water shield around her."

"Yes," Charlotte said, "you are correct, Jackson. It appears that the fires have attacked again, but why? Why make it so plain that they are the ones who did it? They have always tried to make it look like someone else was responsible. What has changed that

24

they are now accepting blame for it, or at least allowing the evidence to point toward them?

"You have been pulled from your assignments until we can figure out what is going on. We will let you know when missions will resume. For now, rest up. I will be in touch."

Charlotte dismissed them. As Abbie was getting up to leave, the High Water Caster spoke again. "Abbie, please stay for a moment." Abbie sat back down.

"Abbie, we need your help," the older woman said. She was in her fifties, but looked much younger. Abbie had never seen gray in Charlotte's hair but thought it would be hard to see, anyway, in the mass of blonde that she usually wore pulled back into a bun. Her dark eyes, somewhere between brown and black—strange looking with such a pale face and light-colored hair—met Abbie's blue. Charlotte's eyes reflected that she was saying something of the utmost seriousness.

"What can I do for you, High Water Caster?"

"We need you to somehow get into the Huntsman Estate to gather information, maybe even take action. Margaret Huntsman is stretching her power and something needs to be done. We haven't confirmed it yet, but we think she had something to do with Liz's death."

"Of course," Abbie said. She had known for years that Margaret killed her mother, having seen the woman in her mother's vision. Convincing the others beyond any doubt was the difficult part. "I'll do whatever I can. How will I get into place?"

"We're not sure yet, but as soon as we can figure it out, we'll let you know. Stand by and be ready to move when we give the word. Things may happen quickly."

And they did. As it turned out, Margaret Huntsman didn't believe in second chances. She overheard one of her maids referring to her as "Maggie" and fired the woman on the spot. The Housekeeper had interviewed dozens of women in the two days following. She picked Abigail.

She interviewed on a Friday afternoon, was contacted that evening, and told to report to work Monday morning. They only had two days until she would start. Isabella Lee, a witch so skilled at research it was almost like magic, got to work immediately. Isabella's preparation and data gathering had taken much of the weekend.

Abbie was a little nervous. Not because she was starting a new job. She was too experienced for that. The anxiety came from starting a new mission, one that could be dangerous if everything she had been briefed on was true. Well, she would get through it. Or not. Stressing over it would do nothing to help.

As always at the start of another assignment, Abigail thought back to something that happened when she was eight years old. She had been at the Wyoming State Fair, and the sights and sounds mesmerized her. She goggled at all the people, so many different types. She was used to groups of people at her home, family and members of the coven, but this was different. These were all strangers.

After staring at the Ferris wheel for a long while, she realized she'd lost track of her parents and her sister, who was only four years old at the time. Swinging her head from side to side and darting about between grown-ups' legs, looking for familiar faces, she started to panic. She had never been alone with so many strangers before. Her heart felt as if it would beat out of her chest and tears pooled in her eyes, threatening to overflow and spill down her face.

In her mad search for her family, she ended up in an alley of sorts between two large tents. It ended at the wall of a third tent. When she turned to go back into the main thoroughfare, a man was standing in her way.

To be fair, the man wasn't mean-looking, nor did he look rough or bad in any way. Yet, she instantly feared him. It was some feeling in her bones, a vibe that he was not someone she wanted to be alone with. His long, sharp face looked like a fox's face to her. When he smiled, she expected to see pointed fangs, but he had normal teeth. From his appearance, he was normal in every way.

"Are you lost, little girl?" Though his tone was not unfriendly, it sent chills up Abigail's back. She was too afraid to answer.

As the man shifted to step closer, Abbie heard her mother's voice.

"Abbie? Abbie, where are you? Abbie!"

The little girl somehow was able to unlock her jaw and yell, "I'm here, Mama. Mama, I'm here!" A look of disappointment crossed the man's vulpine face, but the foot he had lifted settled back down where it had been and he waited calmly for what came next.

Olivia Henderson came into view. She was beautiful. At least, Abigail thought so. Her hair was a deeper red than her daughter's, and it was straighter. It swished in front of her oval face, eyes alight with worry and full lips pursed as if on the verge of speaking, either to scold or to console. She edged by the man with a "pardon me." She swept her daughter up into a hug, holding her tight.

The man dipped his head, said, "Ma'am," and then walked off to join the crowds surging past the alley. Abigail's father, Landon, nodded to the man as he passed him, but looked after him, watching, until the stranger was out of sight.

It was near the end of the day, so the family decided they'd had enough excitement and went home. After they had returned, Olivia sat her daughter down to talk to her. "Abbie, did that man do anything to you, say anything to you?"

"No, Mama," she said. "He asked if I was lost and that's all. He scared me, though. I had a bad feeling in my tummy when he looked at me."

Olivia hugged Abigail's head to her chest. "I know, honey. There is something I have been waiting to tell you, and now seems as good a time as any. Sit down, let's talk."

Abigail sat on the comfortable couch in the recreation room and looked up at her mother sitting on the love seat across from her. For a wonder, there was no one else in the room. Her mother must have told them she wanted to talk with Abbie alone. There were *always* people in the recreation room.

"Abbie, you know that we are a family of elemental witches and warlocks. You know with our magic, we manipulate the power of water, and with that power we do things to help others."

"Yes, Mama."

Olivia smiled at her daughter. "You are old enough now for me to tell you of the other elements, of other elemental magic users."

"There are other types?" Abigail asked. "But everyone uses the power of water. Our family, all of

28

our friends in the coven, everyone."

"Yes, sweet one," Olivia said, "because we have not had you associate with the other types. There are a few other covens in the area, but we don't interact much with them. We only do it when necessary because we all have…ah, different views on things."

"What do you mean, Mama?"

"For starters, let me describe those who are in our coven and use the elemental power of water. Our family, our friends, me, you." She touched Abigail's nose with her fingertip, causing the girl to giggle.

"Water is unique in that it can take more than one form. Like liquid water, we can easily adapt to situations, but we can also be hard, sharp, and dangerous like ice. We sometimes share traits with air elemental witches, too, because water can become gas, like air. The point is that the qualities of the element of water dictate part of who we are. Do you understand that?"

"Yes," the little girl said, nodding.

"Good," Olivia said. "Now, the other elements also affect how the witches and warlocks who use them behave. Air witches are often evasive, ethereal, and insubstantial. Do you understand those words?" She looked at Abbie. "No? It means it is hard to catch them, like trying to grab a handful of air." She demonstrated by swiping at the air and then opening her hand, revealing nothing. Her confused look made Abbie laugh. "It is difficult to pin an air witch to an opinion. Ask a yes or no question and you will get a 'maybe.' This can be frustrating and so dealings with those who use the elemental power of air are often more trouble than it is worth. They are not bad witches, just different than us.

"Earth witches act like the stone of the mountain. They are slow to be convinced of anything, holding to their traditions and to things 'that have always been this way.' It takes time and a great amount of effort to change the mind of an earth witch. They will listen politely, having the patience of dirt and stone itself, but then they will not budge from their viewpoint."

Olivia looked to her daughter to make sure she was still paying attention. Abigail, eyes wide as if she was being told a bedtime story, had her attention fixed on her mother.

"So, you can see that because of our differences, working together with the other elements can be difficult and frustrating.

"But there is one other group that we have not discussed. The fire witches. Whereas earth witches are passively resistant, those who commune with fire are actively aggressive, always trying to impose their will on others. Whereas air witches evade and move out of the way of those who attack them, fire witches begin conflicts and press the attack. Whereas we water witches preserve and nurture, the users of the elemental magic of fire want to consume, to destroy. That man you saw, he was a fire warlock.

"Of the other three elements, fire is most directly opposed to water. They do not like us because they feel weak against us. With our quicksilver evasions and rapid counterattacks, like an ocean wave pulling back and then coming in again and crashing on top of a foe, they are wary of us, but hate us simply for being what we are. There is no negotiation with a fire witch or warlock, not for us."

"Are fire users evil?" Abigail asked. She was thinking of the man who confronted her earlier.

"No, sweetie," Olivia said. "Not all of them are evil, though some definitely are. They are just different, driven by a nature unlike ours. Still, you must be wary of them, them above all."

"I will, Mama. I'll watch out for them."

Olivia smiled down at her daughter and kissed the top of her head. "That's good. It is always good to know what dangers lie out there in the world so you can be prepared for them if they come for you."

The memory dissolved. Her mother had been killed eleven years after that discussion, just over six years ago. She still missed her every day.

None of this would bring Olivia back, of course, but helping to bring the murdering fire witches to justice would help. If she could prevent someone else from losing their mother, all her effort would be worth it. It was why she was going to the Huntsman Estate, working undercover to help bring down Margaret. She would do her best to eliminate dangerous witches, and Margaret Huntsman was as dangerous as they came.

5

~~~

*T*he fire washed over her and incinerated everything, including her own body. She felt her flesh crinkling and bubbling; the sickly smell of it assaulted her nose. Just before her eyes boiled and popped, she saw the face of the dark-haired woman through the red and yellow flames. She was laughing.

Abigail woke with a start. She wiped at her forehead, feeling a thin layer of perspiration there. Her heart galloped as if it was going to bounce out of her chest. She swallowed hard and tried to take a full breath. It took two more tries to fill her tight lungs. Reliving the moment of her mother's death always made her feel like she was having a panic attack.

Of her siblings, she was the only one who had received the entire vision her mother had sent that day. Whether it was because of her power in the elemental magic, an unusual sensitivity, or because she was closest with her mother, she wasn't sure. She had explained it in great detail to the others. She did so repeatedly to her father, searching for any bit of information that could be helpful. Her brother and sister had only received pieces of the sending.

It was unheard of for witches to attack other witches, especially during a festival. There had not been open warfare between different covens for hundreds of years. It was more than unsettling to all who knew about it. And there had been several other attacks since then.

Abigail sat up in her bed. Why had she relived her mother's death yet again? No doubt it had something to do with the mission. She wasn't due to wake up for another hour yet, but she threw the covers off her and swung her legs over the bed, putting her feet on the floor. She couldn't get to sleep again after that vision. She turned her alarm off and got up to start her day.

A hot shower later and Abigail was brushing her red hair, trying to tame it so it didn't go frizzy on her. Where her mother's hair was fire red, Abigail's was more subtle, almost a strawberry blonde color, but not quite. Some called it "dirty red." As she looked at it in the mirror, she couldn't help but to think of the arguments she had in the past about exactly what color it was. Those discussions always ended the same way, with her saying, "It's the color of my hair. Leave it at that."

She smiled at that, laugh lines framing her cheeks. Her large blue eyes—she thought they were too large—blinked as she met her own gaze.

Abigail shook her head. What was she doing studying her own face? She had things to do today to prepare for starting her new job. Her new mission.

She busied herself with putting on makeup and getting dressed.

Abbie picked up the little angel figurine from her nightstand. It was barely an inch and a half tall, small enough for her to carry everywhere in her pocket or purse. She looked at it while running her thumb over the cool, smooth stone. The feel of the smooth sweep of the wings on the back of the figurine always calmed her when she needed it. When she had gotten it after her mother's death, dirty with soot and ash, she had cleaned it, partly with her tears, and had rarely let it out of her sight since then.

"Mother, what am I going to do without you?" Abigail asked the angel. "Even after all these years, there is a hole where you should be, like I am not a complete person. I want so much to talk to you again. I'm going to a place full of normal humans, and maybe a fire witch or two. Do you remember our conversations about those 'only humans'?"

Abigail thought back to the first conversation she could remember on the subject.

"Abbie," Olivia said, "you have to realize that all people, all life, is deserving of consideration and respect. Do you understand what I mean by that?"

"Yes, mother," the fifteen-year-old Abbie had said.

"Do you truly? Do you agree with it?"

"Of course," Abbie said, brow crinkling at her mother's doubt. "I respect life and would never willingly kill anything unless it was the last resort."

"I know that," her mother laughed. "But I'm not talking about killing. I'm talking about everyday life, about treating people as they should be treated, as we would want to be treated."

"I try to treat everyone with respect and

politeness," Abbie said. A twinkle appeared in her eye. "You have made it perfectly clear that you would tolerate no less."

Olivia's smile made Abbie's heart soar. "Yes, that's true. Still, I think you're missing the point. Many of the gifted—most, in fact—have this notion that people who are only human—onlies—are lesser creatures because they cannot use magic. We must not think like that.

"Onlies—and I hesitate to use that term because to some people, it is derogatory—have other skills. Some are gifted physically with athleticism or prowess in battle. Some have keen minds that can develop solutions that even magic cannot equal. Some have other talents. Just because their gifts are not magical in nature as ours are does not mean they are less than us."

"But Mama," Abbie said, "isn't it a bit like humans and apes? Humans have a key thing that apes lack— extreme intelligence—and that sets them apart as surely as it sets apes apart from squirrels. All of them deserve life and deserve to be treated with respect, but apes are not humans any more than squirrels are apes. They are simply lesser forms of life. As are onlies when compared to those who can use magic."

Abigail's mother eyed her, her own blue eyes holding Abbie's, searching. "I would hope that you don't truly believe that you are better than other humans just because you are gifted with the ability to use magic. That is much like saying that people who play sports professionally are a higher species than normal people because they have a gift for playing their particular type of game."

Abbie thought about it for a moment. "Oh. I

never really thought of it that way. It makes sense, though."

Her mother's smile returned. "Think on it, Abigail,"—she always called her by her formal name when driving home the point of a lesson—"and see if you come to the same conclusion. We will talk about it again later."

She did think about it, and the more she did so, the more Abigail saw her mother's point of view. Was she so arrogant that she believed other people were lesser creatures simply because they could not do what she did? She had never thought so, but felt less sure.

After all, the gift of magic use was not constant in successive generations. Where the talent ran strong in families, most of the children inherited the ability to use elemental magic, but not all. Those unable to work the magic were nicknamed "skips." It wasn't exactly derogatory, but neither was it complimentary. Skips were treated in magical families as disabled family members were in typical "only human" families. They were not as capable in some respects, but it was out of their control and no fault of their own. Why didn't she see onlies at least as kindly as that? Yes, she had to think more on it.

Abigail and her mother spoke on the subject a few other times, and if she was honest with herself, she had to admit that her opinion was swinging toward her mother's viewpoint.

Until the day she received the vision her mother had sent just before her death, some four years later.

When Abigail witnessed the way the onlies ambushed Olivia and set her up for the fire witches to kill, she stopped questioning her view of the non-magical humans. She blamed the fire witches, but she also developed an intense hatred for the onlies who were involved. That hatred leaked out to taint her view of all onlies, enough to bring her old prejudice back with a vengeance.

Abigail tried to be respectful and polite, but even as she pretended, she was convinced that those without magical abilities were just not as good as magic users. Whenever memories of the conversations with her mother popped into her mind, she cast them out ferociously. The images of the death of her mother were too vivid, the feelings too raw and powerful. Her attitude would stay. For better or worse, it would stay.

She sighed and gave herself a rueful look in the mirror. It was time she got started. She had things to do and a mission to get underway. Squeezing the carved stone angel in her hand and then stroking it with her thumb, she set it back down in its resting place. She normally kept it with her at all times, a sort of talisman against the bad thoughts and memories, but she couldn't bring anything so personal with her on the mission. It would have to remain there, and her memories of her mother would have to be sufficient in themselves.

She turned and left the room, her steps becoming firmer and her stride more confident as she went.

6

*A*bbie went to one of the meeting rooms. The house, an estate really, had been built by her ancestors and named Aqua Terra more than a hundred years earlier. It had been renovated and expanded several times over the years. The Hendersons were always an influential family, being one of the first to settle in the area that became Jackson, Wyoming, and they later offered the use of their home as a sort of headquarters for the growing coven.

As befit the ancestral home of water witches, the grounds had several water features. A fair-sized lake was nearby, as well as a river, several streams, scattered ponds, and fountains all around the developed areas. It was a gorgeous, green place. At least, that's the way Abigail saw it as she grew up there.

It had been seventy-two years since the coven began using Aqua Terra as their base. Only once in that time was the High Water Caster a Henderson. Abigail's mother.

The family had always been powerful in magic and had produced some gifted witches, but fear of the appearance of favor always swayed the election of the supreme witch so others were named to that office. With Olivia Henderson, though, there was no competition. She was singular in every way. Never once had there been any accusation of favor in electing her to the position. She was universally loved and respected within the water witch community, as well as the earth and air witch communities. Obviously, the fire witches did not feel the same.

Abigail opened the wooden door with a storm cloud carved in it to a chamber that had been renovated into a meeting room. The fireplace crackled with the burning logs within, casting light in a warm circle around it and taking a bit of the chill off the early March morning. The woman sitting at the oval table didn't look up from the papers she was reading when Abigail entered.

"Hi, Isabella," Abbie said, causing the woman to start. "Have you been there all night? It's daylight out, you know." She went to the windows and opened up the drapes, letting the morning light in. It splashed across the room, revealing the bookshelves that lined the wall and the couches and chairs near the fireplace. Paintings of forest scenes with rivers and lakes, with the occasional portrait of some Henderson or another, dotted the walls.

As the light reached her, Isabella Lee squinted and looked up from the papers she was reading by the light of the table lamp. She stood, straightening to her full five foot nine inch height, then arched her back like a cat while rubbing it with her hands and grunting. She sort of looked like a cat. A starving cat. She was the skinniest person Abigail had ever seen. Even her brown hair was thin. Rather, it was fine, hanging straight down past her shoulders and covering the edges of Isabella's long face. Her hazel eyes met Abbie's and a smile split her face. Despite her unhealthy pallor, the smile made her almost beautiful.

"Abbie." Isabella straightened and motioned toward one of the chairs at the table. "No, I haven't been here all night. I've only been here a couple of hours. It was dark when I came in, and I didn't really notice the time. Sit, sit. Let's talk about what we'll be doing."

Abigail smiled back at her and took a seat. "What are you looking at?"

"Some of the information we'll need for the mission." She chuckled.

"What's so funny?" Abigail asked.

"Oh, 'mission.' It makes it sound like we're some kind of big espionage bureau or something, like we're the CIA."

Abigail let loose a little bit of nervous laughter herself. "I know, it's strange when we call these activities missions. Still, that's really what they are, right?"

"I suppose so. I shouldn't laugh. It's serious work. Anyway, this file,"—she handed over a thick file, papers and photos wrapped in a paper accordion cover—"is all the information we have on Margaret Huntsman. You should read it all before you start."

Abigail flipped through the pages absently, but her mind didn't even register what she was looking at until she got to the picture of the woman. She was middle aged with a strong-looking face and dark hair with some gray shot through it. Her beak of a nose was prominent, but it was her hazel eyes that really drew attention. It reminded Abbie of the "thousand-yard stare" that people always talked about with hardened criminals but with just enough softness to keep her from looking like a psychopath. Instead, it made her look strong as iron. The set of her mouth in a tight, thin line didn't make the image any friendlier.

"That's her," Abigail said. "The one responsible for Mother's murder. I saw that woman's face clearly in the vision Mother sent me."

"I know you believe that, Abbie," Isabella said. "And she does seem to be the most likely suspect. I believe you saw her in your mother's memories, but, unfortunately, we can't use that as hard proof. Your brother and sister didn't receive the whole memory like you did, so there aren't even any other witnesses to back it up. We can't confirm it officially until you get in there and find some evidence."

"Evidence."

"Yes. I would go myself, but I'm not up to going out and dealing with things like that. My ability to identify particular witches or warlocks by the residue of magic they have used is valuable, but my magic is generally too weak to handle things like conflict or combat. And, to be honest, I'm a horrible actress and don't do well under pressure. I'm much better in a research capacity."

"That's totally understandable," Abigail said.

"You, on the other hand, are perfect for fieldwork. You're smart, cool under pressure, can make decisions quickly, and you're one of the more powerful witches around here. And you probably haven't even come into your power fully yet. Add to that your talent of detecting magical residue—even if you can't identify the witch who cast it—and you are the perfect choice for this mission."

"Yeah," Abigail said, "except that I'm way too close to it. It's my mother's death we're talking about. Sure, there are other crimes involved, but that's the main one, as far as I'm concerned."

"The Council has decided to overlook that you are 'emotionally invested' in this. There simply isn't anyone better able to do what we need."

Abigail sat silent for a moment, letting what Isabella said sink in. She was being given a chance to take part in this investigation, in this mission, to determine the identity of her mother's murderer, all because of her seemingly insignificant talent. Okay, also because she'd had excellent success in other assignments, but mainly because of her minor ability.

Magic was a strange thing. Different people had different gifts. Some were more attuned to one element or another—that affinity seemed to run in families—and individual strengths varied seemingly without any rhyme or reason. Then there were talents, abilities that were inherent to the magic user, not things that could be learned. Many witches and warlocks, most even, had no additional talent beyond the normal spell-casting that everyone else had.

Everyone but the onlies, and skips.

Talents, though, ranged from the small and trifling—like being able to smell colors—to very useful, like being able to launch fireballs from the fingertips without going through the motions and incantations to cast a spell. Abbie's ability was to determine if magic had been used, the talent to sense magical residue. It wasn't as refined as Isabella's, which could identify the individual magic user, sort of like a fingerprint, but it would be useful during this mission.

Isabella studied Abbie for a moment. "Abbie, it's not an insult that you are getting this opportunity. Several other operatives have useful talents, but you were chosen. It's just one of the factors. You have proven yourself one of the best and, frankly, that's what we need for this mission. It's a good thing."

Abbie sighed. "Oh, I know. Maybe I'm just a little wound up about the mission. I do realize it's a privilege. I'll do my best."

"I know you will." The older witch smiled at Abigail. "So, to be clear, you are to search the house thoroughly, find the residue of magic use, and bring something back to me with magical residue on it. Your primary goal is to bring the item with the residue and to make sure that it is from Margaret Huntsman. I will then determine if it matches the magic that killed Olivia.

"There may be other witches in the household. I can only compare the feel of the residue with others I have encountered, not come up with a witch's name out of the blue. If what you bring back is from another magic-user, chances are I won't be able to identify her, not having encountered the feel of it before. Any other information you are able to obtain will be valuable as well."

"I understand," Abbie said. "Just as I understood the other four times we went over it." She smiled at the other woman and winked to soften her words.

"Yes. I'm sorry, but I just want to make sure we're

clear. We have been trying to get someone into the Huntsman Estate for years. Remember, for me to get a good read, the item had to have been in close proximity to the target of the magic or to have been the target itself. I would think if it is strong enough to trigger your talent, I should be able to trace it, but if given a choice, take the item with the strongest residue.

"And Abbie, be careful. We have heard from a casual acquaintance of someone within the household that a woman disappeared less than a year ago, and it's possible Margaret Huntsman had something to do with it. Do not put it past her to try to kill you if you are revealed."

"I'll be careful," Abbie said. "I always am. I'll be extra careful this time, though, believe me."

Isabella pulled Abigail into a hug. It felt strange because the woman was not affectionate and they were not close. She must have been nervous about the level of danger in the mission.

Abigail hugged her back and waited for the other woman to loosen her grip. It took a long time. Abbie wondered what Isabella hadn't told her. Was this mission more dangerous than she thought? Was it some kind of suicide mission? Even if it was, she'd still do it. She could confirm the identity of her mother's killer. That was worth risking her life for. Margaret Huntsman must pay for what she did, and aside from some rogue vigilante witch or warlock, the only way was to convince the Guiding Council beyond all doubt that Margaret was responsible for Olivia Henderson's death. Then the Council would have to take action.

When Isabella finally let go, Abbie squeezed her

one last time and then stepped back.

"Well, I better get going," Abbie said. "Lots of things to do."

Abigail turned and left before an extended conversation stalled the start of her mission. She had a couple of hours to look over the file Isabella had given her, and she was anxious to get started, to find her mother's killer.

7

~~~~~

"I just don't see why I shouldn't be able to do this."

Benjamin Mason shook his head. His hair moved only a little—he liked to keep it short, with just enough length on top to make it look wind-blown if mussed. His strong jaw was set and his body tensed as if preparing for battle. In a way, he was.

"Benjamin," his mother said, "we have discussed this before. I will not allow you to work as a common laborer. What will people think of you, of our family? You are above such things. No Huntsman will ever perform menial tasks as long as I'm alive."

"I'm not a Huntsman," he said. "I'm a Mason."

"You know what I mean," Margaret said, her hazel eyes glinting, taking on a cast of red from the fire nearby. "It is…inappropriate."

"Mother," Benjamin said, "it's not like I'm planning to dig ditches. It's sampling for environmental pollutants. My degree is in

Environmental Chemistry. The work is in my field."
He tried to keep from sounding like he was whining.

"Oh, Benjamin," she said in a tone that one would use with an obstinate child. "I knew it was wrong to let you choose a major other than business. Your job, if you want to work, is to help run Huntsman Consolidated. That is your proper place. Mucking about with dirt and water and who knows what else is fine for *other* people, those without the wealth, power, and prestige that we—that you—have, but it is not a suitable occupation for *us*. I forbid it."

"Mother, I am twenty-six years old. I will take this job and do the work as long as I find it fulfilling. I have no interest in the family holdings. You are running the company just fine. There's no need for me to get involved."

Ben's mother shifted her gaze from him to her polished walnut desk. He could hear the leather of her chair creak as she turned her eyes toward her friend and business associate Helen Shapiro.

The two women could not have been more different. At least six feet tall with bare feet, Helen towered over Margaret, and her muscular build emphasized Margaret's slimness. With her short blonde hair, Helen honestly looked like one of the East German athletes he'd read about. The one thing both had in common was their presence, which was stronger than their actual physical appearance. They both gave him the sense they were fourteen feet tall.

He didn't like having this conversation in front of Helen, but she was his mother's closest friend and almost a part of the family.

Margaret's eyes met Helen's, and the world seemed to spin for a moment. He squeezed his own eyes shut and blinked several times. The feeling passed.

"So," Margaret said, "what do you think about this situation?"

"I…I'm going to call Dr. Weitz and tell him I can't take the job after all. It's really not something someone of my standing should be considering, anyway."

"Yes," she said. "Yes, that seems like the wise choice. I'm glad we had this talk, Benjamin. You look tired. You should probably go lie down and rest."

Ben turned his head slowly—the edges of his vision seemed to shimmer as he moved—and looked at Helen. She smiled at him. At least, she showed her teeth to him. The woman's blocky face just didn't wear smiles well. When he turned his gaze back to his mother, she was sitting there with her elbows on her desk, her hands steepled together in front of her, silent. When their eyes met, he felt pressure in his temples, as if he was developing a headache.

"That sounds like a good idea," he said, not sure if it was or not. "I feel like I might be getting a headache. Thank you for your time. I know you're busy."

"I always have time for you, Benjamin. You're my son. Now run along and get some rest."

Ben left, still not sure what had happened to make him light-headed. He had to call Dr. Weitz, and then he needed to lie down. Maybe he was getting sick. He'd have to take it easy for the rest of the day, maybe take some vitamin C.

Benjamin Mason made his way listlessly back to his sitting room. No—his rec room, or his playroom. Only his mother called it his sitting room. As he entered, he didn't even pay attention to the pool table, foosball, the line of classic standalone arcade games, the big screen television/interactive gaming rig, or any of the other toys. He shuffled to the couch and allowed his body to fall onto it.

"So, how'd it go?" Lucas King asked him. Ben's head snapped around at the sound, making his vision swim; he had to close his eyes to push back nausea.

He hadn't even realized the man was there. Lucas was Ben's driver and manservant, had been for almost ten years. He was as close to a friend as Benjamin Mason had, though he was careful never to call him that within earshot of his mother.

"I...uh...I'm not really sure," Ben said, squeezing his head with both hands to try to settle out the fuzz in it. "I think it went okay. I'm going to call Dr. Weitz and tell him I can't take the job. It's too menial for me."

Lucas's dark eyes scanned Ben's for a moment. His dark skin creased around his mouth in a smile and then smoothed as the edges of his mouth lowered.

"Wait, what? You're serious?" Lucas rose from the stuffed leather chair and sat on the loveseat across the table from Ben. "You were really excited about that job. You went to tell your mother you were going to take it and that she couldn't do anything about it. Now you've decided not to take it, and yet you're saying the discussion with your mother went well? It sounds like she convinced you to do exactly the opposite of what you were planning."

"Really?" Ben tried to trace his thoughts from before the meeting with his mother. "I don't remember that, Lucas. Maybe I wasn't clear when I was talking to you earlier."

"Dude, you said that this was so important you

were willing to go to battle with your mother, willing to accept whatever punishment she would give you for doing it without her permission, if that's what was necessary."

"No, that's not how it is at all," Ben said. "I'm better than an entry-level, working-class job. My conversation with Mother reminded me of that. Sometimes I get caught up in romantic ideas of being one of the little people. You know, the ones without money."

"You mean, people like me," Lucas said, disappointment evident on his face.

"No, Lucas, it's not like that at all. Listen, I'm feeling kind of dizzy. I'm going to go lie down. I'll talk to you later, okay?"

"Sure. Do you need anything?"

"No, I'm good. Thank you."

Ben went through the door to his bedroom and dropped onto his bed as if his bones had melted. He was asleep within moments, his mind slipping into a confused darkness.

*****

Margaret turned her head toward her friend, confidante, and personal assistant as Benjamin left the study. She smiled.

"Benjie never figured out you got rid of his girlfriend all those months ago?" Helen asked her.

"Helen, please don't call him 'Benjie.' His name is Benjamin. But no, he hasn't come to ask me about it. Yet. I'm sure he suspects I had something to do with her running off without notice but nothing more than that."

"It's kind of risky, making people disappear like that," Helen said. "It could get us attention we don't want."

"Oh, relax. There is no evidence, no real motive. The incompetent investigators at the police department couldn't come up with enough to even interview me, let alone charge me with anything. No, it will be forgotten. Just as our dear Susan will be forgotten. Benjamin will think twice about acting on base attraction for fear of being abandoned again. It will all work out for the better."

"I guess so." Helen smiled. "I never liked that girl, anyway. She was much too good for her own good, if you know what I mean."

"I do. It is unfortunate emotions interfere with mind control. By the time I found out about Susan, Benjamin was already too fond of her for me to manipulate him. In any case, it's done now."

"If you had been working on him consistently, like I always tell you," Helen said, "you wouldn't have to force him to change his mind like that."

"And I have told *you*," Margaret said, "that manipulating someone's mind with magic is tricky. There is a chance I could damage my son, even a chance that the damage would shift his brain to conflict even more with what needs to be done. It's not an exact science. It's magic.

"For the most part, I have to allow my lessons as he grew up to dictate his opinions, just like with everyone else."

"Well, your lessons don't seem to have worked," Helen said acidly. "He seems to balk at everything you want him to do."

"His father impressed his own teaching on the boy

up until he was fifteen. Benjamin clings to his father's ideas. If I had gotten to him to myself earlier, it would have made everything much easier." She pulled a lock of hair back from her face. "These little sessions to correct him will work, for now. Hopefully I can bring him around to the right way of thinking. Eventually."

"He's twenty-six, Margaret. Don't you think if there was a chance, he'd have already come around?"

"Oh, Helen. You really should learn more about the way the mind works. People often change drastically in their late twenties, sometimes completely reversing their opinions. I'll give him another few years. He'll come around, you'll see."

"Sure, sure," Helen said. "And if he doesn't come around? If he continues to be stubborn and resistant and so, so honorable like his late father? What then?"

"He means nothing to me compared to the empire we're building, compared to our grand plans," Margaret said with no emotion. "If he is too much trouble, then he will just have to join his father in the grave."

8

~~~~~

*A*bigail straightened her clothes as she got out of her car in the servants' garage at the Huntsman Estate. In her phone orientation, she'd been advised in no uncertain terms that if her auto was visible at any time, she would be let go on the spot. Margaret Huntsman would not be embarrassed by "dilapidated vehicles strewn throughout her property."

One of the other members of the house staff, a woman named Sadie, met Abigail at the door of the servant quarters and gave her the uniform she would be wearing. She followed Sadie to a small changing room. The clothing Abbie carried was the classic maid's uniform, black dress with white collars and a white apron. At least it was tasteful. She'd been afraid she would be forced to wear one of those God-awful "sexy maid" outfits with a short frilly skirt and a low neckline. The dress came down to her knees and the neck was high enough to wear to church.

Abbie unconsciously wiped her palms on her uniform. Her throat was dry and she cleared it softly. She had gone undercover before for different missions, and each time, the worst part was at the beginning, when she first sank into the role, first made contact with those she'd be interacting with for the remainder of her mission. She didn't show the tension outwardly, of course. If she did, she wouldn't be much of an operative.

Still, her heart fluttered and her stomach jerked as if something within was alive and trying to get out. She took a deep breath, doing so through her nose so she didn't look like she was taking a deep breath. It would be fine. This was just another mission, like all the others she'd done. She would do her job and then move on to her next assignment.

Claire Roberts, the Housekeeper, was maybe in her late fifties. She was short and graying and thick about her middle, but when she smiled she seemed to be a kindly grandmother, making Abbie feel comfortable, like she was with family. She was Abbie's boss and was never called anything but Mrs. Roberts, even by Margaret Huntsman. Her round face swiveled toward Abigail.

"Okay, dear," she said in a soft, sweet voice, "it's really very simple. You are responsible for keeping the second floor tidy, all except the bedrooms. Those will be taken care of by the chamber maids. You will dust, clean, vacuum, keep the linens organized when they come back from the laundry, keep the fireplaces clean and the fires burning, and do whatever else anyone in the household asks of you. All except other maids and laundresses, of course. If they try to give you orders, you come straight to me, and I will sort it out."

"Yes, Mrs. Roberts," Abigail said.

The Housekeeper nodded and then her friendly face transformed into chiseled stone. "One thing you need to remember above all else: Ms. Huntsman is very particular about things in general, but especially about the way those around her act. Your predecessor was let go because she persisted in saying things that should not be said. You will maintain perfect etiquette at all times and will refrain from gossiping or speaking in a negative manner about the household itself or any member of it. Is that clear?"

Abbie put on her best chastised look. "Yes, ma'am." She already knew how strict Margaret was. Ms. Huntsman. She had done her research.

"Good." The kindly grandmother's face came back, and Mrs. Roberts smiled. "Let me show you where everything is, and then I will show you where you'll be staying. I do not expect you to work today, but just to get accustomed to the surroundings and meet the other members of the staff."

When they turned the first corner, another woman was standing in the hall. She was a brunette, with hair at chin length, styled so the ends curled under. Her uniform looked like a cross between a maid's outfit and a cocktail dress, sleeveless and tight across her slender frame, but with the same white apron that Abigail wore. She had a sour look on her face, as if she had just eaten something that didn't agree with her.

"Ah, Harper, good. Harper Addinson, this is our new maid, Abigail Henderson. Harper is Ms. Huntsman's personal maid. She takes care of her rooms and all her needs. If you ever need to interact with anyone on behalf of Ms. Huntsman, she is your contact."

The woman put her fists on her hips and scanned Abbie with her eyes. Abbie felt like Harper was counting the strands of hair on her head. She was not an ugly woman. On the contrary, she would probably be lovely, if she didn't look like she hated life. Harper raised her chin and her pinched mouth moved.

"Pleasure."

"It's nice to meet you, Harper," Abbie said with as much cheer as she could muster. The other woman nodded while somehow still keeping her chin raised. She turned and moved off toward the stairs to the upper floors.

"Ahem." Mrs. Roberts cleared her throat. "Well, that is Harper. You'll get used to her."

The pair wandered through the second floor, Mrs. Roberts pointing out the things Abigail needed to know. As they entered the hall from one of the sitting rooms, they almost ran into a young man striding down the corridor as if he was on an important mission. He hadn't seen them yet, so Abigail took the opportunity to scan him for details. That was her mission, right, to be observant?

He was of average height, maybe five feet and ten inches or so, Abigail thought. His light brown hair was cut short but styled so that it crested and swept back in a wave with just the right mix of styling and chaos. His blue eyes blazed as he looked at the carpet in front of him, mumbling something to himself as he moved. His clothing was casual but would not have been out of place in any situation with the addition of a tie: slacks, a button-down shirt, a nice pair of dress shoes. He looked fit, his appearance enhanced by the clothes that were obviously tailored for him. He was altogether pleasant to look at.

Abigail noticed when he first caught sight of the two women in his peripheral vision. His eyes widened slightly, his mumbling ceased, he stopped walking, and his head snapped up. When her eyes met his, for just a brief moment, she felt as if she knew him somehow. Or, at least, she wanted to.

"Oh," he said. "Sorry, Mrs. Roberts. I was carried away by my thoughts and didn't see you. I almost caused a collision." He chuckled weakly.

"Good morning, Master Benjamin," the Housekeeper said. "This is our new maid, Abigail Henderson. Abigail, this is Benjamin Mason, Ms. Huntsman's only son. You will address him as Master Mason."

Abbie had been staring at those blue eyes—so like the lake near her home—but when they swiveled to meet hers, she dropped her gaze. Not knowing what else to do, she dipped into a curtsy. "I am pleased to meet you, Master Mason."

"No, no, no," he said, a smile lighting up his face. "Please don't give me that 'Master Mason' stuff. Call me Benjamin, or Ben." He reached out and grabbed her hand to shake it. When they touched, a jolt of tingling energy traveled up her arm, dissipating at her shoulder. She barely suppressed a small gasp. It wasn't a metaphorical tingle, not mere attraction. It was a physical sensation as if she'd been given a mild electrical shock. She had never felt anything exactly like it before.

His eyes widened into a surprised look, but it disappeared quickly. He shook his head slightly as he looked down at his own hand, still clasping hers. "It is a pleasure to meet you, Abigail. Welcome to the household. I hope you enjoy it here."

He looked at Mrs. Roberts, still holding Abbie's hand. Warmth spread from the tips of her fingers and crept up her arm, slowly replacing the tingling. He seemed to notice and released it, as if reluctant to do so. When he looked up, his smile returned.

"Well, I better get going. Nice to meet you, Abigail. Be nice to her, Mrs. Roberts." He winked at the older woman and set off down the hall. Abigail watched him go.

"He is very charming," Abbie said, a bit breathless.

"Yes." Mrs. Roberts narrowed her eyes at the young woman. "Don't you dare even think about calling him by his first name. Ms. Huntsman does not tolerate that kind of familiarity from the staff. Master. Mason. Is that clear?"

Abbie had a habit of putting people she met into four categories. She was a keen observer of people and could usually decide within a few minutes if someone was more likely to be of the fire, earth, air, or water personality. From Benjamin Mason, she got a definite water vibe. Yes, he would definitely be a water if he was anything. Strange from the son of a fire witch, maybe a fire warlock himself.

All Abbie could do was to nod in response to Mrs. Roberts's questions, her thoughts entirely consumed by the man she had just met and wondering why she felt as if they'd always known each other.

9

~~~

$\mathcal{B}$en hurried down the hall toward the stairs right after he had almost run into Mrs. Roberts. Abigail. The new girl's name was Abigail. There were fourteen members of the household staff, including Mrs. Roberts's husband, the butler. Or, as the man liked to be called, the Estate Manager. Ben had learned long ago that his mother frowned on his making friends with any of them except Lucas. His mother tolerated that because it was so difficult to determine where duty left off and friendship began. But this girl, Abigail, she seemed...interesting. Even without the tingling when they touched, she fascinated him.

All morning, the confusion from the meeting with his mother the day before swirled in his mind with what Lucas had said. Had he actually changed his mind completely? He was tense and confused and feeling out of it, but when he touched Abigail's hand, it was like she washed all of it away. After the initial burst of electricity, a feeling of calmness, not unlike the one he felt when he and his father had gone sailing, came over him. It surprised him, almost like he had been shocked with static electricity. More sustained and more powerful, though. He wondered if she felt it, too.

Anyway, he seemed to be thinking more clearly now. Whatever had infused him with this feeling of peace, he appreciated it. And he wanted to feel more of it.

As he made his way toward his mother's favorite office—she had three in different parts of the house—he pictured Abigail in his mind. She was slender. Willowy, that was the word. She moved gracefully like a willow in the wind. She wasn't too skinny, though. He noticed some curves under the maid's uniform. He liked that body type, slender and fit but with curving lines he could study…

He mentally slapped himself. What was he doing? He had other things to think about. Things like her heart-shaped face and the way her lips had pursed—just slightly—like she'd been considering something. Her nose was so cute; not too large or small, setting off her cheeks but not drawing attention away from her eyes. And oh, those eyes. He had only met them with his for the briefest of moments, but he felt himself sliding into them, and it took a monumental force of will to keep from being lost. They were blue and liquid, like chips of ice floating in a deep pool with a fire behind them, reflecting out and lighting up the room with their sheer intensity. He wondered if that rusty red was her true hair color or something that came from a bottle. Either way, it was fantastic the way it framed that pretty face of hers.

Ben shook his head to try to dispel the thoughts, not sure if he wanted to do so. She was just a maid, no one for him to get all worked up over. She *was* pretty, though she probably wouldn't be classified as beautiful. But he had other things he needed to think about. With a last image of those amazing eyes, he pushed it all from his mind and quickened his pace.

The second meeting with his mother that day was uncomfortable, as most meetings with her were. Ben had been close to his father when he was still alive but never quite connected to her. She was always aloof, a harsh taskmistress who rarely—if ever—showed affection. He wondered what he would be like if he had been raised by her without his father's influence. He shuddered at the thought.

Henry Mason—his friends all called him Hank—was a great man, as far as Ben was concerned. He was self-made, a hard worker and clever thinker who always seemed to be in the right place at the right time. He made his fortune the old-fashioned way, hard work and persistence, sprinkled with a bit of a gambler's spirit. More, though, he was a great father. Ben missed him dearly.

As hard as he worked, he would still take time off so that the two could go and camp and hike and explore nature. They spent so much time in nearby Yellowstone National Park and the Grand Tetons National Park, Ben considered the areas his back yard. He had thousands of cherished memories of time alone with his father, enjoying the wilderness together.

When Hank died suddenly of a massive stroke when Ben was fifteen, he felt like his world was ending. His mother had always been hands-off with him, and now he was left with only her. He rebelled, of course, as any fifteen-year-old would. He refused to obey her, he slammed doors, he hid from her, and he spent countless hours in his rec room, not even going to meals. No, he had never been close with his mother.

Asking her about Susan was more difficult than it should have been, but he did it. He had tried before, several times, but always found himself done with the discussion with his mother without having brought it up. The conversation only lasted a few minutes, but he left her office feeling like he had been beaten up. He wished he had thought of it the day before and asked then, but that weird light-headed feeling affected his ability to think clearly. Somehow she had given him no information, no answers to his questions, and he was outside the office door before he realized he had even left. He shook his head and aimlessly walked the hallway, not even paying attention to where he was.

"It's really none of your business…" a voice said from down the hall. Ben came out of his reverie and noticed he was near the laundry area at the edge of the building, near the kitchens. He wasn't sure about the voice, but he thought it was one of the laundry maids.

"It is my business," another voice said, cutting the first one off. "If you're overheard complaining when I'm near, it could reflect on me as well. I could get in trouble for it, too. I just started and don't need to be associated with gossip and whining. All I ask is that you do it elsewhere, when I'm not around."

Was that Abigail's voice? Ben moved closer, peeking around the corner to see who was talking.

Sure enough, Abigail was there, but without Mrs. Roberts. The other voice had belonged to Arianna Cox, a laundry maid. Sadie Ellis, a kitchen maid, was there, too. The two women glared at Abigail, their stances rigid, as if they were ready to go into battle.

"Listen, I understand complaining about your job and your employer," Abigail said. "I get it, I really do. Just don't do it around me. I have been told to help out in the laundry for a few hours so I have to be here. Go and whine about Mrs. Huntsman somewhere else. I don't need to get in trouble my second day because of negative speech. Isn't that what the last girl, Samantha, was fired for?"

"Don't get all snooty with me," Arianna said, looking to Sadie, who was nodding vigorously. "I'll say what I like when I like. You can't tell me not to."

"Let me tell you something about what I can and can't do," Abigail said, focusing those eyes on Arianna. The chips of ice looked like diamonds now, and the fire behind them seemed more intense. "I can talk to Mrs. Roberts and tell her I can't work with you two shrieking about how much you hate the lady of the manor. Where would that get you, do you think?"

She waited for a moment to see if there would be any reaction from the women. Both of them fidgeted, glancing at each other. Ben chuckled inwardly. They definitely did not want Abigail to talk to Mrs. Roberts about this.

Abigail's eyes softened and her voice grew warmer. "I don't want any friction, and I don't want to talk to Mrs. Roberts about this. I really do understand the need to complain occasionally, but I don't want to catch any backlash if the wrong person should hear. I'll finish up the laundry. Why don't you two go where you can talk in private?"

Arianna raised her chin and sniffed. Sadie tried to imitate her, but it was ruined by the darting of her eyes, from Arianna to Abigail and back again. "Fine, if you want to do all the work, go ahead. You better do a good job. I don't want to get in trouble for your laziness."

With that, both women strutted out of the laundry room as if they were queens. Ben ducked into a utility closet to avoid being seen. As the two passed, he heard them muttering something about "thinking she's more than she is" and "getting back at her."

As he left the closet to head back to his room, Ben smiled. So, this Abigail had a little fire in her, and some tact, too. She had more going for her than just her amazing eyes, it seemed. Those eyes flashed in his mind again as he walked, making him smile even more widely.

"I just don't know," Ben said to Lucas. "I still don't understand why Susan would leave without saying anything to me. We seemed like we were getting along so well."

"Hey," Lucas said, lounging on one of the sofas in the recreation room while Ben was shooting pool. "Don't take it so personally. Maybe there was an emergency and she had to go. She'll get in touch. She doesn't seem like the kind of girl who just leaves you hanging like that."

"Lucas, it's been almost a year. I've asked everyone else I know. Her parents say they don't know where she went, either. They filed a missing person's report. I knew it wouldn't do much good to ask my mother, but I did. That shows how desperate I am."

Ben looked at his friend. Lucas, at just over six feet

tall when he stood up straight, was gangly and awkward when not behind the wheel. His curly dark hair was normally covered with the little hat Margaret required him to wear to match his uniform. Somehow, he even made that silly hat look cool. He was street smart and smooth in the way only "people of the earth" could be. That's one of the names Ben's mother used to describe those without lots of money.

Lucas's father and grandfather were racecar drivers. Lucas had been, too, for a year or two. Growing up, he was always in and around cars. He could take an engine apart and put it back together before he had learned to ride a bike. Yes, Lucas could drive. Why he took a job as a driver for his family instead of driving racecars or making more money in other driving professions, Ben didn't know, but he was glad Lucas was here.

He had been driving and acting as Ben's personal valet for over nine years now. The young Mason was not interested in being friends with the rich kids his mother wanted him to associate with, and she would not allow him to have friends who weren't rich, not for long. He had no proof, but he thought she had even gone so far as to have the father of one of his friends fired so they had to move away. All for the security of the family and the bloodline, he was sure.

Lucas turned his brown eyes to Ben's blue. "Did your mother know about Susan? I mean, about how much you like her and how much time you two had been spending together?"

"I'm not sure. I don't think so. Why?"

"Oh," Lucas said, "just wondering."

Ben looked at his friend, saying nothing.

"Okay, okay," Lucas said after a long moment. "I

just wonder if your mom may have had something to do with Susan leaving suddenly. She's been gone for so long and her parents have no idea where she went." He watched Ben's face, as if looking for any sign of what he thought about the accusation. "She can be very persuasive, your mother, especially when she opens up the checkbook. Don't look at me like that. You know it's true. Maybe your mother made her an offer she couldn't refuse."

"Be careful, Lucas. People have been fired for saying less. People who had worked here longer than you have at this point."

"I know, I know. I'm just saying it to you, though. You won't turn me in, will you?" He winked at Ben.

Ben laughed. "No, I won't turn you in. I had the same thought myself, to be honest. That's why I wanted to ask her about it. I hope it wasn't that. I'd hate to think she'd just take some money and leave like that. Then again, compared to the alternative..."

"Yeah, well, I'm sure we'll find out eventually. I'm sure it's all a big misunderstanding."

"Maybe," Ben said.

"So, Ben, have you thought about what we talked about?" Lucas said.

"Yes, and I think you're wrong. I think I treat everyone equally."

"Uh, no." Lucas said. "You totally judge people by their money and their upbringing."

Ben eyed his friend. "No I don't. I treat people the way they deserve."

"The way *you* think they deserve, you mean."

"I am not a snob. Mother keeps me from associating with poor people. It's not by choice."

"You look down on others who are not as rich or

influential as your family," Lucas said.

"I do not," Ben countered. "You're my friend, aren't you? You're not rich."

"You're right, I'm not rich, but you don't hang out with me openly, and you won't call me your friend."

"Come on, Lucas," Ben said, sounding to himself to be too whiny. "You know I can't do that. My mother would take it out on you."

"Ben, you don't refer to me as your friend with anyone else. I understand it with your mother, but why with everyone else?"

"I…there's…it's because…" Ben's voice trailed off. "I guess you have a point. Maybe I do look down at people who aren't rich. At least a little bit. I didn't think so, but…"

"An even better question to ask yourself is if you see our new maid as a person or as just another hired helper. Would you be interested in dating her?"

"What? Why would you ask me that? Listen, my thoughts have been frazzled lately. Don't beat me up too hard, okay? Let's talk about it another time."

Lucas patted Ben's shoulder. "Okay, enough said. You really are a good person, Ben. Even if you are a rich guy. Just think about it, okay?"

10

~~~

*A*bigail went about her work, trying to figure out where she could go to get evidence that Margaret Hunstman was the one whose magic killed Olivia. Not being a chamber maid created difficulties because she would have to come up with excuses to be where she could find something that had magical residue and wouldn't be missed. That Harper woman seemed to think she was a guard for the entire area around Margaret Huntsman's rooms. The last thing Abbie needed was to get fired for theft.

She was still irritated with her confrontation with the other two women a few days before. Stupid women. Not only were they petty and unthinking, they were onlies. She hated it that the situation had stuck in her mind and was affecting her even now.

Abigail straightened from dusting under the hallway table on which a small sculpture sat. Out of the corner of her eye, she saw movement and shifted her eyes, leaving her head immobile. It was Benjamin Mason. She allowed a small smile to play across her face before she smoothed it away. He seemed to be popping up quite often since she'd met him four days before.

She saw him look around to see if anyone else was watching. There was no one else in sight, so he started walking toward her.

"Good morning, Abigail," he said, smiling at her.

"Good morning, Master Mason."

"No, no, please. Please don't 'Master Mason' me. It's Ben, just Ben."

"I would get in a lot of trouble if anyone heard me calling you that, Master Mason."

He looked into her eyes as if to see if she was teasing him. The subtle shift in his, along with a tiny crinkle in the skin around his eyes, told her he figured out that she was.

"Fine, then only when no one else is around. Please."

"Okay, Ben." She smiled mischievously at him. "When no one else is around. But only if you call me Abbie."

"It's a deal, Abbie," he said as he reached out his hand to shake hers. When they clasped hands, she felt that little jolt again.

He stood there staring at her, not releasing her hand, looking into her eyes. After a time, he started, and his eyes widened as he realized he was just standing there holding her hand. He released it hastily and color came to his face.

"Well, then," he said, "I...uh...how have things been going? Do you like it here?"

"It's very nice," Abigail said. "I'm still getting used

to things, but I think I'll enjoy being here."

"Good, good. You make sure you let me know if there's anything I can do to help you acclimate and to make you more comfortable."

"There is one thing," she said, leaning in close to whisper in his ear.

"Yes?" he matched her tone and volume.

"There is a guy who's been lurking around. I'm not sure of his intentions, and it makes me a little nervous."

Ben's face went blank and the color left it. "Oh. I'm...I'm sorry Abbie. Have I been making myself a nuisance? The last thing I want is to make you uncomfortable. Please forgive me. I—" Abbie's hand on his arm made his stop speaking and look at her. When he saw her smile, he let out a long breath. "You're teasing me," he said.

"Uh, yep." She patted his arm.

"Whew. Okay." Ben was silent for a moment. "Tell me if I bother you. You don't need that on top of starting a new job and all that."

Abbie laughed. "No, it's fine. You're not bothering me. I do wonder about your intentions, though."

"That's easy enough," he said. "You are fascinating to me. I want to learn everything there is to know about you."

"Everything, huh? That's a lot of stuff."

"I am willing to put in the time," he said, finally smiling and looking more comfortable. "More than willing."

"Why don't we just see what happens and not sweat it too much," Abbie said.

"One thing," Ben countered. "Tell me one thing about you, and I'll let you get back to work. Anything at all.'"

Abbie thought for a moment. She shouldn't be flirting with this man, especially in the middle of a mission, but she felt so comfortable with him, so close already. What harm could one little piece of information do?

"My favorite color is sea foam green."

"It is?" Ben said. "That's good to know. I will definitely remember it. Thank you. I'll let you go back to work now." He turned to leave but stopped when she put her hand on his arm again.

"Hold on a second," she said. What about you? You have to give me some information about yourself. It's no fair otherwise."

"I guess that's fair. My favorite color is blue." He brushed her cheek with his fingertips, causing goose bumps to run up and down her neck. "The exact color of your eyes." He looked deeply into them, and he seemed to shudder as he tore his gaze away. The light seemed to dim when their eye contact was broken, making her sad for the loss. His own blue eyes seemed to hold mysteries enough to explore for the rest of her life.

"I'll leave now," he said, and then he turned and walked quickly away. She giggled under her breath. He looked like he was fleeing.

Abigail settled into a routine, doing her work efficiently and without direct supervision. Mrs. Roberts generally left her alone after the first few days, confident that Abigail knew the rules of the house and that she would do the job she was hired to do. She occasionally saw the Housekeeper, and the older woman would smile at her and ask if she had any problems. Abbie would tell her no and continue whatever task she'd been performing.

She hadn't found anything with magical residue so far in her work, and she had tried. Her talent for detecting the effects of magic was something she needed to focus on, like background noise that didn't make sense until you directed attention to it. She could concentrate and make her detection more sensitive, but she wasn't going to go about the house looking as if she was straining to focus on something. People would think she was strange. Besides, if the residue wasn't strong enough for her to detect without effort, it was probably too weak for Isabella to get a good reading on it. She would just have to keep looking.

A week into the job, she tried to get near Margaret's rooms on the third floor, but every time she came anywhere close to them, she spotted Harper, looking like she was guarding the hallway in front of them. She had to abruptly change the direction she was walking to avoid looking like she was going toward the forbidden area. It was frustrating.

One time, Mrs. Roberts called Abbie to her as she passed in the hall.

"Oh, Abigail, good. Here, take this tea to Ms. Huntsman. She is in the office near her rooms. Harper is currently engaged in something else. Hurry now. Ms. Huntsman does not like to be kept waiting."

It was the break she had been waiting for, a chance to scope out Margaret's rooms and see if she detected anything. As she headed toward her destination, though, she started to worry. Her talent of being able to sense magic and magical residue was fairly rare, but it was not extremely so. In fact, in just her small coven, there were two with such a talent, her and Isabella.

What if Margaret Huntsman had the talent, too? It allowed Abbie to sense magical ability in people. If Margaret could do that, she would pick Abbie out as a witch and know she was a spy. She could seize Abbie or kill her on the spot. She hadn't thought of that. Talents were generally kept secret outside of the covens, so Abbie could not be sure if she was at risk.

On the ten-point scale most covens used, Abigail was almost a level seven witch. Between what she had seen in the vision and heard from other accounts, Margaret was most likely at level eight. That was the same level of Abigail's mother's power. If the woman attacked her, Abbie probably wouldn't survive.

As she passed through the halls, Abbie tried to figure out what to do. She could trip and spill the tea, requiring her to go back and get more, but that would only delay things. She couldn't think of what to do, so she trudged inexorably toward the room. And possibly toward her doom.

When she arrived at the carved wooden door to the office Mrs. Roberts had told her Margaret was using, she knocked twice and opened the door, as etiquette required. Taking a deep breath, she entered, carrying the tray with the full teapot, a cup on a saucer, three wedges of lemon on a plate, a single spoon on a napkin, and a small ceramic container of honey.

"Bring it in, girl," Margaret said, only glancing at her before turning her attention back to the papers on her desk.

Abigail set the tray down on a side table and brought the cup and saucer to her. She filled it with tea as Margaret finally looked up at her.

"You're the new maid, correct?" Margaret said.

"Yes, ma'am. I'm Abigail." She made a small curtsy.

"Abigail. Yes." Margaret looked into her eyes, her dark hazel orbs drilling into Abbie's.

The other woman sat stone still, looking into Abbie's eyes as if trying to read her soul. She could feel her face flush and her scalp started to warm. In another moment, she would have beads of sweat on her forehead. The woman knew. She did have the talent and recognized Abbie for a witch and a spy. Abigail frantically thought of what spells she would use, how she would fight, what she would try to do. She almost cast the first spell to make the odds more even.

"You're pretty enough," Margaret said. "Go on with you. I can put my own honey in. I won't need you further."

Abigail almost sighed as she controlled the exhalation so that the woman in front of her wouldn't recognize her near-panic. "Yes, ma'am." She turned and headed for the door.

"Oh, and Abigail," Margaret's voice followed her.

"Yes ma'am."

"Thank you for the tea."

"You're welcome, ma'am."

Abbie went through the door and closed it behind her. She slumped as all the nervous energy left her body, making her feel like a wet noodle. Movement from the corner of her eye made her turn her head to see Harper coming up the hall. Her face was even more tightly drawn and her mouth even more pinched than when Abbie had met her that first day.

She looked at Abigail accusingly.

"Tea," Abbie said, and walked down the hall toward the kitchens. She could feel the woman's eyes on her until she turned the corner.

It wasn't until she was well away from the room and the hallway that she realized she had been too nervous about being found out to even notice if anything in the room held magical signatures. She had kept her talent searching, at least, and felt the magic in Margaret, of course—that was too powerful to ignore—but nothing else registered.

She thought back, picturing the room, trying to distinguish something that might be important, but she could not. The simple truth was she had failed spectacularly in observing anything useful. She would have to do better next time.

11

*B*en sat in what he considered the most important room in the estate, one that always made him feel closer to his father. It was his father's trophy room, or as Ben had come to think of it: his gun room.

At times, he would go to the room his father had set aside to display the different things he had collected. It was a large chamber, left exactly as it was when Hank Mason was alive. Thickly stuffed leather couches and chairs, a good-sized fireplace, paintings on the wall, sculptures and trophies on pedestals and shelves, books, and of course, there were guns.

There were one hundred thirty-seven different firearms in the room, most in glass cases. The collection held everything from black powder weapons from the time period when the Masons had first settled in the area to high-powered rifles and handguns, now lonely in the room without his father to keep them company. Ben could still feel Hank

Mason's presence here, and it calmed him.

Despite the collection, Ben's father had never hunted an animal in his life, though he did routinely take out one or more of his guns and shoot targets at the range. He had even dabbled in target shooting competitions when he was younger, winning a few awards, the trophies for which validated the formal name of the room.

Ben himself had shot many of the guns he could see as he sat on one of the couches. Those were good days, when his father took him to the range and they shot until the evening came. The boy had become a fair aim with many of them. It was spending time with his father that mattered, though.

He got up from the couch and walked around the room, stopping at guns that had particularly strong memories for him. He ran his fingers along the marble statues of ancient warriors and the bronze statues of horses rearing or galloping. He inhaled the musty smell of old leather from the books neatly arranged on the bookshelves. He sighed at the loss of that innocent, happy time when he really had no cares in the world but, of course, didn't see it that way then.

Ben heard a sound from the doorway and turned in time to see a flash of black and white moving back into the hall.

"Wait," he said, hurrying to the doorway to see who it was. The maid turned to face him, already halfway down the hall with her cart of cleaning tools and supplies. It was Abigail.

"Oh, Abigail, it's you," he said. "Come back, please. Were you going to dust in here?"

She walked slowly back to him, pushing her cart. "I was going to, but please don't let me disturb you. I can do it later."

"No, it's fine. I was just leaving. Really, go ahead."

"I would hate to impose," Abigail said. "It's no—"

"You're not imposing. Please, come on in. I have other things I can be doing, anyway."

"If you're sure…"

"I am." Ben reached for her hand and when his touched hers, he felt that jolt again, like he did when they first met. It almost made him let go, but he didn't. Instead, he tried not to let her see there was anything odd and pulled her through the doorway.

"Have you seen my father's trophy room before?" he asked her.

"Once," she said. "I came in to dust and clean the glass on the cases once before."

"Oh, so there's no need for me to give you the grand tour. Too bad."

Abigail looked at him blankly. She seemed uncomfortable, then he realized he was still holding her hand. He let it go. Slowly. That jolt he felt, it was weaker than it had been. He mourned its loss already.

"Did your father hunt?" she asked.

"No. He didn't believe in hurting things, least of all animals. He told me once that you can find beauty in just about anything. These guns in his collection all sparked his interest and appreciation. The styling, the lines of their design, the way the mechanisms moved, there was something about each one of them. It probably seems silly."

"No, not at all," Abigail said as she walked up to a musket mounted on a stand. "This musket, for example. The way the hammer is curved with just a little bit of ornate design on it and the way the butt sweeps back, I could see calling it graceful, even beautiful. The work it does is ugly, but the object, yes, I can see your father's point."

Ben stared at the new maid, standing there in her black and white uniform, her red hair falling in ringlets and swept back with a piece of pale green hair ribbon. She noticed and fidgeted.

"What?" she said.

"That's almost exactly how my father described that gun. It was one of his favorites. You are something else, Abigail Henderson. I think my father would have loved you."

She looked around, obviously uncomfortable.

"Well, I better get going. I would hate to get you in trouble by holding up your work. Have a good day, Abigail."

"You too, Master Mason. You too."

He thought of insisting she call him Ben, but he had already made her uncomfortable enough. He couldn't help saying one more thing. "Abbie, I'm glad you came here. This room seems…brighter with you present."

He walked away before she had a chance to respond. The last thing he wanted was to embarrass her. As he went through the door, he looked back and saw her looking after him, a confused look on her face. *Yeah, her and me both*, he thought and headed down the hall.

*****

Over the next month Abigail saw Ben more often than chance would dictate. At times, it seemed that every time she turned around, he would be there. She didn't notice at first, reveling in their chance encounters. They would speak a few words, little things about the weather or some bit of news one or the other had heard, then they would go back to whatever they had been doing.

As time went on, though, she got the definite feeling that he was searching her out, "accidentally" almost running into her in the hall as she carried out her tasks and then stopping to chat for a brief time because it was polite to do so. She smiled at the thought. Was he pursuing her?

She didn't have much experience in relationships. She had always been too busy trying to fill the hole her mother's death had left by throwing herself into the work of her coven. She was fairly sure he was flirting with her, but she wasn't positive. All she knew was that she liked it, and that concerned her.

"Hi Abbie," Ben said, looking up and down the hall they were in to see if anyone else was around. "How are you?"

Abigail scanned the area herself and, finding no evidence there was anyone else around, responded, "Hi, Ben. I'm great. How is your day?"

"Fine...now." His smile was so charming and sweet, it made her heart ache.

"Are you off to do anything exciting?" she asked.

"No. I'm just heading down to the gym to work out." He paused as if he had nothing else to say. The silence seemed to stretch and just as Abigail was about to say something, he continued. "What about you, what do you do to keep that body of...I mean, to look so...uh...to stay fit?" He was blushing furiously and it was so cute she wanted to hug him.

"I run from all the guys after me," she deadpanned.

His nostrils flared and his eyes widened, then he blinked. It was a good two seconds before he finally decided it was safe for him to laugh.

"I better get back to work," she said and started to turn.

"Yeah. I better get going, too." His fingertips brushed the skin on her arm as he turned to go the other way. "It was nice seeing you. Have a good day."

"Thank you," Abbie said as she smiled at him. "You too. Don't overdo it and hurt yourself."

"What?"

"You know, during your workout. Don't hurt yourself."

"Oh," he said, "right. I'll try to be careful."

As they went their separate ways, she felt his gaze as he turned to look at her one last time. She smiled.

That was the way of it, chance meetings and awkward conversations. She thought he probably liked her but couldn't convince herself fully it was true. He was, after all, good-looking and rich and part of a powerful family that looked down on those with less money. On the other hand, she herself had a definite bias against onlies and an even stronger one against fire warlocks, but she still enjoyed being near him.

No, there was no future for them, even if, in moments of weakness, she thought about how it might be to be with him. She promised herself she would not get caught up in the little scenarios that played in her mind. Her mission was important, much more important than his blue eyes and gorgeous smile. She would remind herself as often as necessary. No distractions could be allowed.

Still, Abigail did think of Ben. When he appeared

suddenly as she was going about her chores, her heart always did a little dance and she found herself trying to hold down a smile. The last thing she wanted was for him to see her smile. Then he would know how much she enjoyed interacting with him, that she was fond of him. She had to play it cool and maybe he'd get tired of popping up in front of her every time she turned around.

Then again, when she got halfway through the day and he still had not appeared, she found herself worrying that he may have lost interest and moved onto other pursuits. What was wrong with her? She was being contradictory and scatterbrained. How did the man do that to her?

12

*B*en sighed as he tightened the tie around his neck for another of his mother's parties. He hated these things. These soirées were nothing but an excuse for boring people to get together and brag about how much money they made or the amazing vacation they had just taken. He hoped it would end early.

Putting his jacket on—a navy double-breasted suit rather than a tuxedo because this was an "informal" party—he checked himself in the mirror. The sad eyes looking back at him didn't give him much hope for a mercifully quick end to the festivities. Maybe he'd get a chance to see Abigail, though. His blue eyes brightened and the grim line of the mouth in front of him quirked into a small smile.

When Margaret held parties, all the staff helped to serve and do whatever else was needed to make the attendees as happy as possible. Even the part-time staff, those who didn't live at the estate but who covered the days the full-time staff didn't work, were called in to man a tray or take coats at the door. Abigail would definitely be working, but Ben had no idea where. He'd keep his eyes open. It could be fun, like searching for secret treasure.

"Do you like these things all of a sudden?" Lucas's voice came at him from the doorway. "I don't believe I've ever seen you smile for one of these parties."

"I was just thinking of something else," Ben said. "I still hate them. You're lucky you only have to take people's cars and park them."

"Yeah, right. I only have to deal with every one of the guests threatening to have me beaten if there is a scratch on their car when they get it back. That's my idea of fun."

"I guess we both have it bad, huh? I feel like I need a drink."

"Ben, my man, you don't even drink. I don't believe I've ever seen you have more than one, maybe two drinks in a whole evening."

"I might start if there are any more of these parties. Hell, I might start smoking, too. Maybe I'll get a tattoo."

Lucas laughed and slapped Ben on the shoulder. "That would make your mother happy. Try to have some fun tonight, okay? I'll talk to you later."

Ben watched Lucas leave. He thought parking cars and having people threaten him might be a definite improvement over what the night held for him. The men and women his age were the worst. All they talked about was the fun they were having with their parents' money or how they were getting more responsibility in the family businesses or how "poor people" were ruining the country. It's no wonder

Lucas thought him biased against others who didn't have as much money as him. That's all he heard at these social gatherings.

Well, there was nothing to do but to get it over with. With a last look in the mirror, he turned on his heels and headed out of the room. His mother would want him in place before most of the guests arrived.

"Benjamin," Margaret said as he came down the main staircase to the ground floor. "Good, you're not late." She looked him over, fiddled with his collar. "Why didn't you wear the charcoal suit? It looks better on you than the navy blue."

"I just grabbed this one," he said, sighing inwardly. "I can change if you like." He had found it was almost always easier just to do as Margaret wished rather than to argue.

"No," she said, her head tilting slightly as she looked him in the eyes. "No, that's fine. You are presentable enough, I suppose."

Presentable enough. Ben took his place beside his mother and waited. He didn't have to wait long.

As the guests trickled in, Ben and his mother greeted them. It was boring, but at least it was like a finely scripted performance, one he didn't have to think about. "Good evening. Wonderful to see you. You look fantastic. It is good to see you again. You are looking younger every time I see you. Welcome to our home." From the other side: "You are looking well, Ben. What have you been up to, young man? When can we expect to attend your wedding? Have you taken an active role in the family business?" and other intrusive questions. Still, it made time pass without him having to participate in any real conversation.

As he greeted the guests, he scanned the entry area for Abigail. He didn't see her, but that wasn't unexpected. If she was called into serving duty—that's where he would put a beautiful young woman if he were in charge—she would be in one of the larger rooms.

After greeting the bulk of the guests, his mother looked at him coolly and jerked her head slightly toward the main ballroom. He understood. He was to mingle now. Suppressing another sigh, he nodded to her and walked slowly toward his task.

As he made his way to the ballroom, Ben's head swiveled back and forth, eyes scanning the masses of people milling about. His heart sped up with every flash of black and white, but none of the servants carrying trays about were Abigail. Several people spoke to him, but he only made generic statements, not really even thinking about what he was saying, and continued on his way. In the back of his mind, he hoped he hadn't been rude to anyone. If he had been, he would hear about it from his mother, he had no doubt.

He continued to look around when he got to his destination. His mother wanted him to mingle and make their guests feel welcome, but all he could think about was that red hair and those piercing blue eyes. Where was she?

"Drink, sir?" someone said from his left. It didn't register in his mind. He kept up his searching.

"Sir?" the voice said again, insistent.

Ben realized the voice had been talking to him. He absently put his hand out toward the voice to get a drink, his head and eyes reluctantly following a moment later. When his attention was fixed on where his hand was, he almost jumped. He was looking right into Abigail's face.

His eyes widened and his heart leapt. Taking a breath took two tries. "Abbie," he said, and then realized what had come out of his mouth. "I mean, Miss Henderson. I was looking for…that is…you weren't…uh, you look fantastic." He cursed softly under his breath. "I, uh…a drink. Yes. Thank you." He took a drink and emptied the glass in one long gulp. He replaced the empty glass on the tray and took another.

Abigail was silent, looking slightly breathless and completely breathtaking. She had one of the fancier maid uniforms on, one that looked tailored for her, a bit more revealing. She was wearing more makeup than normal, too. She looked like she was ready to go to a party herself. Ben realized his eyes had strayed to scanning her, and he felt himself flush. His eyes snapped back to hers.

"I better see if anyone else needs a drink," she said, her smile at the same time mischievous and pleased, like a cat who had figured out how to get into a bag of treats. She somehow pulled off a graceful curtsy while keeping the tray perfectly level. Tray or not, her fluid movements made the room seem to heat up.

She turned to go but then swung her head around to meet his eyes again. "It was very nice to see you, Master Mason." She leaned in so that she was only a few inches from him, and he leaned toward her slightly, too. "You look fantastic, too." She winked so quickly he wasn't even sure she had done it, and then she was gone.

Ben stood there for a moment, watching her move

among the guests, offering drinks and taking empty glasses. He loved the way she moved, loved watching her move. So graceful, almost like water. He couldn't help but follow her with his eyes. A word popped into his head: sexy.

Remembering where he was, he shook his head and threw back the drink he had in his hand. He surreptitiously flicked his eyes to and fro to see if anyone had noticed him staring at the new maid, but it didn't seem like anyone had. He breathed a sigh of relief. The last thing he needed was for his mother to fire Abigail because he showed interest in her. He'd have to be more careful.

Replaying that smile in his mind, he formed a small smile himself and set about chatting with guests, all the while keeping on the watch for the elusive woman who was so interesting to him.

As he made his rounds, Ben observed the guests and how they interacted. He saw it as a dance. A clumsy one, but a dance all the same. Currents of power and status permeated everything. Those in the higher echelon lorded it over those in the lower and basked in the attention. Those not quite so high scurried around, seeking favor of those above them but stopping occasionally to enjoy their privilege above those beneath them. They all swarmed around those like his mother, trying to curry favor or just experience a small piece of the radiance of the elite.

He couldn't sit idly and watch the entire time, of course. As the son of Margaret Huntsman, many tried to impress him as well, hoping that as his star rose, he would remember them. Ben found it all tiresome, hypocritical, and sad.

"You don't seem to be having much fun," a voice

whispered near his ear. He started and looked over. It was Abigail, somehow right next to him though he had been watching for her all night.

"Yes," he said, "I would like another drink." He made a show of selecting his glass carefully as he whispered back to her. "Honestly, I hate these things. How are you enjoying the evening?" He chuckled a little at that.

"I am finding out the most interesting things," she said, keeping her face neutral but showing her humor in those blue eyes of hers.

"Really?" he said. "Anything I would find interesting?"

"I would think so, especially the talk about the big announcement."

Ben had been keeping his face calm also, scanning the other guests to see if they noticed he had said more than a few words to a servant. At this, though, his face slipped and he showed curiosity. "Announcement? What announcement?"

Abigail shifted her eyes to the side. "That one," she said. She winked quickly at him and flitted off to offer her drinks to a large man whose name Ben couldn't recall.

Ben looked to where Abigail had indicated and saw his mother climbing the stairs. She went up five steps and then turned back toward the mass of guests. She didn't have to clear her throat or do anything else to command attention. Everyone already had one eye on her, so the room quickly quieted when it seemed she would speak.

"Ladies and gentlemen," she said in a normal speaking voice. She was heard easily in the silence that had fallen. "I would like to welcome you to my home.

It is too seldom this house has so many interesting—and influential—people within. I am happy to see you all."

She looked around the room, making eye contact with a few of the guests. When her eyes found Ben, they stopped on him, locked onto his eyes for a moment, then passed on.

"I will not make a grand speech," she continued, "but there is an important announcement that I would like to make." She paused for a moment, looking out over the crowd. Her eyes met Ben's again, and he felt a chill.

"You all know my son Benjamin, of course," she said, pointing to him. The chill intensified as all eyes went to him. "Benjamin, dear, why don't you come up here with me?"

His mother knew people would be looking at him, taking their attention away from her, so moving him next to her would help her to keep the focus near her, if not on her. Ben drank down what was left in his glass and mindlessly held out the empty tumbler. Abigail was suddenly there, taking it from him and putting it on her tray.

"Breathe," she whispered, and then slipped into the crowd.

He did breathe. Deeply. Putting on a smile he was sure everyone could see was fake, he made his way through the parting throng up to the step just below where his mother stood. She reached out and patted him on the shoulder as if he were a prized pet and had performed a trick on command. He swallowed again and made sure his smile was fixed.

"As I was saying," his mother continued, "you all know Benjamin and what a fine young man he is. You also know how hard it is to find a suitable young man these days." She shook her head and put on the most convincing look of sadness he had ever seen her wear. How long had she practiced that look in the mirror?

"Ah, but I promised to be brief. I am happy to announce the engagement of my son, Benjamin Mason, to Penelope Moore. Penelope, please come on up."

13

$\sim\sim\sim$

$\mathcal{B}$en felt like the roof had fallen on him. He couldn't breathe with the tons of concrete and wood pressing down on his chest. He saw, in a sort of fuzzy, dreamlike fashion, a young woman coming up the stairs. Did his mother just say what he thought he heard? Time seemed to be moving more slowly than normal.

He knew Penelope. She was a year or two younger than him and belonged to a wealthy family from Casper, Wyoming. She wasn't ugly, oh no. In fact, she was beautiful, when her face wasn't pinched in disdain over the "little people who seemed to spread like weeds," ruining her enjoyment of life.

She was about five and a half feet tall—a little taller in the heels—and the dress she wore hugged the subtle curves of her body. Her oval face was set off with big brown eyes and full lips and her dark hair fell loosely a few inches past her shoulders. She was definitely pleasant to look at.

Most of the young men present at the party would have killed to be in his shoes. Most had tried, all unsuccessfully, to catch her interest in the past. He had not spent much time with her, disliking everything about her attitude and interests. She was beautiful, sure, but he would rather marry Mrs. Roberts. He was miserable in a five minute conversation with this harpy; he couldn't marry her.

Ben realized that he probably had been standing there for much too long with a blank look on his face. Penelope stood next to him, holding out her hand.

He blinked and when his eyes focused again, Abigail was the first thing he saw. She was in the back of the room, near one of the doorways. Looking carefully left and right to make sure no one was watching her, she motioned to her face with her hand and put on an exaggerated smile. He understood and forced his shocked face into a semblance of a smile, then took Penelope's hand. It was cold and clammy, so different than when he had touched Abigail's hand. The maid's hand was warm and full of life, even delivering that shock or pulse of energy he still wondered about.

"So, there you have it," Margaret Huntsman said. "The newly engaged couple. We'll let them have some time together now. Please, everyone, enjoy yourselves. When a date has been set, you will all receive invitations to the wedding."

Ben's mother left him there, with his new fiancée. He dropped Penelope's hand, said something to her—he could never recall exactly what it was later—and went quickly to the bathroom. He felt like he might throw up.

He washed his face with cold water to try to revive

his flagging thought process. Standing in front of the mirror, palms on the counter, he lifted his dripping chin up so he could look his reflection in the eye. What was he going to do? He didn't want to marry that shrew his mother had shackled him with.

His clean-shaven cheeks, strong jaw, his sand-colored hair that framed his face and contrasted with his blue eyes stared back at him. He wore an expression somewhere between disgust and nausea. He was young and good-looking, he thought. He didn't need his mother to arrange a marriage for him. His image's mouth tightened into a thin line.

His father had always stressed old-fashioned values about marriage and how important it was. And he spoke about being with someone, sharing your life with them, being a part of them. Ben would not cheapen it by marrying for expediency, or for political or business reasons. Isn't that what this was, a marriage of alliance?

No, he wouldn't do it. He *couldn't* do it. When he married—*if* he married—it would be because he loved the woman, not because his mother wanted more business connections. No. He would put his foot down this time. She could not make him marry Penelope. He would just have to discuss it with his mother. After the party.

His mind made up, he toweled off his wet face, checked his reflection one more time to make sure everything was in order, and walked out of the bathroom.

Right into Abigail.

She was standing there, apparently waiting for him, empty tray hanging loosely from one hand. She didn't flinch as he stopped abruptly to keep from running her down. His body came to rest mere inches from hers. It didn't seem to faze her. It made *him* nervous.

"You didn't know," she stated.

"No," he said. "Did you?"

"Yes, I heard some gossip from that…from your fiancée."

He sighed. "Please don't call her that. I'll straighten this thing up. After the party, I am going to talk to my mother and get this resolved."

She eyed him, then looked up and down the hallway to see if anyone was near. "You'll pardon me for saying, Master Mason—Ben, but I don't really think talking to her will do any good. She seems to have it all planned out."

Despite how he felt, Ben allowed himself a small smile. "I like it when you call me Ben. I would appreciate it if you would continue to do so when no one is around to get you in trouble."

Abigail flashed a conspiratorial smile. "I will…when no one is around to get me in trouble."

"Deal," he said and had the urge to take up her hand and shake on the agreement. He didn't, though. "I know she probably won't change her mind, but I have to try."

"Would it really be so bad to marry her?" Abigail asked. "She is beautiful, after all. I've seen how all the other guys follow her around and try to catch her eye."

"She is good-looking, I'll grant that," Ben said, "but that only goes a quarter of an inch down. Underneath, she's all warts and pus and oozing sores. She's a hideous monster."

Abbie giggled softly and Ben felt his body warm. "That bad, huh?"

"Worse. If she could only be more like you."

"Oh, with less warts and pus and stuff?" she teased. "I better get back to work. Good luck on your conversation with your mother. Hopefully you can convince her. No one should have to marry someone they don't want to."

Ben looked into her eyes as he nodded slowly. "Yes, I agree. Miss Hen—I mean, Abbie, I would really like to talk with you sometime. I mean, really talk with you. I—"

"No," she said firmly. "I really don't think that would be a good idea. I'll see you around, though. I understand that you live here." She winked again, turned, and walked off, tray swinging.

Ben watched her until she turned the corner and went out of sight. She looked over her shoulder as she made the turn and smiled at him. When he realized he was standing there with his mouth partway open, staring at where she had been, he shook his head and closed his mouth with a click. He better spend the rest of the night rehearsing what he was going to say to his mother. He was definitely not looking forward to that conversation.

"Come in, Benjamin," Margaret Huntsman said when Ben knocked on her study door late that night, after most of the party guests had departed. His mother had left the party almost an hour earlier and he knew where she would be: in her study trying to get some work done.

Ben took a deep breath and then let it out slowly. He opened the door and stepped into the room. His mother was sitting at the big desk directly across from the entryway. She had her glasses on and looked to have been reading through some reports.

"Let me save you the trouble of asking," she said to him, tilting her head so she could look over the top of her glasses. "I will not reconsider. You will marry Penelope as soon as we can arrange a suitable wedding. I know you don't want to settle down and become responsible, but you have, at most, a year to continue to act like a child. I think it will be closer to six months."

"But," he said, hating the whine in his voice, "I don't even like Penelope. It's not that I don't want to get married. It's that I want to marry someone I love. I will never love that woman."

"Oh, Benjamin." His mother took her glasses off and looked him in the eye. "Love is overrated. You don't need love. What you need is a good solid plan for the future. Penelope's family owns some of the few industries Huntsman Consolidated does not in this state. It's a perfect match. She is young and healthy, not to mention good-looking, and your children will inherit fine traits from both of you. The best part, of course, is that between our holdings and theirs, it makes for a very good alliance."

"I don't care about any of that."

"Benjamin," Margaret said firmly, "you've had enough time being the little boy who thinks only of himself. It's past time for you to grow up and accept the responsibility that comes with being an adult. The responsibility that comes with being a Huntsman."

"I'm not a Huntsman. I'm—"

"Yes, yes, I know. And you know what I mean. You need to set aside your selfish wants and do what is right for the family. The family, the company, is more important than your petty desires and silly, childish dreams. You will marry Penelope, our families' businesses will be strengthened, and we will make more money than ever before."

"Don't we have enough money?" Ben asked.

His mother looked shocked. "Enough money? Benjamin, dear, one can never have enough money. Or power. Your marriage will help us get more of both. It's perfect."

"It's not," Ben said. "I don't love her. I will never love her. I won't marry her."

The fire near his mother's desk was blazing, but the look she gave him made him feel like the temperature had dropped twenty degrees. "You will, and that's final."

Her eyes reflected the firelight, and he could have sworn they glowed for a moment. The room tilted, and he felt another one of those strange dizzy spells coming upon him. Ben closed his eyes for a moment, put his hand up to squeeze his temples, and then opened his eyes again.

"You can't make me marry someone," he said. "I won't do it. Find another way to make an alliance. I'll be no part of it."

Margaret's face changed. Just for the briefest of moments, she showed emotion. Was that surprise? She mastered her expression instantly, and he wondered if he had imagined it.

"Benjamin, you are beginning to irritate me. You will marry Penelope, or I will cut you off. No more allowance, no more credit, nothing. Make too big an issue of it, you will be evicted from this house. You will be penniless and homeless. Do not push me in this. As I said when you came in, this is going to happen, with your cooperation or without. Now leave. I have work to do."

He found himself walking out the door before he even realized he had decided to leave. How did she do that? One thing was for sure, he would not let her win this argument. It was his life they were talking about. He would not let her dictate who he would marry. He would not.

When Ben returned to his room, Lucas was there waiting for him.

"Dude," was all Lucas said.

"Yeah, I know," Ben said as he fell into a chair. "I had no idea. Did you know anything about it?"

"Come on, Ben. If I'd known anything about it, I would have told you. You know that. I wouldn't leave you hanging like that."

"Yeah, I know. I'm still in shock. I can't believe I'm trapped like this. There has to be a way out."

Lucas fixed Ben with a look of astonishment. "Really? You think you'll be able to outsmart your mother? No offense, Ben, but you don't really have all that much experience in laying clever plans that have no escape. Or of defeating them. Your mother is a master."

"I hardly think you bringing that up right now is helping, Lucas."

"Oh, yeah," Lucas said. "Sorry."

Ben closed his eyes for a moment. "I know it will be difficult, but she's still human. We have to think of something."

"I'm with you, Ben," Lucas said. "Just for curiosity's sake, though. If you get married, will I still be your driver and manservant?"

Lucas never saw the couch cushion that hit him in the side of the head.

14

~~~

"We're almost ready," Helen Shapiro said to Margaret.

"Excellent," Margaret said, tipping her teacup and taking a sip. She had found that drinking—any type of drink, but it worked especially well with tea or coffee—allowed her time during a conversation to study others. And to carefully plan what she would say next. Not that she needed it in this case, but old habits were old habits.

Helen was her Executive Assistant, officially, but she was much more. She was Margaret's right hand, the one who controlled the day-to-day operation of her most important work: her plotting to control or eliminate the other factions of witches.

She had known Helen since they were children, and the large woman had one of the most deviously clever minds Margaret had ever known. Sometimes she didn't know what she would do without her.

"Once we have taken care of the water witches, the other two factions will fold easily enough," Helen said. "The air witches will do whatever it takes to avoid trouble, and the earth witches will find that their stubborn, unmoving tactics will not avail them in this case. They will be alone, isolated. We will take them out singly or in small groups. By the time they realize they need to gather together to make a united stand, they will be finished. Besides, our work has already made the different elements suspicious of each other. They may just start doing our work for us."

"Good," Margaret cooed, "very good."

"Frank Gibraltar is doing a great job on his end. You were right about him, I guess. He doesn't look like much, but he gets things done."

"He does. Where is he right now?"

Helen looked at her phone. "I think he's recruiting. He says he'll need more onlies for the next phase of the plans."

"Yes, I believe he is right about that."

Helen's gaze shifted down toward the rug sprawled out on the hardwood floor. "What about the other Council members, and the Grand Flame herself? Many of them oppose your ideas on this."

"What they do not know, they cannot argue against. We must do our job and complete the tasks in front of us. Let me worry about the Council. I have other allies worth far more."

"Fine," Helen said, tilting her head and looking at her friend. "I will let you know when I have a more definite time frame. Like I said, it shouldn't be long now."

"Very well," Margaret said, lifting her tea cup to

her lips again.

"Margaret," Helen said. "Was this the best time to do this thing with your dear son? I mean, I know you want him to have heirs and all that, but now? Things are heating up with our plans. It seems like a distraction."

"Yes, possibly. Benjamin has been becoming more resistant to my magic, for some reason. I need another thing to tie him to me, another source of leverage."

"And you think this Penelope woman will do that? It was obvious to me and everyone else that he's not interested in her. How will that connect him to you?"

"She will not help there," Margaret said. "You're right about that. If he has a child, though, that will be better leverage than I could ever buy."

She took a small sip as she watched Helen over the rim of the cup as she turned to leave. "Oh, and Helen…" Margaret said. When the woman turned to face her, she continued, "…good work on this so far, as always. I don't know what I would do without you."

"You would find someone else to do what was needed," Helen said.

"Mmm-hmm," she murmured as she tipped the cup to her lips again.

*****

The night of the party, after the guests were gone and the servants were cleaning up, Abigail's thoughts ricocheted off the walls in her mind. Just when she tried to lock onto one and inspect it, it zipped away and another came to her attention. Mostly they were about Ben and the announcement that had been made earlier.

Ben—she always thought of him that way instead of as "Benjamin" or as "Master Mason"—obviously had no idea his mother would announce his engagement. Poor guy. Even knowing about it beforehand, it was a shock when Abbie heard it confirmed in public.

She wasn't sure exactly how she felt about it. Sure, she felt bad for Ben, trapped in the scheming of his mother. The woman he was engaged to did seem to be a harpy, a conceited prig with a list of undesirable traits a mile long. She was beautiful, though. That was enough for most men. Most, but not Ben. Abbie knew enough of him to know it wasn't sufficient for him. How miserable would his life be?

Abigail stopped short as she was picking up some empty glasses left lying about by the party guests. She felt bad for herself, too. Why was that? She had no claim on Ben, shouldn't even be thinking about him at all, let alone thinking about having him for herself.

She had never had trouble thinking. In fact, keeping clarity of mind in stressful situations was one of her greatest strengths, one of the things that made her an outstanding operative for the coven. Why was her mind so muddled? Maybe she was getting sick or was just stressed out. She'd have to rest for a few days, take it easy and allow her body to regain equilibrium. Her body and her mind.

Abigail was given the day after the party off from work because she had been up all night serving and then awake during several hours in the morning helping to clean up. She got a full night's—well, day's—rest and awoke feeling less groggy than she thought she would.

She planned to stay in her room, rest, think, and maybe get a little reading done. Maybe she would go out and take a walk on the grounds if the time seemed right, so she could enjoy a little nature, but still, she mainly wanted to relax and do nothing.

Her mind jumped to thoughts of Ben and never really left. What was she doing thinking about him so much? He might be a fire warlock or a skip, and a rich snob to boot. Plus, he was now engaged to another rich snob. Thinking about him would only distract her. She didn't have time for that. She had an important mission to complete.

What was it about him that so intrigued her? Sure, he was hot. He was her "type," if she could be said to have a type. She hadn't really thought about men romantically for several years. Since her mother died, her sole burning thought was to bring justice to the one who caused her mother's death. That left little room for thinking about her own future or a love life.

What if Ben was part of it all? He was, after all, Margaret's son. What if he was a fire warlock? Or what if he was a skip, still part of her plans and her murders, but doing so with guns or subterfuge or another type of mundane method or weapon?

But no, he couldn't be. First, she would sense his magic if he was a warlock. Then, she got a definite feeling, a "bad vibe" when around Margaret—though it might stem from what she knew of the woman— but she got no such feeling from Ben. In fact, it was the opposite. She felt comfortable with him, safe. The excitement, that tingle when they touched hands, and more. She felt down deep in her soul that she could trust him with anything. He was an ally, even if she didn't know how yet.

She wouldn't base her decisions on a feeling, of course. Her mission was too important to let him in on the secret, especially when the purpose of the entire thing was to bring his mother down. He didn't seem to get along well with her, but she was his mother, after all.

Abigail shook her head, putting both palms to it. She needed to think of the simplest of reasons, the most basic of ideas to make her decision. What decision? That question stopped her in her tracks. She had to decide…whether she wanted to pursue a relationship with Ben, or rather, to allow him to pursue one with her.

Okay, plain and simple, that was the best way to do it. He was an only, a rich snob, and he was engaged to be married. *Engaged to be married.* It didn't matter if it was thrust upon him or not, he was going to be married. Abigail was raised to hold honor in high regard. It was not honorable to entertain thoughts of being with him when he was engaged. Therefore, he was unsuitable—or at least unavailable.

It was as simple as that. None of the other arguments mattered after that one. He was engaged and so she would keep him at arm's length. Or farther. She would act professionally and appropriately with him at all times and not allow it to go further than that. She could withstand the desire to look into his eyes and to find out how he felt about things, what he was like down deep. She could and she would, starting immediately. Today.

The days following the party, Abbie was as good as her word. Whenever she saw Ben, she acted with perfect courtesy but treated him like an acquaintance.

Even treating him like a friend would be too personal. She saw how it frustrated him, and it broke her heart, but she was committed. She did miss the conversations they used to have and how she could almost see his thoughts when she looked into those cool blue eyes of his. Truth be told, she missed how they had interacted, like old friends. Or new lovers. Well, not really that, but it almost felt like it sometimes. But no, she would remain steadfast.

He had been trying to chat her up, but she always found a way to stall the conversation and leave him there, bewildered. Sometimes he even looked dazed, his eyes almost glassy. What was going on with him?

She was cleaning the guest rooms one morning when he came around the corner and saw her. He jumped a little and looked around before speaking.

"Good morning, Abbie," he said, putting on the smile he usually wore when he saw her. She loved that smile, loved it even more because she knew it was genuine. His eyes twinkled, and his whole demeanor changed. It made her body warm that he was so obviously fond of her.

"Good morning, Ben," she said while she moved the vacuum cleaner from the hall into one of the guest rooms. She had thought of going back to calling him "Master Mason," but that seemed petty and punitive. She didn't want to crush him or put him down, just not allow him to get close.

"Abbie, is there something wrong?" he asked. "You seem to be avoiding me lately, not talking to me."

"I'm talking to you now," she said. She kept her eyes on the cord of the vacuum as she unwound it. She had already learned, the hard way, that she couldn't maintain eye contact with him. It had almost caused her to give up the entire thing and just drown in them.

"Yeah, I guess. How are you? Is there something you want to tell me? Did I do something to upset you in any way? Sometimes I say things that are insulting to people like…you know, to people not of my social class."

Abbie's mouth dropped open. She was going to call him down for his prejudice, but he spoke too quickly for her to get a word in.

"What?" he said, slapping the side of his head. "Where did that come from? I'm sorry, Abbie. I honestly don't know why I said that. I've been out of sorts lately. Can we just forget about that part? I just want to know if I have upset you."

"No, you have always been very polite to me, very nice. I'm not upset." She plugged the vacuum into the wall outlet. "It was nice talking to you, Ben, but I have to get this done." She switched on the vacuum and started using it on the guest room floor.

Ben stood in the hall, scratching his head before turning and walking away. Abbie's heart sank. He looked as if she had just slapped him. As he walked off, probably headed toward the gym, she wondered for the hundredth time if she was doing the right thing.

15

"*Ahh*," Margaret Huntsman said, "Benjamin, dear. I'm glad you came so quickly, that you were on the estate. I had hoped you weren't on one of your little jaunts."

Ben stepped into his mother's study. He had been relaxing in his rec room, thinking about how to get Abigail alone so he could talk to her when his mother summoned him. It was always best to come right away when she called. He had played little games in the past, delaying and making her wait, but those never ended well. It was easiest—and wisest—just to go with it and see what she wanted.

He never relished going to that study. He could remember no occasions when a visit to the room ended happily. What was it this time? Was she promising someone that he would have children right away? Had she changed her mind and engaged him to someone even more distasteful than Penelope?

He stood there looking at his mother, not bothering to say anything. She would tell him why he had been called to her.

"I have decided that you and Penelope must get to know each other better. After all, you'll be married soon, so you should start spending time together."

Only then did Ben notice another person in the room. It was just a slight motion caught in the corner of his eye, but he knew what he would find when he turned his head to look.

Yes, a beautiful, slender woman was standing there, chin up, back straight, looking like the very image of a young socialite. Penelope *was* beautiful, he had to admit. Her chestnut hair hung down past her shoulders in soft, wavy curls, framing her oval face and brown eyes. She pouted her full, glossy red lips just short of being pinched, as they always were, but that didn't detract from a face any man could happily look at for hours. The only thing that ruined her perfect composure was her hands, which she clasped in front of her. She was not quite wringing them, but it was a near thing.

When his eyes met hers, her mouth shifted up into a smile, and it almost took Ben's breath away. He had to remind himself what bubbled underneath that beautiful exterior.

Penelope drew in a deep breath, causing interesting things to happen to the simple brown dress she wore. Ben made sure his eyes stayed on hers, no matter how much they wanted to scan the fit of the dress over her body. For some reason, he felt guilty that he even wanted to look at her like that.

"Benjamin," she purred. "It is so nice to see you again."

"Hi, Penelope," he said flatly. Turning to his mother, he asked the obvious question. "Mother, what is this all about?"

Margaret had noticed his reaction to seeing Penelope, and a small smile played across her face before she banished it. "As I said, I think it would be good for you two to spend some time together. So, we are going to Europe."

The news hit Ben like a punch in the gut.

"What? Europe? We just went there last year. When do you propose to go to Europe?"

Margaret eyed him coldly. "I do not *propose* anything, Benjamin. I am telling you we are going, and we are going...oh." She looked at her watch. "Now. The jet is fueled up and waiting for us. Don't bother packing. We can get whatever you need there. We'll be staying at our estate in France. At least at first. Who knows where we'll end up?"

Every excuse he could think of ran through Ben's mind. How could he get out of this? He didn't want to go to Europe, and he definitely didn't want to spend hours a day with Penelope. Or his mother, for that matter. As he called any excuse he could think of to his mind and then rejected each one in turn as being too weak to be effective, the moment was taken from him.

"So," Margaret said, "we're all here and ready. Let us go. Europe awaits."

Ben allowed Penelope to put her arm in his as they shuffled toward the waiting car behind his mother. His mind swirled with ideas on how to escape, but it was already too late. He imagined himself a prisoner in shackles making his way to the execution room.

Just before reaching the front door, Ben felt

someone's gaze settle upon him, and he looked up. Abigail stood there, just to the side of the entry hall, looking at him. He stared back, met her eyes with a miserable look, and then he was through the door, Penelope chattering away on his arm.

*****

Abbie was surprised to see Ben. Actually, she was surprised to see him with his mother and that woman, Penelope. She had expected him to track her down and try to talk to her this morning. She guessed she knew why he didn't.

Where were they going? Ben had not spent any time with his fiancée since the engagement announcement. He had told Abbie that he did not like the woman at all, that he was doing his best to figure out how to get out of the engagement. Had he changed his mind? Had her actions caused him to change it?

She realized that she was standing there staring at the closed front door where he and Penelope had passed moments before. Looking around to see if anyone saw her standing there looking longingly toward where Ben had gone, she saw Arianna smiling at her from the other side of the hall. It was not a friendly smile.

Abbie turned and walked away, not looking back. She knew Arianna's eyes followed her as she retreated, but there was nothing she could do. Abbie hoped the other woman didn't see anything or didn't understand if she did see. It hardly mattered at this point. Abbie felt as if she was going to be sick.

While Ben and Margaret were away, Abigail

thought it would be the perfect time for her to get the evidence she needed. Thinking of her mission made her feel a little better, or at least distracted her from what her heart really wanted her to think about.

Okay, Abigail, she thought, *now is your chance. Push all your little childish romantic notions from your head and focus on the mission.* Where could she go to find an item that had been subjected to Margaret's magic?

Her bedroom didn't seem like a likely choice. Abbie herself rarely used magic in her room. There was really no need. Sure, she levitated items to herself occasionally, but little spells like that wouldn't leave any appreciable residue. Where else?

From her observations, it seemed Margaret Huntsman spent most of her time in one of three offices. She called them studies, but it was the same thing. She used one more often than the others, though, one that wasn't in the block of her rooms on the third floor. She had seen Ben coming from that first-floor study once, unhappy at whatever they'd discussed. That was the one she would search.

It wasn't too unusual for the maids to help out in areas they were not assigned, so though she usually cleaned on the second floor, it was feasible that she might be on the floor below. Without Margaret in the house, she should be able to go in, make a quick search, try to find something with residue on it, take it, and leave without being seen. She would wait until the evening when the house became quieter and then do it.

At the appropriate time, Abbie headed over to the study. She didn't bring her cart, only a basket of supplies: furniture polish, a feather duster, some rags, and glass cleaner. She didn't want the presence of the cart outside the room to tip anyone off she was there. She made her way down the hall to the carved wooden doors and turned the knob.

Rather, she tried to turn the knob. It was locked. Damn. She guessed that she would have to try another time. She pushed on the door in frustration and it swung open. The latch hadn't engaged all the way. What great luck. She darted a look up and down the hall and entered the room, switching on the lights as she did so. She also unlocked the door handle.

She knew better than to search the room in the dark. If she did that and someone caught her in there, she would be in trouble for sure, with no way to explain herself. Abbie set about dusting and cleaning, keeping her senses open to any magic she might feel.

As she came around the desk, wiping down the surface with one of her towels, she felt a small residue of magic. Bringing her face closer to the desk, she searched for its source.

"What are you doing in here?" a voice demanded from the doorway. "And what are you doing with your face so close to Madame's desk?"

Abbie didn't jump—thank goodness—and she knew better than to act nervous. She brought the towel up to where her face was, a few inches from the desk's surface, and she rubbed at an imaginary spot. Lifting her head back up, she smiled as if she had solved a problem.

"I'm cleaning," Abigail said.

Harper Addinson stood there in her favorite stance, legs wide and fists on hips. "Who told you to clean in here?"

"No one," Abbie said as innocently as she could manage. "It occurred to me as I passed carrying my tray that it would be a good time to clean, with Ms. Huntsman gone."

"This study was supposed to have been locked. You're not supposed to be in here."

"I'm sorry. I thought my job was to clean. I'll ask Mrs. Roberts about it."

"There's no need for that," the woman snapped. So, she didn't have authority over this room. She figured she'd lord it over Abbie. "Just leave. I will take care of this room."

"Okay," Abbie said. "I'm sorry if I stepped on your toes. I was only trying to help. It won't happen again."

"Hmph." Harper stepped aside as Abbie left the room. The woman made a show of locking the door, closing it firmly, and then trying the handle before stalking off down the hallway.

Well, Abbie wouldn't be able to check that room again. It could have been worse, though. She had already found out what she needed to know. The only residue she had detected was on the desk itself, and probably too weak for Isabella to get a reading. Even if it was strong enough, Abbie couldn't take the whole desk.

Who would have thought it would be so hard to find evidence of magic in the house of a powerful witch? Of course, that witch's house was bigger than some airports. She would keep trying and eventually find what she needed.

When her heart rate settled back to normal and the thoughts of where she might find what she needed faded from her mind, images of Ben came back with a vengeance. She would have to do something about that. It was going to drive her crazy.

16

~~~

*B*en and Penelope were together constantly during the four weeks they traveled Europe. His mother had made sure of that. It wasn't just whisking him away to another continent. She had little trips and visits planned to keep them together and constantly interacting. Sometimes Margaret accompanied them, but most often she had pressing matters to attend to, and the two would be alone. How it grated.

Penelope, for her part, seemed to be enjoying herself immensely. She had been to Europe many times, of course, and had favorite spots she wanted to show Ben. He tried to be polite, but it became harder every day.

"Oh, look at all the shops," Penelope said, pulling Ben's arm toward some expensive clothing establishment. She had not let go of his arm since they left his house. The skin where she grasped seemed irritated and red, as if he had a sunburn.

"Let's see if there is anything in there that will look fabulous on me." She looked at him as if he should say something.

He said nothing.

Her beautiful face morphed into a pout, a common expression for her. Ben merely shook his head. He was not about to feed that ego.

They passed one of the grand fountains in the square in Paris. As they passed it, Ben slowed and finally stopped. Penelope tugged harder on his arm, but he stayed where he was, looking up at the statuary and the complex streams of water coming from it.

The central figure was a mermaid, her torso unclothed and larger than life size. The detail on her tail was fine enough that Ben had the urge to run his fingers over the scales. She held a pot or jar under her right arm, supporting it with her left, tilting it as if pouring its contents into the basin of the fountain. A stream of water jetted out of the mouth of the pot.

Arrayed beneath the mermaid's platform, half a dozen sculpted horses reared and charged, stone waves cascading out from under their hooves or flanks. Jets of water sprayed out to simulate the splashing.

Ben was mesmerized. He had always enjoyed the fountains and sculptures in Europe, but he felt something like a kinship with this one. Abbie's face superimposed itself on the mermaid, and he blinked. It disappeared as quickly as it had appeared, but one thing was certain: this mermaid and the splashing water made him think of her. His heart ached.

"Why are you stopping, Benjamin?" Penelope asked. "The shops are just over there. All these tourists around the fountain are probably all pickpockets and thieves pretending to be tourists. Either that or poor people who saved for years to come here and get in our way. Come on, let's go." She didn't even have the decency to lower her voice. Several people around them gave her sidelong looks.

Ben stayed where he was, looking up at the statue. Had Abbie told him she liked fountains or statues? No, he didn't think so. Still, it made him think of her.

The wind shifted and a little spray blew toward him. He lifted his chin, tilted his head back, and closed his eyes. The tiny droplets were refreshing on his skin. He felt like giggling but only smiled.

"Ewww," Penelope shrieked. "The water is getting on me. It's probably filthy. I don't like getting sprayed." She tugged on his arm so hard, her grasp on it broke and she took two steps before she realized she wasn't holding onto him anymore. "Benjamin, let's go. I want to go to the shop over there."

"You go ahead," he said. "I'll be there in a minute. I want to enjoy the fresh air and the fountain for a little while."

That pout became twice as pronounced as before. Her eyes actually became liquid. She tossed her hair back and Ben wouldn't have been surprised if she had stamped her foot. "Why do you want to stand near a filthy fountain with all these dirty little people? Come with me into the shop, and we can get something pretty for me to wear for you." The look in her eyes went from pathetic puppy dog to smoky.

Ben almost laughed. If it wasn't for the derogatory way in which she described the others enjoying the fountain, he probably would have. "I think I am more comfortable with these people than with some shop clerk who will kneel down and kiss my feet just because he knows I can buy the overpriced goods in his shop."

A sudden look of outrage twisted Penelope's face. "I see. You want to slum for a little while. Very well, I will be in that shop, over there." She pointed to it, threw her hair back over her shoulder, raised her chin, and stomped toward it.

Ben didn't watch her past the first two steps. He turned back toward the fountain and let his thoughts drift to Abigail. He wondered if he would ever be able to bring her here. He was sure she would love the fountain. She wouldn't hate everyone around her, either.

After twenty minutes, he finally turned to go to the clothing shop. Off to the side of the square, he saw a cart selling souvenirs. It was on his way, so he looked it over as he passed. There were little plastic models of the fountain, depicted in intricate detail. He smiled as he bought one. If he couldn't bring Abbie to the fountain, he would bring the fountain to her.

His smile disappeared when he opened the door of the shop. Penelope stood there, pointing, ordering clerks around, telling the dressmaker who owned the establishment which of the dresses she had been offered would suffice. Ben sighed and sat down. He was going to be here for a while.

When they left the shop, him carrying the three dresses and "a surprise" she had bought, Ben wanted to do nothing but take a nap. He had gotten into the habit of doing that while on this trip. Penelope constantly complained about how he seemed to have no energy, but being with her drained it from him. He couldn't wait to go home but had no idea when his mother would let him.

"Don't put that there," Penelope was screeching to one of the maids who had set her dresses on the bed momentarily so she could open the closet door.

Ben heard from the hall and looked in the open doorway to Penelope's room. The maid was scrambling to pick the dresses up from the bed, her face red. She looked like she was trembling.

The woman was small and slight, with strawberry blond hair that hung down to barely touch her shoulders. She reminded Ben of Abigail.

"Penelope," Ben said, "leave the poor girl alone. You're scaring her."

Dark hair flying as she whirled toward him, her eyes ablaze, she seemed barely able to control herself from snapping at him, too. She took a deep breath, and then another, visibly trying to calm herself.

"It is so hard to find good help. I thought that your mother was better at picking servants than this. I want this girl fired, Benjamin. Fired! She is incompetent and has a bad attitude. I do not want to see her face ever again." With that, she swept past him into the hallway and toward his mother's rooms.

Ben tsked. He turned back to the girl, who clutched the dresses to her as if they would protect her, sobbing.

"Now, now," he said to her in a soothing voice. "Here, let me hold those for you." He went to her slowly, so as not to frighten her, and then gently took the dresses from her arms. "It won't do to wrinkle her majesty's dresses. She might explode if she sees a wrinkle."

The woman was not able to hold in a laugh and then looked horrified when it escaped. She clamped her hand over her mouth and locked her eyes on the floor.

"Here," he said, "let's put these in the closet as you were trying to do before she attacked you. Come on, it's okay."

Once the dresses were safely hanging in the closet, Ben turned to the girl. "What is your name?"

"I am called Monique," she said with a French accent.

"Monique, I'm Ben. I am sorry for what Penelope did, sorry she frightened you. You did nothing wrong. She merely…overreacted."

"Thank you, Monsieur Mason. I try to do my job as best I can. It is sometimes difficult to please everyone."

Ben laughed. "Yes, it definitely is, Monique." She had blue eyes, also, though not as amazing as Abigail's. Still, they could have been sisters. He told himself he wasn't being nice to her just because of that. He would have helped her regardless of what she looked like. Wouldn't he?

"Monique," he said, taking her hand with one of his. With the other, he wiped a tear from her smooth cheek. "I'm afraid that we'll have to rearrange your duties for a little while, until I am able to take Penelope out of here. I'm not sure what job you will be doing, but I think it's best to keep her from seeing you again. It shouldn't be long. I'm hoping we can leave soon."

"Do you mean…" she sniffled, "…do you mean that I am not fired?"

"You are definitely not fired, Monique. Penelope is not in charge, though sometimes she thinks she is. I will arrange for you to stay out of sight of her until we leave, and then things will be back to normal after we go. Does that sound all right to you?"

"Oh, yes, Monsieur Mason. That is *fantastique*. Thank you. It is true, what the other staff say, that you are not like all the other rich persons. You are very kind."

He squeezed her hand and then released it. "I try to be, Monique. I do try."

Margaret left the next day, saying something about pressing business she had to attend to back home. Ben suggested that they should all go back home, but she flatly rejected his idea.

"There are other things you two can share here. I have scheduled a few activities, and Penelope is excited about others she wants to do. Another week or two, Benjamin. I know how it is to be homesick but another week or so and then you can come home."

"Fine," he said. "I suppose I can make it another week."

"Or two." Margaret looked at him as if measuring him. "You really are not having a good time? Is spending time with a beautiful woman so onerous to you?"

"Mother, she is not my type. She's beautiful, yes, but we have nothing in common."

"I know," she said. "That's one reason for this trip. You two will find things you have in common, things on which to build a marriage that can last."

"I will never love her, Mother," he said. "It won't happen."

"Who said anything about love? Love is overrated, Benjamin. No, I don't expect you to fall in love with her. I expect that you will marry her and have children with her and continue the family legacy with her.

That's all. Love doesn't even come into it. Stop being such a silly romantic."

Ben remained silent; anything he said would be the wrong thing.

"Benjamin, it's not like you won't have opportunities to make love to others. I heard about you trying to rescue that little maid from Penelope. It's fine. I won't interfere. If you want her to keep her job, so be it. If you want to take her to bed, that's perfectly fine, too. She is attractive. Just remember at the end of the day, your marriage and this alliance are more important. Do not jeopardize that. Do you understand me?"

"Yes, mother," he said. Take her to bed? And that was all right with his mother? That was ridiculous!

"Good. Now come over here and give me a kiss. I'll be leaving soon. I do hope you enjoy your time with Penelope. It will make things so much better if you can enjoy spending time with her. You'll need to do so to keep up appearances."

Ben kissed her on the cheek and went to his own room. He couldn't believe he was trapped in this situation. It was like some kind of horrible dream. He should just leave. Once he got home. On the company jet. It was ridiculous. He was an adult. He could live like other people, with a job and mortgage. He could...could what? Leave the home his father had built, leave behind all those cherished memories, not to mention all his possessions and his way of living. He should, and he would, if he couldn't get his mother to change her mind about Penelope. He would.

On the way to his room, he saw Monique carrying laundry down one of the halls. She was not in her normal maid's outfit but in one of the more functional laundress uniforms. She smiled at him, a genuine, friendly smile and he nodded and smiled back. He missed Abigail so much. He wondered if she thought of him at all. The way she had been avoiding him, he thought she probably didn't. Sighing, he went to lie down. Another week. In another week, he could go home and be done with Penelope, at least for the time being. He wondered if he'd be able to make it.

17

〰〰〰

*A*bigail moved listlessly about the halls, doing her work but not really thinking about it. That was okay, though. Cleaning didn't require her to use much of her thinking or problem-solving abilities. She did her tasks as if by rote and drifted through the day.

If she didn't know better, she'd say she was pining. Or sulking. What did she expect would happen? Ben *was* engaged to Penelope, after all. Did Abbie think he would never spend time with his fiancée?

It was all ridiculous. She had already decided there could be nothing between the two of them, that she would avoid Ben as much as possible, that she would not pay attention to him. Sure, that was fine when he was here at the estate trying to get her attention. But he had been gone for more than three weeks and she missed him. There, she said it. She missed him. His smile, his face, just his presence.

She had no time for this, couldn't afford to get

attached to anyone, least of all the son of her enemy. The son of the woman she had come here to spy on. What would happen if she was a part of Ben's mother being imprisoned or killed for what she had done? What would he think of her then?

There was a bustle of servants and Abigail looked up to see Mrs. Roberts coming down the hall.

"She's back," the round woman said, "she's back. Ms. Huntsman has returned. Make sure everything is in place and perfect. You know how much traveling tires her and makes her more critical. Hurry, hurry." She wasn't speaking specifically to Abigail but to all the servants within earshot. She continued down the hall, repeating the same thing to others she came across.

What? Margaret was back? Ben and Penelope must be back also. Well, hopefully they dropped the woman off at her own home—or out of the plane on the way back—and she wasn't returning with them. But Ben, he should be coming in the entryway within moments. Her heart fluttered despite her insistence that it not. Energy infused her. She hurried to one of the sculptures in the hall and began to dust it, keeping one eye on the front door.

A moment later, Margaret came through. Helen Shapiro was just a step behind her, sweeping through the entryway and into the hall leading to Margaret's study. Abigail waited, holding her breath. Subconsciously, she counted. When she got to ten, she started to worry. The butler had closed the doors immediately after Margaret and Helen came through. Where was Ben?

Hours later, she found out what had happened from Mrs. Roberts.

"Oh, Master Benjamin?" the Housekeeper said. "He and Miss Penelope stayed at the estate in France. Ms. Hunstman had to come back to take care of some urgent business, but the other two continued on with their planned vacation. I have heard the estate there is magnificent. I wish I could see it someday."

"They're not coming back?" Abigail worried the longing in her voice was too evident.

"They are coming back, dear. Just not right now. From what I understand, it will be another week or two. I don't know for sure, of course. Ms. Huntsman hardly confides everything in me."

"Another week or two," Abigail repeated. "I see."

"Oh, dear," the woman said, putting her arm around Abigail's shoulders. "I miss Master Benjamin, too. His smiling face helps to lighten the mood here. Why, when he was a child, every time he showed up, everyone was all smiles. Especially before his father died. He lost a little bit of himself then, I think. Lost a bit of his joy and happiness in life. Still, growing up will do that to you. He is a wonderful man, he is. Penelope should count her lucky stars she was able to nab him. I know other women in wealthy families for hundreds of miles—or even more—who would kill to be in her place."

"Yes, I guess so."

"He'll be back soon, dear," she said, giving Abbie's shoulders a squeeze. "Just do your work and he'll be back in no time."

But Abbie wasn't so sure things would ever be the same. She may have lost the chance she had been given.

"Mrs. Roberts," Abbie said as the Housekeeper turned to leave. "What do you think of Penelope? I mean, do you think she'll be a good wife to Ben…I mean, Master Mason? I only saw her that night at the party, and then once as they were leaving for Europe."

The older woman studied Abigail's face for a moment. "It is not a good habit to talk about friends of the family, no more than it is to talk about Ms. Huntsman and Master Benjamin themselves."

"I'm sorry. I was just wondering. I would like to see…Master Mason happy. He is so kind to everyone."

Mrs. Roberts smiled at her. "Yes, yes, I understand. Don't make a habit of talking about your betters, girl, but I can tell you a little. Miss Moore is beautiful, obviously. Anyone can see that. She is involved with several charities, protecting animals and such, so she has a good heart. She seems polite enough, though she can be a little terse with the staff, as is her right as a guest in the house. Her family is wealthy and owns businesses that are complementary to Ms. Huntsman's own enterprises. Overall, it will be a good combination of two powerful families and two young people who are in the prime of their childbearing years."

She beamed at Abigail. Had Mrs. Roberts just repeated word for word what she had been told by Margaret Huntsman?

"But," Abigail said, "what is she like as a person? Is she kind—to other people, I mean—and is she caring? Does she have a good sense of humor? Does she like children? Does she love Ben…I mean, Master Mason?"

"Dear," Mrs. Robertson said. "I know you have taken a liking to Master Benjamin and want him to be happy, but you really should put out of your head all thoughts about personal matters between him and Miss Moore. He will be happy or he will not be. One thing he will not be is getting out of this marriage. When Ms. Huntsman has decided on something, it is done. Things will work out, if Master Benjamin goes along with what Ms. Huntsman has already arranged. That is about all we can say on the matter. Now run along and get to work. If Master Benjamin is going to be returning soon, you must make sure everything is in order for him. Go now." She made a shooing gesture toward Abigail.

Abbie left, but didn't feel any better about Ben's engagement. Was he falling for the woman? She pictured that simpering little nit hanging all over Ben and laughing her silly, giggling laugh, smiling and shaping him like putty in her hands. A cracking sound, one of the shafts of a feather breaking, made her look down. She was wringing the feather duster she was holding as if it were the woman's neck. She relaxed her hands and took a breath. *He will be happy or he would not.* That had to be the stupidest thing she had ever heard.

One thing the woman had said was correct. Abbie had better prepare for when Ben came back. Their time apart had allowed her to think on some things. The next time he stopped by for a spontaneous talk, she would have some questions ready for him.

*****

"Are we still on schedule?" Margaret Huntsman asked Frank Gibraltar. He wore his typical gray suit and his hair was slicked back. Honestly, he looked like a television mobster. He was competent, though.

"We are." His gravelly voice grew irritating if she had to listen to it for long. Margaret was glad he was a man of few words.

"Our spies tell us the airs and the earths are suspicious of each other, and of the waters," Helen added. "The whole area is ready to burst into flames." She laughed at her own joke. "So to speak."

"Very funny, Helen," Margaret said. "But will it happen soon enough? We are on a schedule here. We have more than just this area to be concerned about, you know. This will just be the start."

"It'll happen soon," Frank said. "But we have run into a little snag."

"A snag," Margaret said.

"Yeah. We have another water witch getting chummy with some airs. In fact, she's romantically involved with an air warlock."

"And that is a problem why?" Margaret demanded. "We're not in the business of trying to stop people from dating, we're trying to start a war."

"Uh," Helen said, "the air warlock is the son of the Galemistress of the largest air coven in the state."

"I see. That won't do at all. Tell me what you will do to unsnag the situation."

"Well," Frank started, "that's why I came to see you. We'll need a little help with this one if we're to take care of it soon."

"I'm listening," Margaret said as she leaned toward the man, focusing intently on his words.

18

"*O*h come on, Peg," Sylvia Moran said.

The two water witches navigated a trail in the cool night air, a trail they had used countless times before.

"Peg Witcher, if you don't stop dallying, I swear we're not going to reach the ritual stones until daybreak."

"Yes, yes," Peg answered, leaving it at that to spare her breath. She didn't remember the trail being this strenuous, but she wasn't getting any younger, either.

Peg looked over at Sylvia. Twenty years younger, more fit, and much more attractive, she was everything a young witch should be. Except patient. Her long blond hair fell in perfect waves to the middle of her back, framing a face like a porcelain doll, pale, smooth, and flawless. Her skin glistened in the moonlight, not from perspiration but just because it always seemed to glow. Her bright blue eyes, button nose, and perfect, full lips caught the eye and wouldn't let go. She was beautiful, everyone thought so, and it irritated Peg to no end.

She loved the woman like a sister, and sister was what she was. Members of their coven were family. Peg just wished the other witch wasn't so perfect. Watching her slender but still curvy body move in the moonlight, she sighed and wished she could find flaws in the other woman's appearance.

She herself was no slouch. People said she was attractive. Men still looked at her, sometimes made comments. Her dark hair shone in the night, in curls and just a little longer than Sylvia's. Her eyes were a light hazel and she had been told, more than once, how beautiful they were. Her own lips, which she thought to be a bit thin, curved into a smile. Yes, there were enough people who had thought she was attractive over the years. Enough. She guessed that everyone had their own strengths and weaknesses. There was no use comparing.

"Thank you for speaking for me," Sylvia said. "It's an honor to be able to take part in the Summer Moon celebration ritual. I know they never would have let me do it without your recommendation."

Peg eyed the younger woman. She really was a good witch. Guilt stabbed her at her petty thoughts from just a moment before. "You deserve it. You are powerful and meticulous in your movements. You should be helping. As one of the two rituals carried out by representatives in seclusion, it is very important to have the right witch performing the rites."

Sylvia smiled at Peg, a sincere, great, beaming smile. The older witch smiled back and picked up her steps. They had a ritual to perform, after all.

The pair continued along the well-worn path and soon they could see by the light of the moon the edge of the lake that was their destination. Their steps became lighter as they neared where they would perform the ritual.

"Do you feel that?" Sylvia asked.

"Feel wha—" Peg started to say, but then she understood what the other woman was saying. A feeling of wrongness permeated the area. She had been to this spot many times, sometimes to perform the ritual they were about to complete. Because it was a nexus of power for water witches, it always felt peaceful, like she had come home. Something was spoiling that peace. To do that on the first full moon after the summer solstice, it had to be a great imbalance.

Too late, Peg realized what it was. "Defend yourself," she yelled before a fist-sized fireball punched through Sylvia's midsection, almost cutting her in half. She knew her friend was dead before she even hit the ground.

Two more fireballs struck the shield of water she called around herself, fizzling into nothingness but still buffeting her with their impact. Turning, she saw no less than five figures coming at her, some waving their arms to call more fiery projectiles into existence. She redoubled her effort on the shield and started moving.

If I can just make it to the lake, I might have a chance. As soon as she thought it, she ran as fast as she could toward the body of water.

More fireballs struck her shield, too many to count. One of the enemies had thrown up a wall of fire in her path. Her shield couldn't withstand that and the projectiles being thrown at her at the same time, so she skirted around it, having to take a few extra precious steps. She was tiring quickly.

The water shield was growing warm, boiling away. If she had the strength, Peg would have attacked one or two of the fire witches, but she barely had enough power to keep the shield from collapsing. Only a few more feet and she would be at the water. There, she could draw on the power within the lake. It might just be enough to survive.

Another wall of fire sprang up in front of her. Peg lacked the strength to dodge around it. She took a deep breath, forced every ounce of magical ability from her tired body, and charged through, stumbling and falling at the edge of the lake. Parts of her skin felt scalded.

Her momentum caused her stumble and fall to turn into a tumble and roll. She found herself face down in a few inches of water. She had made it to the lake. She just hoped it wasn't too late.

Drawing on the well of energy in the deep body of water, she strengthened her shield as a dozen or more fireballs slammed into it with jarring impact. She crawled a few feet until she was in deep enough water to swim. Once there, she dove until she was completely submerged. Already, the water's magic loaned her more power, helping to erase her fatigue.

She floated motionless, suspended in the lifegiving liquid, for a full minute with her eyes closed, concentrating on gathering her power. Then she opened her eyes and looked toward the shore, where the fire witches were still throwing foul magics at her.

Gritting her teeth—they killed Sylvia in ambush— she used the water's own magical energy to propel her forward. She didn't need to swim; she and the water were one. She stopped when she was standing in three feet of water. Her shield glowed in the moonlight, impenetrable to everything the fire witches threw at her.

Peg finally took a look at her enemies. She knew they were users of fire magic, but she had been too desperate to survive earlier to see them clearly. There were four fire witches and three fire warlocks. Luckily, none of them seemed to be as strong as she was.

And now she stood in the middle of a powerful source of water magic. They were about to see how big a mistake they had made.

While maintaining the shield, Peg focused her energies and water jets rocketed out toward half of the attackers. Fireballs, walls of fire, and other spells could not withstand the jets. But those were not her primary attack. As she distracted them with her water jets, she made a sweeping gesture with her left hand and hardened water projectiles, half the length of her moving hand and a quarter as thick, shot out toward three of the witches and one of the warlocks. The missiles were not made of ice, but of hardened water, and when they struck, it was like a bullet from a high-powered rifle.

One of the witches was struck in the chest. The water bullet blew a hole half a foot in diameter through her torso. Another witch's head exploded when struck. The third witch had her right arm torn off, and the fire warlock lost his left leg to two projectiles, causing him to topple to the ground.

Another sweep of her hand and the remaining attackers were incapacitated, two warlocks losing part or all of their heads and the other witch and warlock receiving holes that stretched across most of their abdomens. It would be a matter of a few minutes until they, too, were dead.

Peg looked around for additional enemies. The moans of the dying fire users didn't bother her. In fact, in the rage she was in, she would have liked to have heard more painful cries from them. Still, she didn't think she had finished them all. She had an uncomfortable feeling—

A massive concussion slammed her from her rear left side, not making it through the shield, but throwing her ten feet from where she had been standing. She rolled across the ground several times and then stopped. She tried to regain her breath.

She had been knocked out of the water.

"You very nearly survived," a voice said from behind her. "Nearly, but not quite."

Peg turned in time to see a dark-haired older woman completing a spell. The fire magic she had loosed sped toward Peg, and the water witch knew her shield would not be able to withstand the attack. She tried desperately to jump to the side, but the streak of red-yellow flame followed her like a guided missile.

The last thing Peg knew was the sizzling, whooshing sound of a bolt of fire tearing into her body.

She knew nothing after that.

19

Eight days later, Benjamin Mason returned to the estate. Abigail didn't see him arrive, but heard about it from the other servants. He was alone when he returned, of course, Penelope going to her own home. At least that much was good. What did she think, that the woman would move in to the estate with him? Abigail almost expected it.

Over the nearly four weeks he'd been gone, Abigail did her job, carried out her tasks in exactly the way she always had. She still hadn't found any solid information about Margaret Huntsman and the things she was doing, but that was not what was on her mind. Ben was.

She had expected him to find her the first day, just show up in front of her as he always had, "coincidentally." He did not. In fact, the few times she saw him, it was from a distance and he was busy or seemingly on the way somewhere. She actually thought of searching him out, tracking him down, but she wouldn't do that. She would wait for him.

But she started to wonder. Had he lost interest? Had he ever been interested at all? Did his trip make him fall in love with Penelope? If so, that was fine. He deserved to be in love. But with her? She didn't deserve him. And who did—herself? She needed a break, a place to go and think. She decided to take a little drive on the weekend and clear her head. She knew exactly where to go.

The thin young man smiled widely at Abigail as she pulled up and parked on the circular driveway in front of the large building. As she stepped out of the car, he enfolded her in a crushing hug.

"Hi, Abbie," he said, his voice muffled in her shoulder.

"Hey, Jack," she said. "How's school? How is everything here since I've been gone?"

He released her and backed up a step, his grin so huge she had to increase her own smile until it hurt her face.

"Everything is just like it always is, just lonelier without you here."

"Yeah, right," Abbie chuckled. "Lonely. With only thirty-odd people here. Aqua Terra is many things, but I don't think 'lonely' was ever one of them."

She turned him toward the front door, slipping her arm through his. Jack was only sixteen, thin as a willow switch and as awkward as could be. His mop of dark hair accentuated his eyes, a darker blue than any Abbie had ever seen, like the sky just before dawn's lightening. If he wasn't her favorite cousin, he was in the top three. She loved his youthful exuberance and innocence. She couldn't have chosen a better person to be the first she saw when she returned home.

"Is my father around?" she asked him as they passed through the front door. It was elaborately carved mahogany, identical to its twin right beside it, both with beautiful etched glass windows set in the upper half. Abigail sighed. She had passed through those doors thousands of times. She had only been gone a few months, but it felt good to be back home. She had missed this place.

"I think he may be in his study," Jack said. "Are you going to stick around for a while?"

She smiled at him again. "Yes. I plan on being here all weekend."

"Good. Maybe we can catch up after you talk with your dad. I want to show you some of the stuff I've been learning. Not schoolwork. You know."

"Yes, I do." She hugged him again, and he bounded off. She wished she had his teenage energy level. Not schoolwork. He was talking about water magic. He was a gifted water warlock, as most males in her family were. All the females were powerful, too. There hadn't been a skip in the Henderson females in four generations.

She turned to the left and went down the hallway, trailing her finger along the ornate frames holding the paintings mounted on the walls. She took a deep breath. Even the air tasted sweeter here.

Her knock sounded loud in the quiet hallway. She wondered why there weren't more people moving around. It was just after ten o'clock in the morning. There should have been more activity.

"Come in," an older, yet still strong and deep, voice said from within. Abigail pushed the door open and went through.

"Abbie!" her father said as he rose and crossed the room, almost in a run. His arms surrounded her, and the comfort of his hug made her sigh again.

Landon Henderson was as solid a presence as Abigail had ever met, and not just because he was her father. Everyone thought the same thing. He was tall—six feet three inches—and not at all gangly. He was thick, fit and muscular, even at sixty years old.

It wasn't just his physical attributes, though, that made him so remarkable. He had a charisma, an air of command, a calmness that affected everyone around him. His cool blue eyes seemed to radiate peace like gently rolling waves in the ocean.

With his sandy blond hair and strong jaw, he looked like a leader, though his wife's death had largely sapped his vitality. He had lost some of his spark when she was killed. Still, it was comforting to see him again, to be held in his arms. She felt the tension leave her body.

"How is my little girl?" He gently grabbed her shoulders and put her at arm's length so he could look into her eyes.

"I'm doing okay," she said, not elaborating further.

"Just okay, huh?" He looked more deeply into her eyes as if he was reading her mind. "We'll talk about that later. To what do we owe the honor of your visit?"

Abigail sighed. "I just needed a little break. And I wanted to report how things are going so far with the mission. Are the others available?" She didn't have to say "the other members of the Guiding Council." He knew what she meant.

"Most of them. The Hills are at their own home,

but coincidentally, the others have come to meet here. There has been…a development."

"A development?" Abigail raised her eyebrow at her father's wording.

"Yes. Maybe it's better if you hear it from them, and then you can give your report at the same time. I'll call everyone together. Is an hour from now a good time? You probably want to rest after your long drive."

Abigail smiled at him. "Yes, that's fine. I just need to wash up. I can rest after meeting with the Council. Thank you, Papa." She rose onto her tiptoes and kissed him on the cheek. "I'll see you in an hour in the meeting chamber."

On her way to her room, she pondered what her father had said. "A development." That sounded ominous. Well, at least it would take her mind from her problems with Ben. She wanted something to keep her from dwelling on him, so this was probably as good as anything else. She would still have to figure out what to do about that situation, but for now the new distraction was welcome.

An hour later, Abigail entered the meeting chamber. It was a large room, capable of holding dozens of people comfortably, many at the massive oval of a table in the center of the room. Antique wood flooring, carved recessed book shelves, ancient artwork placed meticulously, and very old and fine rugs dotting the floor made the chamber radiate solemnity and grandeur. It was one of the oldest parts of the constantly-growing structure. Though Aqua Terra had always been her home, this one room had made the entire estate the crown jewel of the water witch coven. Every important matter decided by the

Guiding Council had been discussed and resolved in this room ever since water witches had settled in the area.

She was the first one there, so she busied herself by browsing the books on the shelves. She had read some, but she noted others she'd always meant to read. Every last one of them were either manuals on water magic or histories of her coven and elemental magic users in general. There was even a collection of books on specific histories of the other elemental magic users, those who used earth, air, and fire. It was sparse, though.

Abbie heard voices in the hall outside and turned to see a group of the council members entering.

Ava Martin entered the room first, just a half a step in front of Sophia Hill. The latter must have arrived since Abigail talked to her father. The first woman was short, apple-cheeked, and almost boyish looking in the drab, simple dress that draped over her thick body. She had never cared for fashion and always wore the simplest of clothing. Her hair was short, a simple bob cut. Ava looked easygoing and friendly, but once those hazel eyes locked onto you, she did not seem that way at all.

Sophia, on the other hand, was taller, a good three or four inches above Abigail's five foot, five inch frame, and slender. The blue eyes that were so common among water witches peered out from her brown hair, which fell in soft waves to the middle of her back. She always seemed to have a light in her eyes that said Sophia was about to tell you a joke or do some sort of mischief. She rarely did, but the threat was ever there. Abbie liked Sophia, seeing her as a playful aunt. Still, she too could be stern and serious when dealing with Council business.

Julian Hill, Sophia's husband, was a tall, slender man. He looked as if he could have been Sophia's brother, with his hair and eye color matching that of his wife's and his angular face displaying hints of Sophia's, though hers was much softer and more feminine. He lacked the mischievous look, too.

Julian was talking with Abigail's father, the latter towering over the other man's six foot tall frame. Landon Henderson flicked his eyes up from Julian to meet Abbie's, and he smiled and nodded his head to his daughter, then continued with his conversation.

Finally, Charlotte Whinson, the leader of the Guiding Council, the High Water Caster, stepped through the doorway, looking as if she was pondering something. She almost looked distracted, which shocked Abbie. The woman was the most competent and resourceful leader Abbie had ever met, aside from her mother. At barely over five feet tall, Charlotte was perfectly proportioned. She was not one pound over what was probably the ideal weight for her height, and not one pound less. The dress she wore, elegant yet simple blue silk, swished softly as she moved. Abigail knew she never would have heard it had not the others all moved away from the door, to the table, to take their seats. As they did so, Julian nodded to Abbie, Ava gave her a small smile, and Sophia waved.

Charlotte's light yellow hair, paler than corn silk, was wrapped into a perfect, tight bun on her head, as normal. She was not a beautiful woman, but most would probably call her handsome. Her green eyes scanned the meeting chamber as she crossed the threshold, and any distraction Abigail had seen vanished in an instant. The head water witch nodded and pulled the door closed.

"Let's get started," Charlotte said as she walked around the table to sit at the head. "It is fortuitous that you arrived when you did, Sophia and Julian. We can take care of other business while the entire Council is present. But first..." Charlotte turned to Abigail and gave her a small smile.

"Abbie came for a visit," Landon Henderson said. "While she's here, she thought that it would be good to give you all a briefing on how things are going at the Huntsman Estate. First, though, I would like to share with her the recent developments, if the Council agrees."

"Of course, of course," Charlotte said, as if the question hadn't needed to be asked. "Sophia, if you would? You took the greatest part in the investigation, so you have the most intimate knowledge of the situation."

Sophia straightened in her chair and looked at Abigail. Abbie expected a smile from her, but if anything, the tight line of the other woman's mouth looked as if she was angry. What was going on?

"There has been a tragedy," she started off. "But worse, what happened has implications far beyond the actual unfortunate events. Two of our number have been murdered."

20

*Ab*igail's mouth dropped open, and she stared at Sophia, not believing what she had just heard. "Murdered? Two? Who—" she cleared her throat and swallowed. "Who were they?"

"Sylvia Moran and Peg Witcher," Charlotte answered, her face twisting into a scowl.

Abigail knew the two well. She and Sylvia were friends, being close to the same age, and Peg had always been like another mother to her, especially after her own was taken.

"H-h-how?" she barely seemed able to get the word out.

Sophia's eyes were liquid as she looked into Abigail's. "They were going to Lake Tranquility to perform the ritual for Summer Moon. It seems their attackers were waiting in ambush at the lake itself. We are still not sure exactly what happened. From the residual energy in the area, they seem to have fought back but were overcome in the end."

"Who attacked them?" Abigail asked, her voice still shaky but less so than before. "What kinds of wounds did they have?"

Sophia looked to Charlotte, and the leader of the Council gave a small nod. Sophia's eyes left the older woman's and then snapped back to her, almost as if she didn't believe she had seen the nod. She sighed and looked back to Abigail.

"You must not divulge this information to anyone. Only those in this room know, except two forensics specialists who use magic in their investigations of incident scenes. There were no bodies." Abigail gasped. "Whether taken or destroyed at the battle scene, we do not know. We found evidence, though, a piece of Sylvia's fingernail and some bits of Peg's flesh.

"Also, there is an echo of a large amount of power that was utilized from the lake itself. We're guessing that Peg made it to the water and was able to fend off the attackers for a time. The apparent location of Sylvia's body was much farther from the lake. It had to be Peg."

"Why would they take the bodies?" Abigail asked. "I can see taking the injured or the corpses from among the attackers, but why the victims?"

"We think," Julian said in his deep voice, "that they wanted to hide who attacked our sisters. It's obvious, though, that this was no mundane attack. We scoured the area for shell casings in case there were firearms involved, but no one believed that to be the case, even before the search turned up with no evidence. Those two could have defended against a large number of people with guns. No, it was magic that killed them. But what kind and who? Those are the questions."

"What condition was the skin in, the bits of Peg's...flesh?" Abigail almost choked as she finished her question.

Sophia shifted her eyes to her husband and raised one eyebrow, then returned her gaze to Abbie. "Very good, Abigail. Very clever. The skin was cauterized, like it had been melted."

"Fire witches," Abigail spat. "Fire witches. Again."

"Yes, that's what we believe," Charlotte said. "Isabella is traveling for a few weeks, so we could not have her look for residue at the site. She can try to take a reading of the...remnants when she gets back to see if she can determine anything. We know nothing yet except what you surmised, that it was fires. Which is why your mission is even more important now than ever, leading us to you and your report. What do you have to tell us, Abigail?"

Abbie spent the next hour explaining what she had learned while working for Margaret Huntsman. It was precious little, mainly her schedule and her habits. She mentioned Ben's engagement for the sake of being complete but couldn't see how it would make any difference in the mission, not as far at the others were concerned, anyway. She did not say anything about her feelings for him or her confusion over them. This was not the time or place for that.

The Council listened to Abigail's report, asking a few questions about those who were at the party. Abbie, a competent operative, answered them all without hesitation. She saw her father nodding slightly and wearing a small smile. It made her warm inside that he was proud of her. She wondered what her mother would think of her mission. She had always been an honest, straightforward type of witch, always willing to give someone the benefit of the doubt and disliking deception of any kind. Abbie thought maybe she'd understand the necessity with the current climate.

"We have other witches and warlocks trying to find more information from other angles," Charlotte said when Abigail was finished. "What we really need to know is how large or isolated the situation is. Is Margaret Huntsman acting alone, leading a small group, or are most of the fire witches involved? Is it even isolated to users of fire magic? Are there earths or airs involved? We need to know."

Abigail hadn't thought of that. Just how large was this thing? She had always assumed it was just Margaret and a few rogue fire witches. What if it was bigger than any of them had ever thought? It was a sobering thought.

The Council graciously allowed her to remain while they discussed other Council business. When she raised her eyebrows at her father, he gave an almost-imperceptible shrug. He wasn't sure why they allowed her to stay either.

After the meeting was completed and everyone else had left, giving Abbie fond farewells and wishes for continued success in her mission, she and her father sat in two of the stuffed leather chairs in the meeting room.

"It's unusual for Charlotte to allow anyone to sit through a Council meeting. In fact, I've never seen her do it. I wonder if she is considering adding another seat. After your mother…left us, the other seat was never filled, the one Charlotte vacated to become the High Water Caster."

"Do you really think so?" Abigail asked. "I'm very young to be on the Guiding Council."

"True," Landon Henderson agreed. "I don't know. I'm just saying that it was unusual." He turned his body to face her fully. "Abbie, what's wrong?"

Abigail jumped a little. How did he do that? "What do you mean?"

"You didn't come here just to visit or to give your report. You're running from something, even if just temporarily to clear your head. Don't try to deny it. I know you too well. What's bothering you?"

Abbie sighed. "I don't know. I'm distracted, and I feel like I'm not fulfilling my mission."

"Why would you think that?" her father asked. "Your report was perfect. You had all the answers to everyone's questions and you reported on everything that you could be expected to have found out in the time you've been there. Not being able to find and steal evidence of Margaret's power is understandable. You have to be cautious."

"Maybe," Abigail said. "Still, I'm distracted. What if I'm missing something because I am not as focused as I should be?"

Her father leaned toward her and took her hands in his. "Abbie, you can't be perfect. Not all the time. But I think we're talking about the wrong thing. What we need to talk about is what it is that is distracting you."

She raised her eyes to meet his but said nothing.

"Well?" he said softly. "Out with it. What's going on?"

"There is this guy…" she started and soon she had told him everything.

Abigail got back to the Huntsman Estate late Sunday afternoon. She had talked with her father several times during her short visit once she had confided in him about her feelings about Ben. She still wasn't sure about them, but things were clearer than before her visit home. Her father, always sensitive, caring, and understanding, eased her mind and made her feel so much better.

"Abbie," he had said, "more than any of the other types of elemental magic users, we water folk are in touch with our emotional side. That is, the full range of our emotional side, not just anger like the fires. Listen to your heart, flow with your circumstances, and see how it goes. Don't let your mind overrule your heart, or vice versa. Remember that our entire world is based on smooth, flowing movement. Relax, like a calm lake, and let the wonder of life reveal to you what it will."

She was ready to go back to work and to apply her father's advice.

*****

It felt good to Ben to be home. After more than a month of being gone—and worse, being with Penelope—he was happy to be back where he belonged, back to where Abbie was. Lucas was glad to see him back also. Ben's mother had decided to "travel light," taking no servants with them and relying on those in the estate in France.

He didn't know what he was going to do. He liked Penelope even less than he did before they went on the trip. She thought they got along very well and that he was smitten with her. He shook his head at that.

Ben had seen Abbie a few times since his return. He was barely able to keep up the pretense of not noticing her. He wanted to look at her, stare at her, talk to her, but he didn't. She had shown him well enough that she didn't want him to bother her. She had avoided him for weeks before he left for Europe, and so he would cede to her wishes and keep away from her. Despite how much it caused his heart to ache to do so.

It would all work out. He really shouldn't be spending time thinking about her, anyway. He needed to find a way out of this ridiculous engagement his mother had trapped him in. It was a little uncomfortable seeing Abbie and not talking to her, but it would get easier, in time. It was for the better. Did she realize how much it was killing him?

21

⌇⌇⌇

𝒯he next weekend, Abigail was up more than three hours before dawn and in her car not too many minutes after arising. She had seen Ben only twice during the week and just from afar. She wasn't able to try to converse with him at all. What she needed was some nice peaceful contemplation, away from the hustle and bustle of the estate and the busy servant's quarters. It was Sunday, and she didn't have to work, so she had planned on making the most of it. Starting with one of her favorite things to do.

As she drove the hundred miles or so, she opted for silence rather than the radio. The best thing for her right now was time away to think and commune with nature.

The sky was not even lightening yet as she entered the park. A small group of buffalo crossed the road in front of her, making her wait until they had passed. Two wolves skulked off to the side, their yellow eyes glowing in her headlights. There must have been others in the trees, she knew. As the road neared the river, a beaver waddled into the underbrush, no doubt trying to get an early start on some building project. She loved seeing animals going about their lives despite all the human invaders into their domain. It gave her hope that maybe mankind would not destroy nature completely.

There were no other cars parked at the trailhead to the path she would be going down. Abbie smiled as she strapped her headlamp on, locked her car, and started walking. She was in no hurry. Sunrise was still nearly an hour away. She breathed deeply of the cool morning air and felt more relaxed than she had in several weeks.

The walk didn't take long—it wasn't quite half a mile, though steep—and before she knew it she was at the observation point. She had been hearing the rush of the river for the last several minutes of her hike, but once she arrived at the top of the Lower Yellowstone Falls, the roar drowned everything else out. Her smile, which she had been wearing since starting the trail, grew wider.

Abigail sat on the weathered wooden bench and waited, thinking of everything and nothing. She was lost in the sound of water falling and crashing to the rocks below, the smell of the damp foliage, and the feel of the chill mist on her face as it wafted up from below. She was so entranced by it all, she didn't notice another person coming down the trail until he was nearly on top of her. How had she not been paying enough attention to see the light of his headlamp?

She started and jerked upright, in turn frightening

the man who was only ten feet away from her. No, not just a man. It was Benjamin Mason. Looking around for a way to escape, she wondered if she could survive jumping into the river and riding the waterfall down.

"Oh," Ben said. "I'm sorry, you startled me. I didn't know there was anyone else here. My apologies."

She just nodded, not trusting her voice.

"Abbie?" Ben said, peering at her and blinding her with his headlamp. "Oh, sorry again," he said as he angled the light downward so it wasn't shining in her eyes.

"Uh," she stammered, "yes. Fancy seeing you here, Master Mason."

"Oh, please, don't call me that. My mother insists on etiquette and titles and all that, but I don't. Please call me Ben. Not Master Mason, just Ben. I thought we were done with that."

Her heart fluttered. *What was wrong with her? She wasn't fifteen years old.* "Okay. Ben. I wasn't sure if this was considered a public place."

He smiled, and she was thankful she was sitting down, because if she had been standing up, her knees would have given out. The way his smile was just slightly lopsided made her want to stare. So sexy. "Thank you, Abbie. May I share your bench? I'm assuming we're both here to see the sunrise. I'd like to share it with you."

What was going on with her heart? It was beating a mile a minute. She would have to go to one of the healers in the coven to see if she was ill. No one had ever done this to her, no matter how fond she was of them. "Yes…yes, of course. It's not really my bench.

I'm just sitting on it." She dropped her eyes to the ground and felt herself flush in embarrassment. *What was that?* Where had her brain gone?

He narrowed his eyes at her, as if wondering if she was making fun of him, but nevertheless came and sat down near her. Much too near her. She could feel the heat coming off him in the morning chill. *Did he have a fever or something? Or did she?* She was feeling warm, too.

They sat in silence for a time, the roar of the falls unbroken by speech. Ahead of them, the sky was beginning to lighten, casting strange twilight shadows around them.

"This is one of my favorite places to watch the sunrise," he said, jerking her out of the spell she had been in. "It's so peaceful here without all the people."

"Yes," she agreed.

"I've always had a special fondness for water," he continued. "It's amazing, when you think of it."

"Really?" Abbie said, wondering about his reasoning. He was from a fire family, after all. "How so?"

The light spreading across the sky was enough that he turned off his headlamp, and she followed suit. They could still see each other dimly, more than a silhouette but less than distinct. He turned on the bench to face her more squarely. There was a light in his eyes, no doubt just a glimmer of a reflection of the lightening sky. It almost looked like he was excited to talk about it, but that would be ridiculous. Why would he be excited about water?

"Well, besides all that stuff about being the cornerstone of life and in addition to all the very cool things that make it almost unique chemically—I won't even go into detail about that—it's kind of an anomaly. I mean, it's soft, but can pack a wallop as a wave or if you fall into it from too high. It flows into any shape, making its way through even the tiniest of crevices but is still solid in its natural form for part of the year in many locations. It is soothing to listen to or to watch but can be dangerous and deadly. I just think it sums up nature perfectly."

He stopped, as if suddenly realizing he was getting caught up in his own voice. He dropped his eyes, and Abbie could have sworn she saw his cheeks redden in the dim light. "Anyway, I've just always liked water. Lakes, streams, falls, the ocean, all of it. I've always felt a connection. You probably think it's silly." He chuckled and raised his eyes to hers. "Maybe it is."

"No," Abbie said, looking deeply into his eyes and marveling again at their color. They were the color of a deep lake in the bright afternoon sun. "It's not silly. I understand exactly what you're talking about."

"Oh," he said. "That reminds me. I got you something when I was in Europe. It's just a silly little trinket, but I was at this magnificent fountain and it made me think of you and…" he fished around in his pocket for something. "Anyway, I thought how much you would probably like the fountain, but it was there and I couldn't very well bring it back for you, so here." He handed her a small plastic model of a fountain.

"You have been carrying that around since you went to Europe?" she asked.

"Uh, yeah. I was hoping to give it to you, but you know, I haven't really seen you around."

She took it from him, turning it in her hands. A slow smile spread over her face. "It's beautiful. You're right, I would love to see a full-size version of this."

He looked into her eyes and started to say something again but cut himself short. Eyes darting toward the source of the brightening sky, downriver from the water fall, he said, "Sunrises. I love them, too. Much more than sunsets. I mean, sunsets are beautiful and everything, but sunrises to me hold the promise of a new day and all its possibilities. A sunset is the end of a day, sort of like the death of the light." He fidgeted with his hands and chuckled. "You came here to enjoy the quiet and the sunrise, and I'm talking your ear off. I'll just be quiet and let you enjoy it now."

They looked into each other's eyes for what seemed like hours, neither one speaking. Her heart was beating overtime, but she didn't feel nervous. She just felt…comfortable. After putting the little fountain in her pocket, she fidgeted on the bench so she had an excuse to break their eye contact. She almost didn't have the strength to do so.

As she moved, she felt a sharp pain in the index finger of her right hand. "Ouch!" she said.

He shook his head as if coming out of a trance. His eyes, which had gone soft and dreamy, snapped into focus. "What's wrong?"

"Splinter," she said. "I rubbed my hand along the bench and it bit me."

"Let me see." Before she could react, he lifted her hand in his. A tingle went up her arm and settled at the back of her neck as goose bumps.

He squinted at her finger in the dim light. "I can't see it." He ran his own finger lightly—like the faintest of fairy kisses—over hers and she felt the sliver snag and pull. "There it is."

He turned his headlamp back on to inspect the

finger he was still holding. "Hm. I don't have any tools here for the job, so I'll need to improvise." She wasn't sure what he meant by that, but as long as he kept holding her hand, she was more than willing to find out.

Ben shot one quick look to her and slowly brought her hand to his mouth. She watched in surprise as he gently took her finger in between his lips. Her body went wild. The tingle from before became fire racing up her arm, though her chest, and into her heart, which started pounding at twice the speed as before. She almost pulled her hand free but couldn't quite force herself to do it. Fine. If she was going to die from an exploding heart, then she could think of no better way to go. She peeked at him to make sure he wasn't looking at her, and then she closed her eyes and sank into the feeling.

Ben used his teeth to pinpoint the splinter. After a few false starts, he finally snagged it, all the while causing the most delicious suction on her finger. When he finally yanked the sliver free, the pain was nothing compared to the loss of his mouth on her. He unceremoniously spat the tiny piece of wood onto the ground.

"I think I got all of it," he said.

She opened her eyes to find him staring into them. *How long has he been looking at me?*

"I...uh...thank you." She jerked her hand away, missing the contact with his almost immediately. Why did her hand suddenly feel cold, incomplete? "I think you got it. It feels much better."

He smiled at her in a way she had never seen him smile before. His eyes were liquid, half-glazed. "Well, I better check," he said, taking up her hand again. His soft skin caressed where the splinter had been and nothing snagged this time. "Yeah, I think I got it." He kissed the back of her hand but did not release it. Instead, dragging his eyes away from hers, as if it was the hardest thing he had ever done, he looked toward where the sun was about to break the horizon.

Abbie didn't try to pull her hand away, but sat there, afraid to move in case it would break the spell, too afraid he might let her hand go. She turned her head to see the sunrise with him. While she looked, the reds and oranges lit up the morning sky and the wispy clouds it contained. The light shone down on the canyon, making the Yellowstone River below the falls glitter like a snake covered in diamonds. The canyon walls were afire with the reflected light, the sharp rocks splitting it and causing a dazzling display for the audience of two. Abbie's breath caught in her throat.

"Oh, it's beautiful," she said.

"It is," he agreed. The odd tone in his voice made her look over at him. He was staring at her. His hand had started to absently caress her hand and palm. The fire shot up her arm again.

Her blue eyes looked into his as he leaned closer, ever closer. When she thought they might bump heads, he angled his slightly and then their lips met, soft as butterfly wings.

Abbie couldn't form a complete thought, but what echoed in her mind was that she didn't want this to end. Ever. She wrapped her arms around him and drew him closer, even as he did the same. The brush of his lips over hers made the heat she had felt before burn even hotter, and she met his kiss hungrily. She lost the sense of time when their tongues touched, lightly at first, and then more insistently. She felt like they were one person, separated in all but that tiny spot, their lips and their mouths. They kissed, desperately and passionately for a long time, and then they parted. When they did, it was like the newly risen sun had gone out.

Abigail took in a deep breath, trying to slow her heart and trying to minimize the light-headed feeling. She looked at Ben, his eyes glittering in the new day, and wanted nothing more than to continue kissing him forever.

"Wow," he said, breathing heavily himself.

And then it all came crashing down.

She couldn't do this. She had a mission to perform. He was merely a human, or worse, a fire warlock. She couldn't get involved with him like this.

"I...I...have to go." She got up abruptly and turned from him.

"Abbie," he said, a pleading in his voice. "Please, don't go. I'm sorry. I shouldn't have done that. Please, don't go."

She started walking up the trail. "Please leave me alone, Ben. Just stay here for a little while. I can't...I won't...I just need to go." She all but ran up the trail and away from him.

What was I thinking? Abbie thought as she fled Ben. Master Mason. She brushed her lips with her finger, still feeling the heat of his lips on her. *I can't do this. I can't. Oh, Papa, I understand what you were trying to tell me, but this can't possibly work.*

Her car sped along the roads in the national park, going well above the limit displayed on the traffic signs. She paid it no attention, navigating the winding roads by instinct, using all her thought process for the current dilemma.

Benjamin, Ben, was an only. Only human. At best. She was more than human. How could she think of being with him?

But she did think of him. Often. And she thought of being with him. That was the reason she came out to the park in the first place, to seek the solitude and beauty of nature, to watch the sunrise near the water, to try to forget about her feelings for him for a short time. Why did he have to show up?

She knew he didn't do it on purpose. He was just as surprised to see her as she was to see him. Still, that time they had spent, the feel of his lips on hers, the strength of her body's reaction to him...it was all too much. She was confused. She needed to be alone to think things through.

Abigail wondered if she should abandon the mission, leave the estate, and never come back. Her feelings were already affecting her performance. She had caught herself more than once daydreaming about chancing upon Ben while she should have been listening or watching to get information for her coven. What if she was distracted at a crucial moment? She could not only ruin the mission, she could be killed. Margaret Huntsman had killed before. There was a rumor about the woman last year, Ben's friend. *Master Mason's friend.* This was not a game she was playing.

Abbie pulled up to the servants' garage and parked. She sat in her car for a long time, running through everything in her head yet again. The question remained. What would she do? She had thought she had things fairly well under control, but that kiss shattered all her reasoning and fuddled her brain. What would her mother do?

Letting out a heavy sigh, she got out of her car and went to her room. Maybe she could take a nap. Things always seemed clearer after a nap. She hoped she didn't dream; she knew who the dreams would be about.

22
〰〰〰

*B*en stared as Abbie hurried away from him. She had asked him to wait before he got up and left, so he sat there looking after her until she made another turn on the trail switchback and he lost sight of her. What had just happened?

He played back through the scene in his mind. Was he too aggressive? Did he scare her, make her afraid he would attack her? He hoped not. He would never want that. He wished she would let him talk to her, but forcing the issue wouldn't help. When she was ready to talk, maybe she would. Maybe.

As many times as he went over what had happened in his mind, he couldn't see what he did that would make her run away like that. He scratched his head. "Women," his father had told him when he was fifteen, "are the last great mystery in the universe for men. I'm pretty sure we'll figure out time travel before we figure them out." Ben would have to agree.

He checked his watch. It had been twenty minutes since Abbie ran off. He got to his feet and started slowly up the trail. It only took about ten minutes to reach the parking lot at a normal pace, so she would be miles away. Other people were starting to come down the trail to see the waterfall. He put on a polite smile and said good morning to each as they passed him. His heart wasn't in it, though.

Why did he feel so guilty, like he'd done something wrong? He hoped she would talk to him about this. He couldn't handle it if he was never able to talk to her again.

When Ben reached the parking lot, he looked around in vain for Abbie's red hair. She wasn't there, of course, and neither was her car, the only other car that had been in the parking lot when he arrived. With a sigh, he climbed into his own vehicle and started back home.

Lucas was sitting on the couch in the rec room when Ben walked in. He waved to Ben. "You know," he said, picking up the remote and turning off the television, "you ought to go and have quiet time to yourself more often. When you drive yourself, it's like a mini vacation for me. I sat around and—" He noticed the look on Ben's face and stopped talking. Tilting his head to the side and narrowing his eyes as if inspecting Ben, he said, "What's up? You look like your favorite puppy just died."

Ben raked his fingers through his hair and blew out a breath. "You know, this engagement thing has really got me down. I have to do something about it."

"Yeah," Lucas said, "I hear ya. But what are you going to do? What *can* you do?"

"I don't know, I just don't know. Mother has me

over a barrel here. I'm an adult, but to her I might as well still be three years old. She has all the power." Ben looked at the floor, thinking. "Maybe I'll just run away."

Lucas's scoff brought Ben's head up again. "Dude, that's something a five-year-old would say. What do you mean, 'run away'? Where can you hide? You're Ben Mason. Everyone in the state knows what you look like and who you are."

"That's an exaggeration, and you know it," Ben said, but the point was valid. "She would probably just have her goons drag me back here, stuff me in a tux, and drag me to the altar to marry Penelope. Ack, Penelope."

"True, true," Lucas said. "It's too bad you're not already married. Then all this would be moot."

Ben's eyes lit up. "Lucas, you're a genius! That's it, that's what I need to do. I need to get married before they can set up this farce of a wedding with Penelope." He broke into a grin.

"Whoa there, partner. What do you mean, get married? Susan is still missing, and unless I've missed it completely, you haven't been dating anyone else. Who are you going to marry?"

Ben deflated. This going back and forth from hope to despair was exhausting. Then, an idea came to him. "Abigail."

Lucas's brows drew down, and he tilted his head to the side. "Abigail? That new maid? What about her?"

"I'll marry her," Ben said, triumphant.

"Now Ben, I know things seem desperate and that this would be an easy way out, but think, man. She's a maid. You're rich. I mean super-rich. You can't just go and marry a maid."

"Sure I can. It would be perfect. It would get Mother off my back. I'm sure Abigail would love to have people serving her instead of her serving others. She'd do it."

"Ben," Lucas said, "you don't really think this will work, do you? It sounds like trouble to me."

Ben was out of his chair, pacing as he spoke. "No, it's perfect. Sure, she's only a maid, but this is the kind of chance not everyone has. I'll ask her, and I bet she'll say yes. We'll get married and keep it secret from everyone at first. I'll tell my mother when the plans for the wedding to Penelope are coming close to fruition. We'll have to figure out what to do with Abigail's job here, though. She can probably just keep working until we reveal our marriage to everyone. She'll understand. Yeah, that's what I'm going to do. It's perfect."

"Ben, my man," Lucas said. "Do you remember our conversation about how you see people who are not rich as being lesser than yourself?"

"Yes."

"Well, you just can't use people like this. You can't try to lure the poor girl into marrying you to solve your problem. You can't buy her. It's not cool, man."

Ben looked askance at his friend, but then he understood. "Oh, right, I never told you. Lucas, I'm crazy about that girl. I want to marry her. I mean, seriously want to marry her. It's not just solving a problem, it's what I would do even if there was no engagement. The timing just fits in perfectly now."

He told Lucas about the sunrise and their kiss and the little chance meetings he'd been arranging for the last few months. "I think I knew the first time I met her, but now I'm really sure. This is the girl I want, and if the timing helps with other problems, then what's the harm?"

"You're crazy about her?" Lucas asked. "You really felt like this even before you came up with your lunatic idea?"

"Yep."

"You do know that once your mother finds out, she'll cut you off, right? Even if you weren't doing it to spite her, she'd close the wallet on you because you went and did it without her permission. And with someone as 'lowly' as a maid."

"Yeah," Ben said sadly. "I know. I'll tell you, Lucas, I don't really think I was cut out for all this." He swept his arm out, including the entire room and estate. "I think I'd rather work for a living and just make ends meet. None of this money or luxury makes me happy. I'm miserable."

"That's just because you don't know how it is to have to 'just make ends meet.' I understand the sentiment, though."

Ben smiled at his friend. "Okay, so I need to plan this thing out. You're going to help me, right?"

"You bet. I am your manservant, after all." Lucas grimaced when he said it. He had always hated that particular title. "Besides, I'm your friend, so I won't even charge you overtime for it." He winked.

"Great," Ben said, clapping him on the back. "Let's get started."

*****

Arianna Cox silently moved away from the door to Master Mason's recreation room and down the hall.

She had heard enough, she thought. Enough to get that new girl, Abigail, in trouble. She deserved it for calling her and Sadie down that day.

It was unfortunate that Master Mason would get in trouble, too. He was a kind man, and *so* nice to look at. He had always been polite to her. Still, if she could get the new girl fired, it would be worth it.

She had to time it perfectly to get the best price for her information. Too soon or too late and she would miss out on a reward. It was enough to get this Abigail fired, but why not get something for herself in the bargain? Yes, she would hold her tongue for now, watch and wait until the time was right. With a wicked smile, she continued her work, dusting the picture frames and sculptures in the hall.

23

~~~~~

*B*en thought he was doing a good job maintaining his sanity even though he knew Abigail was in the house somewhere. He wasn't sure what she was thinking, but she had fled from him at the waterfall, so he was determined to let her come to him when she wanted to talk about it. Whenever he thought about it, pain engulfed him and threatened to steal his breath. He kept as busy as he could and did his best to stay away from the areas he thought she would be in at the times he used to find her there. He could survive this if he never saw or heard her.

He thought about the pure ridiculousness of it. He was essentially a prisoner in his own house, afraid to move about freely. The last thing he wanted to do was to make things weird for her, and she had made it clear that she wanted nothing to do with him. So he skulked around in his own house and trod carefully lest he run into her.

It worked for four days.

He came around the corner in a hallway and almost ran into her. They both stopped in their tracks and looked at each other. They were silent for a moment. Ben wasn't sure about her, but he didn't know what to say.

"Um, hi," he finally got out and stepped to the left to go around her.

She stepped to the right so they were still face-to-face. Color bloomed on her cheeks as she stepped to her left.

Ben stepped to his right at the same time. He felt his face burning, too.

They both laughed, and he stepped back, sweeping his arm out and bowing to let her pass. She touched his arm, and he thought he would lose his mind.

"Thank you, Ben," she said, her voice as sweet and perfect as he remembered it. "Do you think we can talk?"

"Definitely," he said.

"I…miss talking to you. I wasn't thinking straight before, and I think I was rude to you, but while you were gone, I missed our little chats. And since…the waterfall, I miss them more." She forced a chuckle. "Silly, huh?"

"Oh, Abbie, it's not silly at all. It's been driving me crazy that I haven't been able to talk to you. I thought you didn't like me or decided you didn't want to talk to me, so I tried to leave you alone. It was very hard."

"For me, too," she said. "Maybe we can forget all that stuff and just go with whatever seems to work. How about that?"

"That sounds fantastic to me. Thank you."

She flashed him her gorgeous smile, stepped

around him, and continued down the hall. He watched her until she was out of sight. Looking around to make sure no one else was there, he let the smile that was trying to get out leap onto his face. The world wasn't such a bad place, after all.

Over the next several weeks, things between Ben and Abbie eased back to how they were before the kiss. The furtive glances, the chance meetings, the conversations that seemed forced at first but then became more comfortable, all of that became a regular routine.

Ben also found himself doing little things for her. One time, he made a little origami flower he learned how to make on the internet and put it on her cart as she was inside one of the rooms cleaning. He wanted to stay to watch her face when she found it, but he was afraid it would ruin the surprise.

He did other things, too. Little notes, some with only a smiley face, some with sly turns of phrase he made up to make her smile. He thought of sending her flowers but didn't want to call attention to her, and, to be honest, he didn't want her to think he was just like every other guy. Sending a dozen red roses may show that he was in love with her, but how original was that? No, she deserved creativity. She inspired it in him.

So, he continued his little romantic overtures, chatting with her and smiling at her when the chance arose, and generally tried to keep things light. He never told her, in notes or in person, that he loved her. He was afraid it would scare her away, especially because he knew it was true.

Ben was still thinking about how to bring up his idea to Abbie. She seemed to have forgotten about fleeing from him, and he had not brought it up for fear of a relapse. The time for him to act finally came four and a half weeks after they watched the sunrise together at the waterfall. Abbie was dusting the artwork in the main hall on the second floor—there was always someone dusting something—and Ben came up the stairs.

He looked around to make sure no one else was around, even opening the door to a guest room to make sure there wasn't anyone close enough to hear. Abbie looked at him quizzically.

"Abbie," he said, a little breathless from his anxiety, "I wanted to ask you something."

Abbie swiveled her head back and forth to check for eavesdroppers. "Okay?" It came out sounding more like a question than a statement.

Ben took a deep breath, looked around again, hastily dropped to one knee and launched into what he had rehearsed. "Abbie, would you marry me?" He held out a ring to her.

The look on her face was difficult to read. It was shock, happiness, suspicion, and even a bit of anger mixed in. He wasn't sure what it meant. She bit her lower lip and looked around again.

"Ben, get up off the floor," she hissed. "If someone sees you, we're both in trouble."

He did as she asked, standing there gazing at her in expectation.

"Is this some kind of joke?" she asked, looking at the ring he still held in his hand and narrowing her eyes.

"No, no," he said. "It's no joke. I'm serious. I want you to marry me." He paused, then continued. "If you want to, that is."

Her eyes softened a little. "Are you crazy?" It was said gently.

"I am," he said. "I'm crazy about you. I have been from the first. That kiss clinched it. I want to be with you."

"You know that's not really how these things work, right?" she said. "Typically, people spend a lot of time together, date, get engaged, and then get married. Over a period of time."

"I know," he said, eyes dropping to the floor. "The thing is, Mother has engaged me to Penelope, and there isn't really much time. I can't...don't want to wait. It's you I want, not her." He proffered the ring again. "Marry me and make me the happiest man in the world?"

A smile tugged at the corners of her mouth, but she exerted her will and smoothed her face into a neutral expression. "You are crazy." A soft chuckle escaped her lips and her eyes widened.

He continued to hold out the ring.

"Oh, give me that," she said, snatching it from him and closing her fist around it. "Someone seeing you holding that out to me will be as bad as you being on your knee." She opened her fist slowly and peered at what was in her palm. It was ornately fashioned in white gold with a large diamond solitaire and intricate swirls around the band. It was somehow fancy and yet still simple. "Oh, Ben, it's beautiful."

"It pales in comparison to the one who is holding it," he said, and she rolled her eyes at him.

"Too much?" he asked.

She shook her head. "No, just enough. But don't go saying things like that all the time, or I'll think you're trying to sway me with pretty language."

"Okay," he said.

Abbie looked at the ring again. "It looks like an antique, an heirloom."

Ben hoped that didn't mean she felt insulted that he had offered her an old ring. "Not quite so old as that. It was my grandmother's, on my father's side. My father carried it around in his pocket after she died. He had it with him when he passed away. It means the world to me, a tie to him, and to my nana, who died when I was ten years old. He said that it was too simple for my mother to wear. When he proposed to her, he didn't even bother to offer it to her, instead buying a very expensive and gaudy ring."

"Oh, Ben." She closed her fingers over the ring again. "Can I think about it for a day or two?" she asked, worrying that bottom lip in her teeth again. "Is that okay?"

Ben felt something in his middle wriggle as if he had swallowed a live eel. "Um, yeah, that's fine."

"It's not that I don't like you or anything," she said. "It's just that it's so sudden, so unexpected. I need to sort things out." She shook her head. "I'm not making any sense. Just please give me a day or two, okay?"

Ben looked around yet again and then took Abbie's hands in his. "I understand. Take as long as you want. You know where to find me. After all, you know where I live." He winked at her, brought her hands up and kissed them and then turned and went downstairs.

24

*F*or two days, Abigail thought of nothing else but what her answer would be. The ring, a fine necklace looped through it so that it hung between her breasts, was a constant reminder. As if she needed one.

As she went about her work, she ticked off pros and cons of each of her two options. A simple yes or no answer didn't seem very simple at all. Abbie was grateful that Ben wasn't there every time she turned around. He was obviously making an effort to stay clear of her to allow her to make a decision without his influence. That went into the "yes" column as a pro.

Her mother and father had always taught her to be mindful of her feelings, and it had always been implied that if she decided to marry, it would be for love, not for expediency or because she felt she had to because she had simply been with someone for a period of time. They also believed, she knew, that real love was worth sacrifice. But was it worth all sacrifice? Were some things more important even than true love? Was it even love that she felt? She wasn't sure.

Her mission was the most important thing in her life. A chance to help to bring her mother's killer to justice was not something she took lightly, even if she took her responsibilities to her coven lightly, which she didn't. If she said yes to Ben, her mission would be over. The chance of sneaking in another operative was slim. The water witches might lose any chance of getting inside information about Margaret Huntsman. Others might lose their lives.

Then again, her mission had not yielded anything worthwhile in months of her being in the household. She knew that she had to be patient when gathering intel undercover, and even more so, it seemed, to find evidence of Margaret's magic use that would not be missed, but she wasn't sure she would ever find out anything that would bring the woman down. She could spend two years being a maid and not have anything to show for it. If she was married to Margaret's son, she might actually have a better chance of uncovering something.

But all these things were not what she should be considering. When it came down to it, the success or failure of her mission might be a wash when comparing the two scenarios. What she really needed to think about was if she wanted to marry Ben.

She had only known him for a few months, but she did care for him. She cared a great deal for him. But was it love? She'd never really been in love, at least not that she knew. She'd been infatuated when she was younger, but she was an adult now.

All Abbie knew was that when she looked into Ben's eyes, nothing else mattered. It was unnerving how he took over her thoughts when he wasn't around and how she felt that anything was possible when he was. He was an only, just a normal human, but for some reason that didn't matter to her. Did it?

Most witches, no matter which element or coven, saw normal humans as being not quite as good, not quite as elevated, as magic users. It was a prejudice like any other, she thought, and she tried not to dwell on it, but in the back of her mind, way down deep, she thought that maybe she did believe it. At least a little. Could she reconcile her bias with marrying a man without magic? She didn't know.

Children. Would they have the gift of magic? Did Ben even want them? She didn't want any right now, but she could see in the future wanting to have one or two. Or maybe three. She enjoyed interacting with young people, and she adored babies, as did most sane people, she thought.

She shook her head, muttering to herself as she walked down the hall on the second floor, right past the spot where Ben had gotten to his knee and proposed. She could picture him there. What was she going to do?

She stopped cold in her tracks. What if he was in on what his mother was doing? What if she got married to one who was complicit in her mother's murder? But no. Ben was an honest, honorable man. He wouldn't be part of his mother's schemes. Would he? Was he a fire warlock? Not all children of witches and warlocks had the gift. He might be a skip. It was too bad she didn't know more about his family; the covens tended to be secretive about their powers and their personal lives.

It was interesting to her, yoo, that she normally thought of him as an only, not a skip. She was almost positive he was not a warlock, or she would have sensed his power, but if he was powerless and from a fire family, he would be a skip. Strange.

When two days had passed, Abbie found Ben, who had made himself easy to find. He seemed to be doing slow laps of the mansion. He didn't approach Abbie, but he was available if she wanted to talk to him.

"I have thought about your...question," she said. She made her expression unreadable. His eyes were tense, his mouth a tight line. He obviously had no idea if she was going to say yes or no. He waited for her to finish.

She just stood there looking at him.

"And...?" he finally said.

"Are you sure this is what you want? I—"

He put his finger on her lips, stopping her. He looked into her eyes, and she couldn't have averted her glance if she had wanted to. She didn't want to.

"Abbie. It's you I want. It's you I have to be with. There is nothing on this Earth as perfect as you are for me. Yes, this is what I want. More than anything. The question is, is it what you want?"

He removed his finger and goose bumps raced up her back. Ben looked around, eyes darting to find anyone who might have seen them. There was no one.

That's right, there was no one. No one else. She had made her decision, but it had not been as firm as she would have liked. It was now. What he said was exactly how she herself felt.

"And I have decided," she said, stepping closer to him to put her mouth next to his ear, "that I would love to marry you." She gave his earlobe a quick kiss and then stepped back, looking around herself to make sure no one had seen. It would be so wonderful not to have to worry about others seeing them interact after they were married.

Ben relaxed immediately, his shoulders dropping a little and a sigh escaping his lips. She wished he could take her in his arms, but he couldn't, not here. He smiled at her, nodded, and looked deep into her eyes. "This weekend, let's meet away from the estate and we can talk about it, figure things out."

"Yes," she said, matching his smile. "That sounds nice."

She walked away, but she could feel his smile follow her as she went. She tried to temper her smile so people wouldn't ask her about it, but quickly realized there was no way she could keep it off her face. She would have to try to avoid others until the smile lessened on its own. She thought a year or two might do it.

That weekend, Abigail met Ben at the brink of the Lower Yellowstone Falls, the same place they had their first—and only—kiss. They remedied that little detail immediately. This time, Ben arrived earlier, waiting on the same bench they'd shared before.

She ran the last few steps as he got up from the bench. He enfolded her in his arms and squeezed. She felt his warmth through the jacket she was wearing, or maybe it was just her own flush. As she leaned her head back so she could look at him, he moved his head closer and kissed her.

She let herself be swept away this time, not

fighting and not thinking, just enjoying their closeness, the softness of his lips on hers, the way they connected. Their tongues danced and the world spun.

When the kiss finally ended, Abbie put her head on his chest and breathed deeply. She was out of breath as if she had run for miles.

"Whoa," he said, as if he had taken the word directly from her mind.

"Ditto," she said.

They sat on the bench until the sun rose, his arm encircling her. He nuzzled her hair, kissed her ear, and pulled her tight to his side. She could have spent the rest of her life in that moment and been perfectly happy.

After the sun was up and other people started to show up at the falls, they walked back up the trail together, heads close, talking about what they would do.

"I have a friend who can legally marry us," Ben said. "Well, he's not really a friend, I guess, because I can't really hang out with him. Mother would never approve. Anyway, he got ordained as some kind of holy man or shaman or something a few years back just on a lark. He's legal, though." He looked her in the eyes. "That's if you don't mind. We can have a big wedding to renew our vows when the timing is better. Right now, we don't have the time or the opportunity. Is that all right with you?"

Abbie had never been one of those women who cared about a big wedding. It wasn't the Day that mattered to her. It was what it stood for, and the time after that day was what really mattered. "That's fine with me. I understand the time constraints and…other concerns."

"You are fantastic!" Ben said and kissed her on the cheek while walking, almost tripping over himself.

"Just pay attention to the trail," she said. "The last thing we need is you falling over the edge, bouncing down the slope, and going into the river."

"I can rent a place where we can live, though I still haven't figured out how the logistics will work at first. I mean,"—he scrubbed his fingers through his hair—"I'm not sure when or how to break it to Mother. She's still set on me marrying Penelope. Ugh. I'm not really sure what she'll do when she finds out about you. I do know that I want to be married before breaking it to her. She has ways of getting what she wants."

"It's better to wait at least a few weeks, I think," Abigail said. "It'll give me a chance to give notice and find a job." As she said it, a lump formed in her throat. It felt like she was starting their relationship, their marriage, with deception. "Ben, there are some things I need to tell you about."

"There are things I need to tell you about, too." His phone chimed, and he pulled it out of his pocket. "Damn! It's my mother." He looked at Abbie, his expression pained, and then he silenced the phone and put it back in his pocket. "So, let's talk about these things—" The phone rang again.

Abigail took Ben's hand. "Go ahead and answer it. I appreciate you being polite and not taking the call, but she'll just keep on calling you."

He sighed and took the phone out again, answering it. "Hello? Yes. No. I'm in Yellowstone trying to clear my head. Yes, I know. Yes. All right. Bye."

He turned toward her, his mouth set in a frown. "She needs me to come back home right away. Something about a tailor and some suits for some special occasion. I'm sorry, Abbie."

Abigail hugged him and gave him a quick kiss on the mouth. "It's fine. I understand. Once you're mine, though, she is going to take a back seat, so help me."

He smiled at her. "Definitely. I wouldn't have it any other way. Let's figure out a time and place to talk about those other things and to figure out the schedule for us getting married." His smile grew wider. "We're actually going to get married."

Her face split into a smile to match his. "We are. Now get going before you get in trouble."

Ben pulled her close, kissed her thoroughly, leaving her breathless, and then headed toward his car. "Thank you, Abbie." She didn't ask what the thanks were for but headed toward her own car to make the long drive back home.

It took two more meetings to finally get everything set up for the marriage. With the limited amount of time they had and all the preparations to make, there wasn't time to talk about the other things Abbie wanted to talk about. She was anxious to confess to him what she was doing at the estate and who she really was, yet when there never seemed to be time to discuss it, it was almost a relief. Still, her conscience bothered her.

She decided that the real reason she hesitated was the small chance he was complicit in his mother's wrongdoing. It would break her heart if he was, but more, it could put her in mortal danger. Even thinking that made her feel guilty, too. He couldn't be part of it. He just couldn't.

They agreed she could give notice after they got married. They would pretend nothing had changed, continuing their normal routines, until they were able to get a better handle on what they would do, where they would go. They simply didn't have the time to do all that first. If Margaret Huntsman found out before they were actually married, she would do something to prevent it. They had to get it done as soon as possible. They set a date two weeks from their last "logistics meeting."

"I rented us a house in Cody," Ben told her as they shared a final kiss and were getting ready to leave in their separate cars. "I prepaid the rent for a year, in cash. That should give us time to figure things out."

"You know, this isn't the typical romantic wedding story," Abbie said. "All this sneaking around makes me feel guilty, and I haven't done anything wrong."

Ben took her hand and kissed it. "I know, Abbie, and I'm sorry. It's just the situation with my mother and the stupid engagement to Penelope and all that. Once we get married and settle into a routine, I'll make it up to you. I promise."

She eyed him as if weighing him and his motives. "Okay, but you have a lot to make up for. I hope you're prepared to do what it takes."

"I am, Abbie." He pulled her into a kiss and then released her. "I *so* am."

"You better be. For a few weeks, I can go and stay at our house on the weekends, at least until I have given my notice and leave the estate. Will you be able to spend the weekends with me?"

"Absolutely," he said. "My mother is used to me being gone during the weekends, so it won't be suspicious at all. We'll make it work."

She smiled at him. "I know we will." Looking at her watch, she sighed. "We better get going." She ran her fingers through his hair—she loved doing that—and kissed him one last time before walking toward her car. She stopped, turned around, and came back to him as he was standing there watching her. "I...I love you, you know. I just wanted to tell you that."

His gorgeous blue eyes went liquid and he pulled her into a hug. "Oh, Abbie, I've been wanting to hear that for so long. I am totally, incurably, outrageously, head over heels in love with you." He kissed her.

"Sure, try to one-up me," she said, sticking her tongue out at him and then laughing. "I'll see you around."

"You definitely will," he said.

25

~~~~~

*F*riday afternoon, as Abbie was finishing up her work, she pondered what she would do. She seemed to be spending a lot of time doing that lately.

I can't just leave them ignorant of what I am doing, she thought. *I have to tell them, and sooner is better than later. But what if they try to talk me out of it? What if they forbid me to go through with it? At least I'd have a resolution and then I wouldn't be so torn.*

She argued with herself for hours and finally came to the conclusion that she had to go home and tell her father, at least. She felt guilty in abandoning her mission, but down deep, she thought it was the right thing to do. Didn't he tell her himself that love was worth sacrifice? She did believe that, but then why did she feel like she was being irresponsible?

Still arguing with herself, her stomach tied in knots over it, she left early the next morning to drive to her home. It was the longest five hours of her life.

"Abbie!" her father said as she showed up in his study. He rushed to her to pull her into a hug. "Twice in a month's time. What's the occasion?"

He must have felt her tense because he released his embrace, grabbed her shoulders and moved her to arm's length, studying her face. "What's wrong?"

"Oh, Papa," she said. Her eyes welled up, but she was determined not to cry. "I have to tell you something, something I am hoping won't disappoint you."

"Disappoint me?" he said. "Never. Come on, let's sit, and you can tell me all about it." He led her to the leather sofa and drew her down to sit next to him. He turned his body to face her.

Abbie looked into his gentle eyes, but that made her feel worse. She dropped her gaze, watched her hands fidgeting in front of her. There was nothing else to do but just rush through and get it out. She could sort out the details after the initial surprise.

"I'm getting married," she said. She looked up to watch for her father's response. There was none. He sat, relaxed, just as before, looking into her eyes.

"...to Margaret Huntsman's son."

Landon Henderson sat exactly as he had been. Nothing changed. Nothing. He was waiting for her to continue.

She didn't.

After a full minute of silence, he spoke. "Do you love him?"

"Yes," she said without a pause. "I do."

Her father's face finally showed some expression. He smiled. Smiled!

"Then that's what you should be doing, isn't it?"

"It means I will have to abort the mission,

obviously," she said.

"Yes."

"It will be difficult or impossible to get another operative in there without arousing suspicion."

"You're right."

"I'll be joined in wedlock to the son of our greatest enemy, the woman responsible for Mother's death."

"I understand that," he said. "Abbie, in the grand scheme of things, the effects of what you are doing on the mission are insignificant."

Abbie looked at him, mouth hanging open. "What…" she cleared her throat, "what do you mean?"

Her father took her hands in his and kissed them. "Abbie, your mother and I always told you to trust your heart but to use your mind to make sure of things. Finding a person with whom you want to spend the rest of your life is one of the most important things you can ever do. These other things, they pale in significance. We'll get by without a spy inside the estate.

"We also do not judge one person by another person's deeds. What matters is that you are choosing to live life. In all important things, there is sacrifice."

"But," she said, "I'm abandoning an important mission. I am being unreliable."

"Abbie, Abbie, don't you understand? If you were to stay there and not marry the man you love, would you be able to do your job effectively? Would you be a good operative?"

"No, I guess not."

"Then the mission is already compromised—through no fault of your own—so you can take that part right out of the equation. Like I said, we can get by without an internal spy. It was always a slim chance that you'd be able to find anything important, anyway. Margaret is too cunning to allow even her staff to find incriminating evidence. We gave it a shot, but it was just about time to pull you out of there, anyway. As you leave, maybe you can take a piece or two of evidence. It won't matter if they miss it. At worst, they'll think you're a thief.

"So you see, you really have nothing to be ashamed of, but you have everything to look forward to."

Abigail looked at her father, eyes and mouth wide. Then she charged him and wrapped him in a rib-bruising hug. "I love you," she said.

"I love you, too, honey. I don't suppose the wedding is going to be normal in the sense that there will be guests or anything?"

Abbie could feel her face getting hot. "No. With everything going on with Margaret and the sham engagement she's trying to force on Ben, we're just going to go and do it. We do plan on having a wedding to renew our vows once things cool down, though."

Landon sighed. "I guess that'll have to do." He smiled widely at his daughter. "I hope you will be happy, Abbie. Keeping a marriage good is a lot of work."

"I'll work hard for it, Papa. We'll be happy. At least, we will once all this craziness with Ben's mother is over."

Abigail talked with her father for several more hours before going to her room. As she drifted off to sleep, she thought over what she and Landon had talked about. She was happy that he was so supportive. She wished her mother could be here to share it all with her. She knew her mother would love Ben. But now she knew something else, too. She knew that her mother would be supportive of her decision, not just because she loved Abigail but because she believed in love itself. Her father made her see that. Smiling, she drifted off to sleep.

*****

While Abbie was off doing whatever she was doing for the day, Ben had gone to Yellowstone, as he always did when he wanted some alone time to think. The habit had been ingrained in him early. He and his father used to go to the park and just relax, spending time together and, more importantly, spending it away from the world and all its problems and stresses. Building an empire as his father did from scratch was more than a full-time job. It was an all-consuming project that left little time for anything else. His father worked hard, harder than Ben had ever seen anyone else work, but he occasionally needed some quiet time to decompress. Even as a child, Ben knew how special those times his father shared with him were.

He missed his father. Hank Mason would have loved Abbie. A smile spread across Ben's face as he looked out over Artists Point, all its colors dazzling in the morning sun.

It was such a contrast, the relationship between Ben and his mother and the one he shared with his father. He had read about the special bond between boys and their mothers, but he had never felt it. They just didn't connect. Maybe it was because she was so aloof. The part that bothered him was that he didn't even really want a close relationship with her. That embarrassed him and made him feel like a jerk, but it was true. You didn't get to pick your family, but if you did, he wouldn't have picked Margaret Huntsman. That might make him a horrible son, but he couldn't help it.

He did try to be a dutiful son, though. He hoped that once everything settled down, she would accept Abigail. In the meantime, she would be angry and vindictive. He fully expected her to cut off all his money and to do whatever she could to make his life miserable. He had planned on it, in fact. He prepaid the small home he and Abbie would live in, he had socked away a little money for emergencies, and he had spent a good deal of time trying to figure out how she would act against him so that he could counteract what she did. It all made him nervous, but it would not deter him. He would see this through.

He almost couldn't believe it himself. He was going to get married...and by his choice. There was something about Abigail right from the first time he had met her, something that told him she would be important. Little did he know that she would become the most important thing. Important enough to give up the family fortune for. He hoped he had not misjudged her. If she was at all attached to material things, she would be upset that they would have no money.

That started him wondering. What was her family like? What did her father and mother do for work? Did they have money? Were they comfortable or just making ends meet? He had never asked her. He never really had the time and opportunity to talk about things like that. He hoped that would change soon.

He wanted to know everything about her.

There were less than two weeks left until the wedding. He hesitated to even call it a wedding. It was just going to be him, Abbie, Lucas—as a witness—and the guy marrying them. Regardless, it was the most important day of his life so far. He would go over everything one more time to make sure it would go without a hitch. He couldn't let his mother ruin this.

He reached into his pocket for his phone. Whenever he started to feel stressed, he looked at the pictures he had taken of Abbie. That always calmed him down. He patted his front pocket, then his back pocket, then all his others. Damn. He had left his phone at home. He couldn't remember the last time he had done that. Well, he would just have to pull up the thousand pictures of her in his mind. He closed his eyes and saw those gorgeous blue orbs of hers looking at him. He sighed, leaned back against the bench, and enjoyed the show.

26

Abigail went about her work with half a mind. Less than two weeks until the secret marriage ceremony Ben had arranged. She still couldn't believe it was happening. While it was romantic, she wasn't thrilled about having to do it in secret. It would be okay, though. They could do a big formal ceremony once all the heat died down. If it ever did.

Ben was feeling his nerves, she thought. To be honest with herself, she was feeling them, too. He had been almost aloof lately, preoccupied with all the arrangements and constantly looking over his shoulder, afraid his mother would find out and stop it. He had even made a few comments that were totally unlike him, slightly derogatory things he said in passing about "little people" and the poor. Just a little while longer and the stress of waiting would be over. They would be legally married, and then there was nothing Margaret could do.

But that wasn't true. The woman could have Abbie killed. She had done it before. That was the reason Abbie was here to begin with. She would have to have a conversation with Ben to tell him about that. She had not had a chance to tell him all she wanted to. They had so little time alone together.

She could picture it now. They would be sitting by the fireplace, cozy in each other's arms and she would casually mention it. "Ben, did you know that your mother is a murderer and that she has killed several people that I know of, including my own mother?" Yeah, sure. It would happen exactly like that.

"Abigail," a woman's voice said, breaking her from her daydreams. "Can I speak with you for a minute?"

Abbie turned to find Arianna Cox standing next to her. With her tanned skin, brown eyes, and dark hair, she was a visual opposite of Abbie. A smile played across her face, but it wasn't sincere. They'd hardly spoken since Abbie called Arianna down that day, the first week on the job.

"Arianna," she said. "Of course, what is it?"

The other woman took a breath and steeled herself to speak. Abigail noticed something odd about how she did it, as if she had been practicing looking like she was nervous. What was she up to?

"I just want to let you know I have noticed your...interactions...with Master Mason. I have seen how you look at him and how he looks at you. I know you're planning to be with him."

Abigail felt herself flush. *No, don't go red now*, she thought. *It will give me away.* "What are you talking about?" There, her voice hardly quivered. She wanted to say more, but refrained.

"Oh, come on Abigail. Anyone with one eye could

see there's something there. Plus, I have heard things. It's a big estate, but it can be a small world sometimes."

"Arianna, what is the point of this? What do you want from me?"

"Want?" the other woman said. "What do I want?" She put her hand to her chest and widened her eyes as if she didn't understand what Abigail was saying. "I want nothing but to help a fellow staff member. I just want to try to keep you from getting your heart broken."

Abigail narrowed her eyes and searched the other woman's face. She had to hand it to Arianna, she was a good actress. Abbie couldn't pick up anything in her expression that told her what was going on. "And how, exactly, are you going to keep my heart from being broken?"

"Abigail, dear, why are you so suspicious? I'm trying to help you out. I heard some things, as I said, and I want to let you know. That's all."

"You heard some things," Abigail repeated flatly. "Okay, tell me these important things so my heart does not get broken."

"Very well. I'll just come right out and say it. I overheard Master Mason talking with Lucas. You know Lucas, his driver and manservant?" She waited for Abigail's nod, as if she needed it. Everyone knew Lucas. The estate wasn't *that* big.

Arianna continued, "They were talking, and Master Mason said, 'I need to find a way out of this engagement.' Lucas said, 'It's too bad you're not already married.' Master Mason jumped on that idea and said, 'Lucas, you're a genius. That's what I'll do. I'll get married before my mother has a chance to marry me off to Penelope.'"

"I know this, Arianna," Abigail said.

"Hear me out. I'm almost finished. So, Lucas said, 'And who are you going to marry to make this thing work?' And Ben said, 'I'll marry Abbie. She's just a maid, so she'll be happy to marry me.'" When Abbie flinched, a small smile crept onto Arianna's face before she smoothed it away.

"Lucas asked what would happen when Ms. Huntsman found out, and Master Mason agreed that she would be livid that he had married such a commoner, a low-class maid. They talked about it for a while, making plans and deciding exactly how it would be done. I just wanted to let you know that he's using you to escape the situation he is in and that he will most likely ditch you as soon as the coast is clear."

"I…" Abigail said, "…you heard them say exactly that? 'Just a maid' and all the rest of it?"

"I'm afraid so," Arianna said, her mouth turning down into a frown. "I wanted to let you know. I'm sure you already know how all the rich people feel about those of us who work for a living. I just wanted you to know what Benjamin is really up to. If you planned on using him for his money, then it's all fine and good, but if you thought he really cared about you, well, I just wanted to set you straight. We 'little people' need to stick together, right?"

Abigail hardly heard that last part. She was reviewing in her head all the conversations she had with Ben, the different times he had said things about "little people" and how he—one of the rich folks— was different than what he assumed she was used to. Could it be true? She would have to take some time to think about this.

"Abigail?" Arianna said, false sincerity flowing through her voice as if they were close friends. "Are you okay? You didn't know *that* then, did you? I'm sorry to be the one to break it to you, but it's better that you found out now, before it's too late. You know, in case you wanted to change your plans."

"Yes," Abigail said. "Yes, it is better. Thank you, Arianna. I'll think about what you said."

Arianna Cox turned her head and coughed softly into her hand. "Okay, then. I'll see you later. Good luck." As she left, Arianna added, "Honestly, I'm surprised he hasn't had you fired yet to get you out of the way, now that the Penelope crisis is over. Ms. Huntsman has called off the wedding. I guess you can count that as luck."

Abigail didn't have an answer for that.

*****

"Did you tell her just as we discussed?" Margaret Huntsman said to Arianna a half an hour after the woman had talked to Abigail.

"Yes, Ms. Huntsman, just like we talked about."

"And?"

"Well, ma'am," Arianna said, "she seemed upset. She covered it quickly, but she got a sour expression and turned a little pale."

"Did she confirm anything, give you any more information than what we already had?"

"No, ma'am. She just acted like it didn't matter." The laundress wrung her hands, unable to meet Margaret's eyes. "It affected her, though. It definitely did."

"We will see," Margaret Huntsman said. "Thank you, Arianna. Let me know if you overhear anything else useful."

Arianna didn't move to leave. She raised her gaze to look at Margaret's face, if not her eyes. "Ma'am?"

"Yes, what is it?"

"This won't get Master Mason in trouble or anything, will it? He has always been kind to me and all the other staff. I would hate for him to be in trouble."

Margaret's mouth quirked into a small smile. "No, Arianna. He is not in trouble. You have helped me so I can talk to him about that woman trying to take advantage of him. You saved him from making a serious mistake. You have done well. Now be off with you. I have work to do."

Arianna curtsied and then quickly turned and left the room.

"Really?" a voice preceded the woman who entered the room from a hidden side door. "'You saved him from making a serious mistake'?"

"That might be the truth," Margaret said. "If we take care of this now, then yes, this one—" she nodded her head toward where Arianna had been— "has possibly just saved his life."

"Do you think it will be that easy?" Helen asked.

"I certainly hope so," Margaret answered. "If not, I might have to take more drastic action. People have been known to disappear before."

"Yes," Helen smiled. "They certainly have."

"So you see," Margaret Huntsman said to Abigail less than an hour later, "we have found your work to be sub-standard, and so you are to be relieved." She waved an envelope at the girl. "I am paying you for the rest of the week, but you will leave immediately."

"I don't know what to say," Abigail said. "I worked hard and Mrs. Roberts didn't seem to have any complaints."

"Mrs. Roberts works for me. Remember that. You are fired. Take your check, pack your things, and leave. Don't make me have to call security. Harper will assist you in departing with the least disturbance. Enjoy your day."

With that, Abigail was dismissed from Margaret's presence, and from her employment. Harper hustled her to the servants' quarters and watched as Abbie packed her things.

"Change out of the uniform," the shrew said. "That does not belong to you."

She did so, still dazed by what had happened. She was soon in her car and heading out the main driveway. The lights of the estate shrank in her rear view mirror, and they soon quivered and took on a watery appearance. Abbie pulled to the side of the road and sat there, weeping.

What had just happened? Was it as Arianna said? Did Ben no longer have need of her, so he had his mother fire her? She couldn't believe it. She would ask him, right out. She couldn't have misjudged him that much, could she?

She picked up her phone and selected his number. The distinctive tone sounded, followed by, "I'm sorry, the number you have dialed is no longer in service. Please try again."

Abbie held the phone out and stared at the screen. He had changed his number? Maybe it was true, then. She put her head on the steering wheel and tried to breathe. A crushing weight sat on her chest. It took five long minutes to regain her ability to breathe. Then she wiped her eyes, pulled out onto the road, and headed back to her home at Aqua Terra.

She didn't know what she would do, but whatever it was, she would do it at home, surrounded by people who loved her. Actually and sincerely loved her. The tears began again immediately as she headed down the darkened road.

27

"*E*nough," Ben said aloud to himself. "It has been long enough." He realized he was talking to himself and looked around to see if anyone had noticed. It had been almost a week since he had talked to Abbie, and he had never memorized her phone number, just using it as a preset. He kicked himself for that. Without his contacts list on his phone, he couldn't call her, hadn't even caught sight of her in the halls. His patience was at an end, and he charged toward the servants' quarters to talk to her.

Ben gritted his teeth. When he had returned from Yellowstone, he couldn't find his phone anywhere. He had been feeling out of sorts, but he had never misplaced it so badly. He finally gave up and figured he had dropped it somewhere in the park and went to the phone store to replace it.

"What do you mean my account has been closed?" he said to the clerk. "I didn't close my account."

The young woman behind the counter tapped out something on her iPad. "Yes, Mr. Mason, it says right here that your account was closed and locked." Her eyes narrowed. "That's strange."

"What's strange?"

"There were special instructions to delete all information connected to this account. I didn't even know we could do that."

Ben scrubbed his hand through his hair. "Who authorized that? Does it say?"

"I'm sorry, sir, but I'm not allowed to give you that information. It appears that the account is a business account, one for Huntsman Consolidated. Were you recently fired? That could be the reason."

It took every ounce of willpower not to yell at the woman. It wasn't her fault, though. Obviously his mother was pulling his strings. He simply bought a new phone, this one under just his own name. That didn't allow him to retrieve what he'd lost though, like Abbie's phone number and the pictures he had taken of her. He would have to get her number—and memorize it this time—and take more pictures of her. It was strange not being able to see images of her anytime he wanted.

Ben came around the corner in the main hallway and almost ran into a tall, slender, brown-haired woman carrying linens. He seemed to almost run into people in that particular part of the hallway quite a bit. They both skidded on the floor from their abrupt halts.

"Oh, I'm sorry," Ben said, noticing that the girl wore a maid's uniform. "Pardon me."

"No, it was my fault," she said. "I should have watched where I was going."

Ben looked into her hazel eyes and then scanned her face. "I don't believe we have met. I'm Benjamin Mason." He put his hand out but then noticed that hers were both full with the linens she was carrying. He let his hand drop. "Oh, sorry."

"It is a pleasure to meet you, Master Mason. I'm Candace Fuller. I'm the new maid. I just started yesterday."

"I see. I didn't know we were adding to the staff. Welcome."

"I'm not so much an addition," she said, "as a replacement for one of the maids who left."

"Really?" Ben was curious now. "Do you know who you are replacing?"

"Yes, I believe her name was Abigail. She left abruptly, didn't even give notice." She wrinkled her nose and frowned to indicate what she thought of acting in such a way.

"Abigail?" Ben said, his heart sinking into his stomach. "I hadn't heard she left. Well, as I said, Candace, welcome. I hope you like it here."

Ben started off toward his room to lie down. Abigail was gone? He wondered if she went to the little house he had rented.

It only took two steps before he changed his mind about going to his room. He did think he needed to lie down, but he needed answers more. And he thought he knew where he could get some, if answers were to be found anywhere.

"Mrs. Roberts," Ben said as he found the Housekeeper after searching for a half an hour. "I wonder if I could talk to you for a minute."

The squat gray-haired woman turned at Ben's voice and a smile came across her face. She always had liked Ben. "Master Benjamin!" She could call him that because she basically raised him from infancy. "It's a pleasure to see you. I haven't had a chance to talk to you since you returned from your trip. Did you have a good time overseas?"

"Uh, yes, it was fine, thank you. Mrs. Roberts, what happened to Abigail? I just found out she has been replaced."

The Housekeeper's face fell. "Oh, Abigail. I'm not really sure. She has been acting strangely, as if she was mourning someone or heartbroken or something. Don't misunderstand me, she did her work, and did it well, but she wasn't her same happy self during the time that you were gone. A few weeks ago, though, she snapped out of it and was her normal perky, cheerful self. I didn't ask her what was going on in her life. It was really none of my business. As long as it did not affect her work, I left her alone.

"Like I said, I thought it was all done and over with, but then, just three days ago, something happened and she apparently went to Ms. Huntsman and quit. She didn't give notice or a reason. I am really sorry to see her go and even more sorry that she's having a rough time and couldn't trust me to speak to me instead of Ms. Huntsman. I hope she gets through it okay."

"She was upset and just left?" Ben asked. "That doesn't sound like her at all. She seemed so much more reliable than that."

"That was my opinion, too. It's too bad, it really is. The new girl, Candace, seems to be a good worker, though, so don't you worry about the work getting done. We will soldier on." She smiled at Ben, and he forced a smile also. Turning on his heel, he headed toward his room. He felt a headache coming on and that was just fine. His heart already ached fiercely, so why shouldn't his head, too?

28

Margaret looked over her desk at Helen Shapiro, still so physically intimidating after all these years. Helen was just, well, large. She was not fat. In fact, she looked to be solid muscle. If Margaret wasn't so powerful, so confident, in her own right, she might be a little intimidated herself. She had known Helen for more than thirty years—from even before she had met Henry Mason—and had worked with her closely. They were friends, but they were also business associates. Not just in the mundane business of making money, but also in all the business related to fire magic. They had been through a lot together.

"I'm telling you, Margaret," Helen said. "He's more trouble than he's worth. Why don't you just arrange an accident? Things happen all the time. No one will be the wiser if it is done correctly."

It was an old argument, one that would continue until the subject of the discussion either threw his part in wholly with Margaret's plans or defied her so strongly that she was forced to take action to eliminate him.

"Oh, Helen, give it a rest. One would think you had a personal vendetta against the boy the way you are always calling for me to kill him."

"He will never come around. He has too much Boy Scout in him. Some people are not meant to be in control, they can't make the tough decisions. He's a lost cause."

"He is my heir," Margaret said. "I still think I can get him under control. With a bit more patient work, he'll come around."

"Are you going to use more of your mind control tricks, then? Will you finally squeeze him to force him to submit to your will?"

Margaret sighed. "Helen, for someone as intelligent and clever as you, you seem to have trouble grasping the simple fact that my 'mind control tricks' are very delicate and dangerous to use. If I push too hard, too quickly, I can do damage to him—"

"So what?"

Margaret put her hand up to stop her friend from interrupting her again. "It is not just the damage I'm concerned with. It's the type of damage. The process is inexact. I could kill him." She raised a finger toward Helen as the woman opened her mouth to interrupt again. "Or I could cause changes that would make him completely unpredictable, totally insane, or just aggressive and violent. If he displayed any of those things, don't you think it would call attention to us? Don't you?"

Helen, for once, remained silent, looking abashed.

"I am working on it," Margaret continued. "I do

not want to waste him. He has his definite uses and, honestly, I'm getting too old to start over with another adopted child. It would be at least twenty years before he or she is suitable for my plans. No, I will continue to work on Benjamin until it is clear he will turn on me. Rebellion is one thing, betrayal another. There is time yet. I have been exerting more control over him, using more of my power. As much as I can afford to use right now. His mood and focus are already being affected."

"But what about this marriage scheme of his, wanting to marry the maid to foil your plans with Penelope?"

"That has been taken care of. The girl is gone, and he has no cards left to play. He will bluster and throw a tantrum, but he will marry the one of my choice. My plans will unfold as I have developed them."

"I don't really think—" A knock at the door to Margaret's study interrupted Helen.

"That would be Benjamin," Margaret said. "This will be delicate, so I would like you to leave through the hidden door. You can stay just inside the passageway and listen, if you like, but I think your presence will make the situation even more tense for him."

"I understand," Helen said, moving behind the desk to the door hidden on the wall there. "Good luck. He is a stubborn one, I'll give him that. Just like his father."

Margaret only nodded and showed her teeth. Whether in a smile or something else, her friend would have to decide for herself. As the secret door closed, she called out, "Come in."

Benjamin opened the door and entered. He looked

around to see if Margaret was alone and when he saw that she was, he nodded while closing the door behind him. "Mother."

"Benjamin, what a pleasant surprise. Come in, sit down. Would you like something to drink?" She lifted her cup as if to show it to him. "This tea has the most delightful hint of mint in it."

"No," he said. "Thank you. I was wondering if I could talk to you."

"Of course. What is it?"

"I'll get right to the point. I will not marry Penelope. I don't like her, and I can't even think of spending my life with her."

"Benjamin," Margaret said, "we have discussed this before. You don't have to like her. You don't even have to lie down with her. Well, not more than once or twice, hopefully, just enough to make some heirs. If she is too repulsive for that, there are ways, artificial insemination and such, that can accomplish the same thing."

"No, you don't understand. We are not in the thirteenth century. We are not going to negotiate my freedom and my marriage like it is some commodity. When I get married, I want it to be to someone I love. I want it to mean something. Why can't you understand that?"

"I understand much more than you know," Margaret said, beginning to feel the anger being stoked within her. "I understand your childish need for romance and to feel like you belong somewhere. You want to be the protector, the hero, for your damsel in distress. For your maid in distress, as it were."

"What?" Benjamin's eyes snapped to hers and in

them, she saw a fire she had not seen but once or twice in his life. If she could harness that passion, he would be a fine ally in all she did, a fine heir to take over when she decided to step down. "What did you do to Abigail?"

"Me?" she said. "I didn't do anything to your little playmate. She decided to leave—without giving proper notice, I might add—and those who spoke with her could not convince her to stay. From what I understand, she was adequate at her meaningless and menial job but she was easily replaced. Perhaps something you did to chase her away? Maybe your little wedding plans were not suitable for her?"

She felt the tingle of victory when his face went from anger to shock and then to suspicion. It was so easy to manipulate people. Dangle what they desired in front of them and then withhold it and you controlled them and their world.

"How did you chase her away? Did you threaten her, bribe her, tell her lies to make her hate me? What?"

Margaret leaned back in her chair and steepled her fingers. "Benjamin, she didn't confide in anyone here, so there is no telling, but she obviously is running from something. From her work history, leaving without giving notice is not something she usually did, so it must have been something serious to cause her to leave like that. My advice is to forget about her as she has no doubt forgotten about you already. Move on. You have a wedding soon. To Penelope. Focus on that."

By the look on his face, that was a minor mistake. She should not have mentioned it so blatantly, so soon. His jaw clenched, the muscles twitching on the side of his face, and his mouth became a tight, straight line.

"I'm serious," he said. "I will not marry Penelope. I'm done with this farce. Find another way to make your alliances."

This was not going at all how it should be. Margaret sighed. She had no choice but to give him a little nudge in the direction she needed him to go. While pausing in her speech and reaching for her cup of tea, she called forth her magic.

She had learned when still young how to use the magic to manipulate people. She developed the ability over years of practice, sometimes accidentally harming her subjects. She had learned to be very careful when touching magical energies to someone's mind. One little slip here or there and, as she told Helen, she could cause irreparable damage. All her experimentation had taught her to use the power with a light touch. Therein lay the problem. When she wanted to use her abilities to cause someone to think or act in a certain way, patience and care were the last things she wanted to deal with.

She had never heard of another witch with her abilities and had kept them secret her entire life. No one but Helen knew what she could do, and even her friend did not know it all. Still, there were limits. There were definitely limits.

She sipped her tea while watching Ben's face, a thunderhead. She laid the magic lightly on him, suffusing his skull, going straight to his mind. His resolve seemed to slip, just a little. That would be the effect of her suggestion taking hold. One of his eyebrows raised slightly, but that was all. She tightened her control, fine-tuning the thread of magic she was using. He was hers now.

"So, Benjamin," she said, calmly and conversationally, "what will you do? Are we agreed that you will be getting married as soon as I can arrange the wedding?" She would have to give him "refresher" doses of the magic over the next few weeks to make sure the suggestion took hold firmly. He had proven to be more resilient lately, for some reason.

"No."

Margaret almost dropped her cup halfway to the saucer on her desk. "What?"

"No," he repeated. "I told you, I will not marry Penelope. I'm serious, Mother, I am done with this. I won't play this game any longer."

It must be his heightened emotional state. Yes, that was it. The mind was powerful and mysterious. Perhaps his strong feelings on the matter were helping him resist her manipulations. No matter. She would increase the power by a hair. His resistance would surely buffer him from harm with a little more magic. She looked into his eyes and willed the fire energy to increase in strength.

"There is simply no way you can make me marry that woman," Benjamin continued, as if nothing was happening, as if she wasn't flooding his mind with magic.

It was unthinkable. She dare not use any more of the magic. She was already using more than she had ever used with any other subject, even those whose minds she had burned out so completely as to render them a shell of a person. If she was going to kill him, she would kill him more cleanly, not in that way. Never in that way. She did have her limits.

"Benjamin," she said, trying to act as if nothing was amiss. "Think about what you are saying, what you are doing. You cannot defy me. I am your mother. And I am the one who holds the purse. Do you understand what I'm saying?"

"Oh, I understand you perfectly," he said. "If I don't go along, you will cut me off, stop the flow of money. I understand and I don't care. Take my money away. I can work for a living. I am not like all your society friends. I'm not afraid to get a job and pay my own way."

"Pay your own way?" she laughed. "You have no idea what the world is like for someone without money. You don't know how it is to live not knowing if you will be able to eat the next day or whether you will have a home next week. Do you think it's so easy? If so, go into any city and look at the homeless, the destitute. Talk to them—heaven forbid—and see how easy it is."

"I would rather live like that than to have all the money in the world and be trapped in a marriage with someone I don't care for. I won't do it. Do your worst."

"I am warning you, Benjamin," she said. Anger built in her, not only because of his rebellion but from the failure of her magic. "Do not push me on this."

"This conversation is over. Do what you will. I am no longer your little pawn." He turned on his heels, left the room, and slammed the door behind him. Margaret could not recall when anyone had ever stormed out of her presence in that way. Not even her ex-husband.

A soft click and a draft from her right let her know

that Helen did stay to listen and was now coming back into the room.

"I told you," she said. "Why didn't you control his mind? Still afraid to fry his little brain?"

"No," Margaret said. Should she tell Helen? She did not like to admit weakness or failure of any kind. She would tell her part of the truth. "His emotional state makes it difficult to use the magic on him. When he calms down, I will use it and things will be fine."

"So, you're going to just let him get away with telling you to your face that he will not do what you want?"

"Yes."

Helen looked at her, silent. The woman had never seen her defeated. In anything.

"But to help him decide," Margaret said, "I'm going to cut off his money, freeze his credit cards, the whole thing. It will make him see how much he relies on it."

Helen smiled at that. "It will be interesting to see how the little boy handles life without Mommy's money. He'll be begging you to let him marry that snooty girl."

Margaret Huntsman nodded. She hoped so. There was more than one way to change a person's attitude. She sincerely hoped this would work. In the back of her mind, she considered what had happened, how he had withstood her magic. She didn't like that. If she couldn't convince him in more conventional ways to join her, she might just have to eliminate him after all.

29

*B*en had spent the rest of the day after the conversation with his mother trying to forget all about it. He went to the fitness room and worked out, he spent some time in his recreation room, he took a nap. Through it all, her words kept echoing in his head. "I'll cut you off," they said in her voice.

Surely she was joking. Well, no, his mother didn't joke. Bluffing, maybe. Yes, bluffing. She was angry at him, but it would pass. He would not relent, though. He simply couldn't see spending the rest of his life— or even a few years—with Penelope. He had no respect for her. Respect was important, and required, in any serious relationship, as far as he was concerned.

The next day was clear and warm, and Ben decided to take a drive to clear his head. On his way through Cody, going out toward the national park, he pulled into a drive-through to get some coffee.

"I'm afraid your credit card has been declined, sir," the barista told him.

"What? That's ridiculous. Run it again."

"I did, sir, three times. It has been declined."

Ben scratched his head. Was this a mistake? Could his mother have actually cut him off? "Try this one," he said, handing over another credit card.

The man returned. "Nope."

"Oh, fine," Ben hissed. "Here." He handed over a twenty dollar bill. He seethed while waiting for his change. Did she really, actually cut him off?

After tipping the barista—it wasn't his fault, after all—he drove off. Right to the bank. A quick check with his ATM card gave evidence that Margaret had not been joking. His account was frozen. There was money in there still, he thought, but he was unable to get at it. He was in a lot of trouble.

Ben scrapped his plans for the day and went back home. He needed to find out how complete his mother's plans were. The kitchen was his first destination. He waved to the cook as he opened the door to one of the refrigerators, poking around for some kind of snack. He felt his shoulder blades itch, waiting for the cook, Evelyn, to tell him he couldn't have any food. She didn't.

"How are you this morning, Master Mason?" she said cheerily.

"Oh, I've been better," he answered, trying to be upbeat, "but I've been worse, too." He continued looking for something that looked appetizing, but didn't really feel hungry.

"Can I make you a sandwich or get you something else?" the cook asked, eyeing him with what he thought might be suspicion.

He began to tell her no but then changed his mind. "Yes, that would be fantastic, thank you."

She set about whipping up a sandwich to his specifications—a simple turkey and ham on rye would do—and was done in no time. He took the offered sandwich from her and headed out the door. "I think I'll eat this in my room. Thank you, Evelyn."

The cook smiled at him. "It was my pleasure, Master Mason. Always a pleasure."

He mechanically chewed the sandwich as he went to his rec room. He was allowed to eat, so that was good. He assumed he'd be allowed to stay in the house, though he half expected his rooms would be empty. They were not. So, he had at least a little time. Good.

As he ate the rest of his sandwich, Ben thought about what he would do. His mother would expect him to relent, to agree to go along with the marriage to Penelope. If he continued to refuse, she would tighten the screws. He would be expelled or not be allowed to eat, probably both. She would take his cars...

Thinking about cars, he realized that he hadn't seen Lucas. The man was his manservant and driver. He was always around. Where was he this morning?

Ben picked up his phone and called his friend.

"Hey, Ben," Lucas said. "What's up?"

"Where are you? Did you take the day off?"

"Well, sort of. Today, tomorrow, and every day after that."

"What?"

"Your mom fired me yesterday," Lucas said, "told me that 'my services would no longer be required.' She paid me for the next month so I wouldn't make a big deal about it but told me not to say anything to you until you asked or I'd forfeit that extra pay."

"Oh, Lucas, man, I'm sorry. I told her yesterday I wouldn't marry Penelope and she said she'd cut me off. I didn't think about it affecting you."

"You know what?" Lucas said, "It's not a big deal. I'm crashing at my parents' house until I figure something out. If you had asked me before you talked to her and told me what the consequences would be, I would have still told you to go ahead and tell her to go to hell."

"Thank you," Ben said. "I'll try to figure something out to help you. Just as soon as I figure out how I can help myself. I'll get back to you."

"Sure, no problem. You know where I'll be." His friend paused for a moment, and then continued. "And Ben?"

"Yeah?"

"Good luck. Your mother has a lot of influence and power. If you have really pissed her off, you might have a hard road ahead."

"I know. Thanks, Lucas. We'll talk soon."

Ben thought of confronting his mother, but that would do no good. It might actually irritate her enough to cause her to do even worse things to him, like kicking him out of the house. He had to think this through and do things logically. Besides, he thought he remembered her saying she'd be out of town on business for a few days.

He sat there, tapping his cell phone against his bottom lip as he thought. Letting his hand drop, he dialed and put the phone to his ear.

"Yes, Dr. Weitz, this is Benjamin Mason. I was wondering if that job we spoke about was still available. My circumstances have changed, and I would very much like to take your offer."

He listened to the man on the other side of the line. "Okay. Yes, I understand. I'm happy you were able to fill it with someone else. I appreciate your time. Yes, please do let me know if you need help in the future. Thank you. Goodbye."

Damn. Well, he would just have to do things the old-fashioned way and go job hunting. It was obvious she wouldn't let him stay in the estate for long unless he gave in. He had that house he rented for himself and Abbie, paid up for almost the next year, so at least he would have a place to live, but he needed to eat and pay for utilities and all the other stuff he had never had to deal with.

A job first, those other things after. He could move out of the house in a few days and be out of his mother's control.

Things did not turn out to be as easy as Ben thought they would be. He wasn't used to the process of going out and trying to sell himself to employers for jobs that he—honestly, in the back of his mind—felt he was too good for. It wasn't that snob mentality he had been accused of in the past. He had thought what with his degree and how well he got along with people, he would be able to obtain a position within the first few hours.

It didn't happen that way.

The problem was that forces seemed to be working against him. And when "forces" came to mind, a picture of his mother appeared in his head. He had a feeling that there was something going on when a number of businessmen refused to see him at all. Even people he knew, ones he had met several times and knew were friends of his father were "too busy" to see him. It wasn't until one particularly honest individual told him straight out, though, that he was sure.

"I'm sorry, Ben," one of the business owners he'd seen a few times at his mother's parties said. "I can't go against your mother on this. She has told the entire community that you are not to be given a job or to be helped in any way. Defying her would be suicide for most businesses. She just has too many connections, too much power. I hope you understand."

He did. He understood that his mother had him over a barrel and he was powerless to do anything except complain about it. He had to hand it to her, she was effective. She wouldn't make him change his mind, though.

He kept trying. There had to be at least one person in Cody, or even in the outlying areas, who would stand up for what was right. Ben just wasn't sure how to find that person.

After that first day, it became clear he would not be able to get a job in the conventional way, so he went to an employment agency. Maybe he could get temporary work, something to get started.

"I know who you are, Benjamin Mason," the smartly dressed woman said to him. She was one of the agency reps. "I'll be honest with you. No agency within a hundred miles will have anything to do with you. Your mother has too much influence. Even the mayor wouldn't go against her."

Ben looked at her blankly, quite a feat considering the disgust he felt. "Thank you for being honest. I knew it was a long shot, but I wanted to try, anyway."

"A little bit of advice," she said. Her name tag read

Adrian Rowley. "If you still don't want to do whatever it is that she wants you to do, you might want to try getting a job out of state, or at least far enough away that her influence isn't so great. I can't blatantly help you by referring you to anyone or anything like that…" she looked around to make sure she wouldn't be overheard, "…but that's my suggestion, for what it's worth. Look for something away from here. You're wasting your time trying to get employment locally."

"I appreciate that, Adrian," Ben said, standing up and putting his hand out to shake hers. "I will consider your suggestion. It's the most promising thing I've heard all day."

Disgusted, Ben drove back home. He had thought about going to Yellowstone to sit and think, but he couldn't muster up the motivation to do it. All he felt like doing was taking a nap. Sulking, some would call it. He preferred the term "regrouping."

His mother was indeed away on a business trip for a few days, so he had no fear of being summoned to her study during that time. Still, as he walked through the halls of his home, he felt an outsider for the first time in his life. Were the maids and the butler looking strangely at him? Was that sympathy or disappointment in their faces? Scrubbing his hand through his hair, he headed for his rec room. Lucas wouldn't be there, of course, but at least he could take refuge in his solitude. It was all he had left…until his mother took that, too. First Abbie was taken away from him and now everything else. He hadn't felt this badly about life since his father died. He wondered how he could find her to talk to her. He thought about how his mother was controlling matters, destroying his phone and having his account deleted, and it made him want to bite something.

Just before he reached his rooms, Claire Roberts came around the corner and caught sight of him. He really didn't want to talk to the Housekeeper, but he couldn't be rude to her either. Her face had a soft expression, her eyes lidded and her mouth in as close to a pout as he had ever seen. It reminded him of the look she had when he had found a baby bird when he was a child, one that had fallen out of its nest, and he brought it to her to nurse back to health.

"Master Benjamin," she said.

"Good afternoon, Mrs. Roberts," he said politely, trying his best to smile though his misery.

"I was just thinking of you this morning," she said. That was a strange thing to say. Her job was basically to take care of him. Well, his home, anyway, but still. It was strange.

"I remember," she continued, "when your father was not too much older than you. He had a friend, and those two were inseparable. His name was Jacob Johnson, but Mr. Mason always called him JJ. You probably don't remember him."

Why is she telling me this? "No, I'm afraid I don't recall. I don't really remember any of my father's friends. I always just assumed he was so busy working that he didn't have many."

"That's true, yes," the Housekeeper said. "But that was only later. Before he met Ms. Huntsman, he had friends, and among them JJ was the closest." A pained look came over her face, but she smoothed it away and continued. "Ms. Huntsman did not like him spending his time with his friends and neglecting her, and she seemed to take a special dislike to JJ. But I fear I am being inappropriate in speaking about this." She patted her gray hair, curled up tight in her typical bun.

"That is interesting, Mrs. Roberts," Ben said, "but I am not feeling well right now, so if you will excuse me, I think I'll lie down."

"Of course, of course," she said. "I do ramble on. The point. I'll get to the point. When your father was given a choice, he cut off ties with his former friends. Because of some support and good advice he had given your father, JJ was given some starting capital to develop a business. He chose to open a restaurant in Custer. You know, in South Dakota. He is still there, according to the last information I had about him."

She reached into the pocket of her uniform and drew out a small piece of paper. "Custer. JJ never blamed your father for choosing his wife over him. He would probably love to see Mr. Mason's son, maybe enough to help him out if that son ever needed anything. I just thought maybe you would like to know a little bit about your father's past. For no particular reason, you understand."

Ben took the note and scanned it. A name and address, even a phone number. He looked down at the woman who had been in his life for almost his entire twenty-six years. When it finally hit him what she had done, the risk she had taken—she could easily lose her job for this—his eyes became liquid. Impulsively, he reached out and wrapped his arms around her. "Mrs. Roberts, you are an angel. You don't know how much this means to me. Thank you so much."

The round woman seemed flustered, no doubt because of the impropriety of him hugging her. "Not at all. Just an old woman thinking about the past and sharing little stories of a boy's father. A man's father. How you have grown." She shook her head and sniffled, looking like she might cry. "Well, Master Benjamin, I have work to do. I hope the rest of your day is better than the first part."

Ben smiled at her, the first genuine smile he had for days. "It definitely will be. Thank you so much, Mrs. Roberts. I will miss you."

"I will miss you, too, Master Benjamin. You remind me so much of your father. Good luck to you. I hope to see you again soon."

Ben hugged her again, and she hurried off. He looked at the paper in his hand. Custer. Well, that was as good a place as any. He had things to do. For the first time that day, he felt like there may be some hope left for him.

30

⌇⌇⌇

*B*en packed some clothes and a few personal items into a suitcase and walked out of his room. As he made his way to the front door, memories of every inch of the house assailed him. Running through the halls as a child, parties his father used to throw, dozens of other little insignificant scenes flashed through his mind. No, not insignificant. Just mundane. He cherished every one of them.

He would miss this house; he had lived here all his life. The hope that he would be able to come back some day pulsed in him. His mother couldn't hold a grudge forever, could she? Not with her own son. But he wasn't so sure. Some of the stories he'd heard about her business dealings made him even warier of his mother than he was from his personal experience. He'd have to see how it turned out. For now, he had to leave.

He reached the door and took one last look

around at the grand entryway. Then he turned and went through the door to his waiting car, closing it behind him.

Ben had decided a phone call out of the blue wouldn't be appropriate. If he was going to ask a man he didn't remember ever meeting for help, he would do it in person. That was the respectful thing to do. It was quite a drive, but he figured he had nothing if he didn't have time.

The drive to Custer was about six hours through rolling hills, mountains, and plains. He had traveled those roads before, but not in years, and he enjoyed the open road, the thought that he was doing something for himself, something that wasn't tied to his mother's power. It made him feel—how could he describe it?—grown up. Maybe things wouldn't be so bad.

When he finally reached Custer, he was tired from his job-searching earlier in the day and from the long drive. He thought of getting a motel room, but it was the last week of July, right in the middle of tourist season, so he probably wouldn't be able to find a vacancy. Besides, he had a limited amount of cash and didn't really want to spend it on a room unless he had to. If, after he found JJ, the man couldn't help him, he'd just sleep in his car or make the long drive back home.

Custer was a small town with most of its businesses apparently based on the tourist trade. With Mount Rushmore and several other major attractions nearby, it seemed logical. He drove down Highway 16, Mount Rushmore road, his head swiveling to take in the scenery.

The word he would have had to use for the city

was "quaint." Many of the buildings were rustic and life-sized statues of buffalo stood at just about every intersection. Some of them were painted wildly, in stars and stripes or even solid purple. Ben laughed at that. With an eye on his GPS, he headed toward his destination.

He had briefly entertained the thought of sleeping in his car and trying to find JJ the next day, but he was hungry and needed to eat, so he figured he would kill two birds with one stone and find the restaurant. No time like the present.

Ben followed the GPS directions and made it to the restaurant JJ owned. It was called "JJ's Place," a steakhouse, with the dishes mainly centered around cuts of red meat, but they had chicken, some different international dishes, and even a vegetarian meal or two.

A kindly older woman named Mabel, according to her name tag, greeted Ben. She looked at him strangely, as if she recognized him, but just shook her head and led him to a table. When she had him settled and started to walk away, Ben asked her about the man he had come to see.

"Is JJ around?" he said.

The woman narrowed her eyes and looked at him as if she was trying to figure out if he was teasing her. Her expression became more pleasant, but still curious. "Yeah, he's helping out in the kitchen. One of the cooks called in sick."

"Could you please let him know that Hank Mason's son, Ben, is here? I'd like to see him, if he can spare a few minutes."

"Ben Mason?" the woman said, a smile breaking through her previously suspicious expression. "Little

Benjie?"

"Please," he said, face reddening. He hadn't heard that name in more than twenty years. "Just Ben."

"You don't remember me," she said. "But of course, you wouldn't. The last time I saw you was when you were three or four years old. I should have recognized you. You look just like your father when he was your age. It is so good to see you."

She shook her head and rolled her eyes. "But I'm blabbering when you want to talk to JJ. Let me go get him. We can catch up after you two talk. Ben Mason. It is so good to see you." She hurried off toward the kitchen.

Ben hadn't even ordered yet when an older man, tall and skinny as a scarecrow, came up to his booth. His age worn face looked as if he had been through a lifetime of challenges but had come out victorious. There was a regal aspect in how his steady gaze met Ben's eyes and scanned him briefly before lighting up. His face, wrinkled but still firm, broke into a smile. Swiping a lock of gray hair that had fallen from his cook's hat, he reached his hand out to Ben.

"Ben Mason," he said, shaking Ben's hand firmly. He had a strong grip. "I couldn't believe it when Mabel told me you were out here. Just look at you. All grown up and looking as good as your father ever did."

His smile faltered. "I'm so sorry to hear about his death. I figured he'd live forever, and I'm not the only one who hoped he would. He was a saint, that man, a true gentleman and humanitarian. The world lost something the day he left it."

"Thanks, JJ," Ben said. "I feel the same way. I have never heard anyone say anything negative about him. I only hope I can be half the man he was."

"I'm sure you will be, Ben. With his blood in you, I'm sure you will be. So, then, what brings you to my neck of the woods?"

"Well, that's a bit of a story. If it's not too much trouble, could I stick around until closing time and then we can take the time to talk? Mabel told me that you were covering for one of the cooks, so I know you're busy. If you don't mind me taking up a booth, I can eat and then wait around until you can really talk. Is there anything I can do to help out?"

"That sounds great," the old man said. "Thanks for the offer to help, but we'll be fine. Just like your father, always thinking of others. Sit and enjoy your dinner. We'll be done in no time. It's only an hour until closing time."

"Okay," Ben said. "You're sure I can't do anything to help?"

"Young man," Mabel said, "trying to help is one thing, but don't overdo it. You are to sit there and eat your dinner and patiently wait until we are done. Not another word out of you."

"Yes ma'am," Ben said, smiling at the old woman. She reminded him of Mrs. Roberts.

After ordering and receiving his food, Ben sat there eating it, thinking about his situation. He wasn't sure how JJ could help him out, but just talking to someone who knew his father lightened his mood. He still thought of Abbie with every other thought, but at least he was doing something productive. He hoped he was.

When the restaurant closed and everything was cleaned up and put away, JJ and Mabel bid goodnight to the employees who were still there helping to close and then came to sit with Ben.

JJ lowered himself to the seat with a grunt. "I'm getting too old for this," he grumbled.

"Oh, hush," Mabel said. "You've been saying that for years. You still work circles around all these youngsters." She patted his hand and smiled at him.

The man turned to Ben. "So, young Ben. Do you like to be called Ben or Benjamin? I've heard everyone calls you Benjamin."

"I prefer Ben among friends," Ben said. "Please call me Ben."

The old man's face crinkled into a smile. "Ben it is, then. So, what brings you all the way out here?"

"I'm kind of in a tough spot," Ben said. "My mother decided I would be married to a woman in another family with money, but I don't love her. In fact, I can't stand her. She's beautiful and everything, but she's a horrible person. Well, maybe that's too harsh, but I don't get along with her, and I don't like her personality."

A look passed between the two, as if they knew something about the situation but didn't want to say so. He disregarded it and continued.

"I finally got fed up with it all and told my mother I wouldn't marry Penelope—that's the girl's name—and there was nothing she could do to make me. She threatened to cut me off if I didn't change my mind. I told her nothing would change my mind and I wouldn't marry Penelope and that was all there was to it. I figured she was bluffing about cutting me off.

"She wasn't. I tried to find a job locally, but she has made sure that I can't get a job anywhere. She's too powerful for any of the businesses to defy. I was trying to figure out what to do when Mrs. Roberts told me about you."

"Claire is still there?" Mabel asked. "She's a lovely woman."

"Yes," Ben said. "She told me about you and where to find you. I didn't remember you. She said maybe you could help me get a job or something."

JJ sat silent, considering, for a moment. "I just might be able to help you at that. It's a shame that you are in such a predicament, but I agree with you. Marriage is one of life's greatest pleasures, if you marry someone you love." He reached out and took Mabel's hand in his own and patted it with his other. "There's no better reason to stand up to adversity. Your father said almost those very same words to me once.

"Truth is, I've been wanting someone to manage the restaurant for me. I'm trying to spend less time here, but I haven't been successful so far. I think a smart young fella like you would probably do a good job, allow me to forget the place for a day or two, get some fishing in."

"JJ, that's very nice of you, but I don't know anything about restaurants. I wouldn't know where to start."

"Oh, it's not all that hard. My head cook and some of the others have been here for years. They can let you know if you're confused. I can teach you all I know in no time. What do you say? Would you help an old man out?"

"I...I don't know what to say," Ben said. He looked over and saw Mabel smiling and nodding her head. "That would be great. I just can't promise how long I'll be here. I'm not sure what will happen with my mother. I may be here a long time or only a few months. I don't want you to spend all that effort teaching me and then have me leave."

"We'll worry about that if and when it happens," JJ said. "I know you're not going to make a career out of it. I heard you went and got some fancy degree at the university. Even if your mother never comes around, you'll want a higher-paying job eventually. We'll help each other out now, and it'll all settle out eventually."

"Thank you so much for this, JJ. It really helps a lot. I'll take you up on it."

"Good, it's settled then." JJ looked him up and down. "You really do look an awful lot like your father. Brings back memories. Do you have a place to stay?"

"Uh, no," Ben said. "I just got to town. I'll find something, though."

"Nonsense," Mabel interrupted. "You can come and stay with us. We have a couple of extra rooms since the boys moved out and you are more than welcome. You may want to get your own place later, but for now, it's one less thing you have to worry about."

Ben felt warm in a way he hadn't felt in a long time, except for when he was with Abbie. It felt like...he didn't know...family. He agreed and the three closed up the restaurant and headed home. It wasn't an ideal situation, but it was much more than he had expected earlier in the day. He had time now. Time to figure out what he'd do, time to think. Time to decide how to survive without Abbie.

31

Abbie took her time driving back home. She wasn't much in the mood for people, even family. She drove through Yellowstone National park, the shortest distance between the Huntsman Estate and Aqua Terra, enjoying the trees and the occasional sighting of an elk or a buffalo as she went. Tears came and went until her eyes felt crusty and her face puffy.

How could she have been so stupid? Why would she think that Ben would actually be interested in her? She was, as far as he knew, just a maid. He was rich and handsome and such a great guy. Of course he had ulterior motives in asking to marry her so soon. Still, she had believed he was trustworthy and that he really cared about her.

When Arianna told her about what she had heard, Abbie didn't believe it at first. She'd always had a small doubt and that doubt had been confirmed as valid. She felt like a fool. She felt betrayed. She felt...lonely.

Anyway, it was over. All she had to do was to wait until time smoothed it all away, until every thought that came into her head was not of Ben. Wasn't that how it worked with her mother leaving her? She should have known that falling in love so quickly was not possible. For him, anyway. Her love was true, she knew. False love couldn't hurt this much. Oh, what was she doing even thinking about it? It only made it all worse.

Nearly five hours later, she pulled up into the circular driveway of her family home. There was no one outside to greet her this time. It was just as well. Maybe she could make it to her room without having to talk to anyone. It suited her mood.

The house was quiet as she ghosted her way through the hall toward her room. The photographs and paintings of her family lined the walls and seemed to cast accusations at her. She had given up her mission only to find out she had been duped. Was Ben part of Margaret's schemes or was he just selfish in using her to escape the marriage that had been set as his prison? She looked straight ahead so she didn't meet those accusing looks.

Reaching her room, she closed the door and threw herself onto the bed. Maybe sleeping would help. A month or two of slumber might do it. She took the little angel carving from her nightstand and squeezed it in her hand. In a few minutes, she was asleep.

A gentle knock at the door made her start. She looked around, disoriented at first, and determined that it was still daytime. Beams of light slid in between the window's shutters.

"Come in," she said to the door as the knock

repeated.

Her father opened the door slowly and entered the room. He looked tired, worn. She was sure she looked worse. He walked slowly to the chair next to her bed and sat.

"I saw your car in the driveway," he said. "I figured you would search me out eventually, but I waited a couple of hours before deciding I would check up on you. There must be something wrong for you to avoid everyone. No one saw you. I asked."

"I was really tired when I came in," Abigail said. "I thought I'd lie down for a few minutes. I must have fallen asleep."

"Oh, Abigail, such a sorry excuse for an explanation. We both know you would have told someone you were here if everything was all right. That's fine, though. I'm here now, so maybe you can tell me what the problem is. Are you okay?"

She felt the tears gathering in her half-lidded eyes. She sniffled and looked toward the carpeted floor. "I...just have some things to think about."

Her father was silent, waiting, allowing her time to gather her thoughts.

"Oh, Papa, it's such a mess!" She got to her feet, walked the two steps to him and threw her arms around him. "I gave up my mission, placed my future at Ben's feet, and he broke my heart. He never loved me. He just wanted me for a convenient way to get out of the marriage arrangements her mother had made for him."

The tears came, then, hot and fast. She had thought there were none left, but she was wrong. Her father held her tight as she cried. Soon, they stopped and she lifted her head from his shoulder.

"Sorry," she sniffled. "I seem to have made your shoulder wet." She laughed, though it was a sad thing.

"That's fine. I'll dry off. Do you want to tell me about it?"

She did. Abigail told him about her doubt and how it had made her feel guilty for doubting, about the conversation Arianna had overheard, about everything that had occurred since she had last talked to her father. When she was done, she collapsed as if all the energy had been drained out of her.

Landon Henderson listened without saying a word. When Abigail was done, he sat in silence, stroking her hair, still saying nothing. Abigail felt better for having told him and the silence seemed a comfort.

"I made a mess of things, huh?" she said.

"Not at all. I won't argue that it is a hard situation. I do understand the feeling of having your heart broken, so I do not underestimate the pain you are in right now. I also won't try to tell you you'll feel fine anytime soon. You're too smart to fall for that."

He paused, looking her in the eyes, his blue orbs catching her up, holding her, soothing her. "But I have to ask, what if Arianna was lying to you? Your doubts aside, what if she was just trying to drive a wedge between the two of you with some carefully crafted lie?"

"I don't think that's the case," Abbie said. Her voice sounded weak in her own ears.

"You don't *think* that's the case? You don't *know*?"

Abigail put her head in her hands. "I don't *know* anything, except that my heart is breaking. Ben was raised to have the attitude that those who aren't filthy rich are not as important, not as good, as those who are. You can't live with that every day without believing it on some level."

"Abigail," her father said. "Has he ever done anything to indicate that he thinks less of you than his society friends? Has he ever treated you like you were a lesser person?"

She thought for a moment, scanning her memories of all the interactions she had with Ben. "No." It came out almost as a whisper. "But..."

"I see." Landon rubbed his chin. "It's something to think about, then, isn't it?"

"I know it sounds stupid to believe someone I don't know well and who doesn't like me, but her story only confirms a feeling I've had throughout our getting to know each other. I wouldn't make a decision based just on the word of someone like her. He has said some things, just in passing, but they sounded like he did look down on those who aren't rich."

"Oh, Abbie," he father said. "The mind and emotions are treacherous things. We can talk ourselves into just about anything. It may be possible that you're looking for things that aren't there, and then when some piece of evidence to back up your beliefs is presented, you take it and run with it. Or it could all be true. Take some time, think it through. There is no schedule here. Once you decide what the actual situation is, you'll begin the healing process, either by reconciling with him or by purging him from your thoughts. Either way, I'll be here for you." He paused for a moment, and then added, "Abbie, I know you struggle with your feelings about onlies. You are not immune to a little prejudice yourself. None of us are. But maybe you can ask yourself if the stray thought that onlies are not as good as witches or warlocks really means that you believe that's the truth of it."

He leaned over and kissed her forehead. After he had gotten to his feet and left the room, Abbie threw herself back on the bed and sighed. He had given her something to think about. She felt a little better, but she knew her ordeal was far from over.

She slept fitfully that night, waking from dreams and nightmares she hardly remembered when she finally dragged herself from her covers to go downstairs to find something to eat.

It was not even 7:00 AM yet, so the only people she saw were the servants beginning their day. The cook, Jared Scott, whipped her up some eggs and pancakes and she settled into eating mechanically. She was very hungry after not eating much at all the day before, but as she shoveled the food into her mouth, she barely tasted it. Her thoughts were on her problem.

"I thought that was your car in the driveway," a voice said, breaking into her thoughts. She knew that voice, and her heart jumped.

"Zoe?" Abigail turned to the other woman walking into the small dining room. "You are a sight for sore eyes!"

Abigail sprang from her chair and rushed over to hug her friend. It felt good to hug someone. She was feeling a little needy of human contact. With those who meant the most to her, anyway.

"Hey, hey," Zoe said. "Don't crush the life out of me. Have you been working out or something? Gads, but you're strong."

Abbie dropped her arms and stepped back to look at her best friend, Zoe Reyes. The two had known each other since they were toddlers and had been inseparable most of their lives. Until recently, when Zoe had been traveling while Abbie took spying missions.

Zoe was only five feet two inches tall, but she seemed to stand much taller. She was slender and moved with a dignity that Abbie admired, as if she were royalty and the world would move out of her way. She wasn't haughty, just...regal. Her dark brown hair reached a few inches below her shoulder and it flowed loosely as she moved her head, the light catching the highlights in it. Abigail had always been a little jealous of her friend. She was beautiful and got attention wherever she went. Her large brown almond-shaped eyes fixed on hers and a gorgeous smile that brightened any room she was in beamed.

"I've missed you, Abs," Zoe said, calling her by the nickname only she used.

"Oh, I've missed you too, Zo," Abigail said. "How long are you back in town?"

"Just a week or so. You know, busy, busy." Zoe rolled her eyes.

"How is your research going? How many countries have you been to since we talked last? Have you found any cool records or spells?"

Zoe was a researcher. The coven itself covered the expenses of sending her around the world to research ancient records and to find not just histories but spells that had been lost. During the heyday of magic, it was rumored that witches could do things that boggled the minds of their modern-day counterparts. She had found enough interesting information to justify continuing her hunt.

"I have found a few interesting things. Even to a homebody like you." Zoe winked at her friend.

"Ooh, tell me all about them. I could use some distraction."

"I'll tell you all about them," Zoe said. "Briefly. Then you will tell me what's going on with you." Abbie nodded.

"Well," Zoe said, "I've been searching all these ancient records, all over the world. I'm close to something, I know it. I can't tell you about it just yet, not until I piece things together, but it's big Abs, very big. I mean, so big that it'll be talked about in every water witch coven worldwide. I can't wait to be able to tell you more."

"That's it?" Abbie asked. "You're just going to give me, 'it's big and I can't tell you about it?' Come on, Zo, I need more than that."

Zoe looked around, as if someone else would be in the room. "Okay, fine. Some of these ancient records talk about a library even older than they themselves are. I am so close to finding the location. When I do, we may have the first real records of the history of witches from well before Christ walked the earth. Maybe as far back as the first civilizations in Mesopotamia."

"A library? That's…pretty cool, I guess."

"Abs, it could solve mysteries that have been stumping us for hundreds of years, if not thousands. And think of the spells. Spellbooks that no one has seen in ages, from the golden age of magic, before civilization watered it all down and killed the most promising magic users."

"I see your point," Abbie said. "Actually, that is pretty cool, now that you mention it."

"I know, right? So, I heard you were on a mission trying to infiltrate the household of your mother's murderer. Is it over? Did you get the information you needed?"

Abigail took a drink to get down the lump in her throat. How could she explain to her friend how the world had lost its light?

"No. I abandoned the mission. There were…complications."

Zoe sat down and took a piece of bacon from Abigail's plate. Munching on it, she waved her hand for Abbie to sit. "Sit down. It sounds like this is going to take a little while for you to tell it all to me."

A nervous giggle escaped Abbie's mouth. Same old Zoe: right to the point. She sat down and began to tell her friend all about her troubles.

After she was caught up, Zoe leaned back in her chair. "Hmmm. That sounds rough. Are you sure you love this guy?"

"I do. The Elemental Powers help me, but I do. This thing is crushing me, Zo. I need to just scream. The feeling is building up in me, begging for release, but there's nothing I can do to make it go away. Sometimes I think it's going to make me explode. It hurts. It hurts so badly. There is a constant ache and spikes of pain on top of that. Nothing helps."

Zoe waited, silent. Abbie wasn't sure if she had said something wrong or why else her friend wasn't speaking. To fill the silence, she continued.

"I know enough to recognize that just loving someone isn't the answer to everything, though. I love him, but I'm not sure if that's enough for us to be happy together. I mean, what if he's part of Margaret Huntsman's plans? What if he took part in the murder of my mother? What if he has secrets that make it impossible for us to be together? What if he doesn't love me?"

"Ah, now we come down to it," Zoe said softly. "Do you believe you love him more than he loves you?"

"Yes."

"And that scares you?"

"Yes."

"Why?"

Abigail sighed. "You know me, Zo. I don't just give my heart away. But I have this time. I have given it away completely. What if I love him more than anything else on earth, but his personality doesn't fit with mine? What if he is selfish, and he's involved in things that go against everything I believe in? Love can't cover over those things, not for more than a short time."

"Oh, Abbie," Zoe said through a laugh. "You always did make problems for yourself when there weren't any there. We're water witches. We go with the flow, like the waves in the ocean. Go with this. Don't create reasons why you can't be together before you know if any of those reasons are true.

"If it ends up that you and he cannot be together—sometimes love just isn't enough for two people to be together forever—then you will deal with it then. Don't jump to conclusions and cause problems now when you don't even know if there is a real reason."

Abbie looked at her friend. "I guess you're right. I need to think about it some more, try to figure out if I'm just talking myself into something or if all my reasons are valid. Thanks, Zo. You always did know how to cut through all the mess and get to the main point."

"I am a researcher, after all," Zoe said. "It's kind of what I do. And I do it very well, I might add. We'll talk more about some of the things I've found lately. After you have some alone time to think about your situation. I'll be around, okay? Let me know when you want to talk again."

"I will. Thanks." Abigail hugged her friend and then Zoe left with a little wave.

Abbie looked at her phone lying on the table. Why hadn't Ben texted her or called her? She had left abruptly and he didn't even try to get in touch with her? She would put that in the con column. If he didn't care enough to find out what was wrong, then that answered the question. Right?

Of course, maybe he was just being compassionate. From all appearances, she had rejected him and fled. Maybe he wanted to call her but he didn't want to pressure her or take the chance he would irritate her. That would go in the pro column. Why was this thing so hard?

She reached for the phone to call him, but then realized she had done that before. His number was no longer valid. Had he changed it to keep her from contacting him, or was it another coincidence? He could have just blocked her instead of changing his number. Oh, she didn't know. She felt like throwing the phone, but refrained.

She thought for a minute about going back to the estate but forcefully shoved it out of her head. She would not act without thinking things through. That would only make matters worse. She didn't know what was going on, but she wanted to. She would have to try to figure out a way to get the information she wanted. The information she needed.

A dozen scenarios came to mind. Ben hated her and never wanted anything to do with her again and felt so strongly about it that he changed his number. His mother had canceled his phone so he couldn't contact Abbie. He had been kidnapped and the ones who abducted him canceled his cell service and destroyed his phone so he could not be tracked...

Okay, she needed to calm down and think rationally. She was being ridiculous now and that was getting her nowhere. She went back to her room to lie down. She lay there for a long time, rubbing her angel carving with her thumb and staring at the ceiling.

32

~~~

$\mathcal{B}$en kept himself busy working at the restaurant for nearly two months. The Johnsons even felt comfortable enough with him running the place to take a short fishing vacation. The hours were long, which suited him. When he was working, learning how to manage the place, he had less idle time for his mind to dwell on Abbie. Instead of thinking of her twenty-four hours a day, only half his thoughts were of her. He couldn't push her out of his mind completely, but sometimes if he was concentrating on something else, she didn't monopolize his thoughts completely. It would have to do.

There was no shortage of women who flirted with him. He was young, in good physical condition, and better than average looking, he figured, so it was natural. Wearing a tie also made him look important—if they only knew—so that lured the gold diggers. He was polite, though at times it happened so many times in one night that it irritated him. The nagging thought that none of the women trying to get his attention were of his social class stuck with him, but that old prejudice wasn't what made him disinterested.

He didn't want a girl. He wanted *the* girl. None of them were Abbie. At times, his emotional pain must have shown through when someone who reminded him of Abbie flirted with him. Their eyes would widen like he had just slapped them or said something rude, and they'd hurry off. He felt bad that he was grimacing at them, but he couldn't bring himself to care too much. They would find someone else to flirt with. There was no one else for him.

All of it reminded him of the time he had spent with Abbie, how they seemed to fit together so well, how much a part of him she felt. He didn't even feel like a whole person without her.

What was he doing so far away from where she was? He still didn't know exactly where she lived, but he knew it was relatively close to his home. His former home; the estate.

"You seem preoccupied," JJ said to Ben as they and Mabel were sitting around one of the tables after a particularly busy Saturday, a few days after they had returned from their vacation. "Something wrong?"

"We don't want to pry, mind you," Mabel said. "You don't have to talk about it if you don't want to, but it's obvious there is more bothering you than an argument with your mother. If I were to bet, I'd say there's a girl involved."

Ben watched the kindly woman's mouth as she spoke to him. He was so tired, it seemed to echo surrealistically. "I'll talk about it. It couldn't hurt.

There's this girl, Abigail—Abbie. She was one of our maids. She hadn't worked there long, only a few months—"

"Worked?" JJ interrupted.

"She kind of quit, or she was fired, or something. I'm not really sure what happened. I'm still trying to figure it out. Anyway, there was something about her, right from the start. We just sort of fit. When I first met her and shook her hand, there was a jolt, like electricity."

Ben saw Mabel clasp JJ's hand on the table as a wide smile lit up her face. Her eyes sparkled and she looked as if she was about to speak. He continued before she could utter a word.

"I know all the old clichés about a spark or electricity or chemistry and all that, but I'm talking actual, real, live electricity. As if she had been rubbing her feet on a thick carpet on a very windy day and held a lot of static electricity. I could almost hear the 'bzzztt' as it arced from her hand to mine.

"That was just part of it, though." Ben ran his fingers through his hair and sighed. "We just seemed to have a connection. I've never felt anything like it before. I enjoyed it, but it was a little scary, too. But I'm dragging this on…"

Mabel still had that smile on her face, and JJ's eyes told him that he understood completely what Ben was describing. He was nodding slightly.

"My mother had engaged me to this girl, Penelope. It was a marriage that would have helped the families financially, made alliances that would help both. I didn't want Penelope. I wanted Abbie. Then mother brought the Penelope and me to Europe for a few weeks. When I came home, things weren't the same, as if Abbie had lost interest in me.

"I worked on her, just little things to show her how much she meant to me, and she warmed up to me a bit. When my mother tried to push the schedule up for me to marry Penelope, I saw my only chance was to already be married and so I asked Abbie to be my wife."

Mabel sighed and JJ just stared at him.

"I know, it was kind of silly. I had only known her for a few months. Still, it seemed right." Ben stopped and went to run his hands through his hair again, but dropped his hand to his lap instead.

"And she told you no?" Mabel asked, her eyes lidded and her mouth turning down into something that was not quite a frown, but close.

"No," Ben said. "She said yes."

Mabel's mouth instantly turned upward into a smile. JJ nodded and wore a small smile himself.

"But that's not the end of it," he continued. "We planned to get married in secret and reveal it to everyone when the wedding to Penelope had been planned. Things seemed to be going well.

"But I became...distracted...for a while. I don't know what it was, but it seemed like I was constantly in a daze. Maybe I was getting sick or something, or maybe the stress was affecting me. I don't know.

"The next thing I knew, Abbie was gone. I was told she quit, that she didn't want to talk to me anymore. I didn't believe it. At least, not fully. But she had been distant...

"My mother took my phone when I wasn't looking and destroyed it. She also canceled my service and changed the phone number on my account. I lost my contact information and couldn't call Abbie to find out what happened. She can't call me either because I don't have the same number. If I had memorized her number, I could have talked to her."

Ben put his head in his hands. "Then when I told Mother that I wasn't going to marry Penelope, she made it impossible for me to get a job locally, and she canceled all my credit cards and froze my accounts. But you already know that part. It's not knowing about Abbie, if she cares about me or if I was the reason she left, that's what's killing me."

JJ and Mabel were silent for a moment, looking at each other, looking around the restaurant dining area, looking anywhere but toward Ben.

Finally, Mabel spoke. "Dear, please don't think this is too harsh, but you're acting like an idiot."

Ben's mouth dropped open as he met the old woman's eyes. He began to speak, but she continued.

"I understand trying to find a way to survive, to make money to live. Your mother put you in a bad position and you have to do your best to get out of it. The thing with Abbie, though..." She blew out a breath and took another deeper one. "You have to find out. You have to know where you stand with her. What if she thinks you don't want her and you're here thinking that she doesn't want you and it's all just a big misunderstanding? Are you willing to lose her forever because of something so silly?"

"I...what if she does hate me?" Ben said. "I don't want to irritate her or make her even madder at me. I don't want to hurt her feelings. Plus, I tried to find her number, but it's unlisted. Maybe Abigail isn't even her real name. I don't know."

"Son," JJ said, "you know as well as we do those are just excuses. What is it really? Are you afraid you might find out it's true, that she really doesn't want you? Isn't it better to know for sure and move on if that's what the situation calls for? Besides, I think the chances are good that she feels the same as you. She may feel like you abandoned her. Do the right thing. Track her down. Talk to her, and see what the situation is. No matter which way it goes, you'll have some closure."

This was nothing Ben hadn't thought of himself since she left. Maybe he was just scared.

"You know, you're right," he said. "Not knowing is worse than being sure about where we stand. I will find her. Somehow."

Both of the Johnsons smiled, at Ben and at each other. They stayed up for several more hours talking about what he could do and how he could go about his search. When he finally got to bed, he had hope, for the first time in weeks.

The next morning Ben rose even earlier than normal. He went to the restaurant to help the servers and the cook open up. After two cups of coffee and an hour of chores, he put his mind on autopilot and tried to figure out what he would do to track down Abbie. Even without the coffee, he felt refreshed, his steps lighter and his outlook more optimistic than it had been for quite a while.

Abbie might have rejected him after all, but just the fact that he was doing something other than hiding made all the difference.

Once the restaurant was up and running and he was no longer needed—after he had made his greetings to the regulars who came in for breakfast— he got on the internet and tried to search out where Abigail might live.

It wasn't as easy as the movies made it seem.

Ben kicked himself for never asking where she was from or where her family was. He knew her favorite color—sea foam green—and the things she liked to do. He knew her best friend's name was Zoe— though she had started when she told him, surprised she had said it. But somehow, whenever they started discussing family, she was able to distract him or change the subject. He didn't know if her parents were alive or dead, where they were, if she had any siblings, or any other information about those close to her. Was she hiding something?

Without even an idea of where she was from, he couldn't very well track her down. A Google search of Abigail Henderson in Wyoming brought up no matches. When he searched for the last name Henderson, there were 508 matches, too many to be useful. She could be from Cody, just a few miles away from his home, or she could be from New York or California, trying to start up a new life. He didn't think so, though. He thought she was local. But how local?

He finally sighed and threw up his hands. He would have to try a different approach.

"I don't want to try to tell you how to go about it," JJ said to him later that day when Ben explained the trouble he was having, "but when I hire a new person, I have a service do a background check on them. You know, look for a criminal record, bad credit, things like that. It helps me to know what kind of person they are and what I'm getting into."

Ben smacked his forehead with his palm. "Of course. I'm an idiot. There are lots of services out there that do that kind of thing."

"Yep. There are even private investigators that do that kind of work. Expensive, though."

Ben thought for a moment. "I think maybe I can make it easier than that. All that stuff was probably done when Mrs. Roberts hired her. I just may be able to go straight to the employer. Excuse me, I have a call to make."

Two minutes later, Ben heard Lucas's voice on the phone.

"Hello."

"Hey Lucas, what's up?"

"Hey, it's my long-lost buddy Benjamin Mason. How are things way over there in Custer?" They had talked a few times since he had started working at the restaurant.

"They're about the same as the last time we talked," Ben said. "There's not much going on here. Listen, I wonder if you could do me a favor."

"Sure thing," Lucas said. "What do you need?"

"I need you to go and ask Mrs. Roberts for her phone number."

"Come again? Isn't she a bit too old for you?"

"Very funny, Lucas. I need to ask her where Abbie lives, or at least where she did live before she started working for the estate. I need to track her down. I need to talk to her."

"You're finally coming around, huh? It's about time. I'll do my best to either get her number, to have her call you, or to give the information to me directly so I can tell you."

"Thanks, Lucas," Ben said. "You'd be doing me a huge favor. Give me a call as soon as you can to tell me what's up."

"Will do. And Ben?"

"Yeah?"

"I really hope it was all just a misunderstanding. I think Abigail is good for you. I hope things work out."

"Thanks, buddy, me too. I'll talk to you soon."

"Yes you will. Talk to you later."

As Ben ended the call, a small ray of optimism flashed within him. It might be stupid to think things would go well for him for a change, but it seemed he had turned a corner and his luck would start to be good. He pocketed his phone and headed back to the restaurant to look for something to do. It would take Lucas a day or two to get to Mrs. Roberts, and Ben had better distract himself or it would seem like weeks.

33

Two days later, Lucas called Ben back. As expected, Mrs. Roberts would not tell Lucas anything. His former driver gave her Ben's new phone number, and she promised to call at noon on the following day. Waiting another twenty-four hours was excruciating, but he survived it and waited anxiously as noon approached.

Ben left the restaurant and waited in his room for the call. His cell phone rang at exactly 12:00 PM. Mrs. Roberts was one of the most efficient and reliable people Ben had ever met.

"Hello," he said into the phone.

"Master Benjamin?" Claire Roberts's voice said.

"Mrs. Roberts, it's so nice to hear your voice. How are things at the estate?"

There was a slight pause. "They are fine. We all miss you, though. It's a regrettable situation, it is. All the staff hopes that you can reconcile with your mother and return." The last word seemed clipped, as if she was going to say more but decided not to.

"I miss you, too," Ben said. "Hopefully things will pass. My mother and I are both stubborn, though, so it may take a while." He meant it as a joke and tried to insert a chuckle, but it came out as a strange noise instead, like an animal whose tail had been stepped on, surprising it but not really causing pain.

"Lucas tells me that you need my help?" She turned the statement into a question.

"Yes, I do. I need to find Abigail. Can you tell me where she lives or at least where she lived before coming to the estate?"

The line was silent again. Ben was about to ask in another way when Mrs. Roberts spoke again.

"I can't tell you information that was in her application, Master Benjamin. Not only is it disloyal to Ms. Huntsman but it is illegal as well. I'm very sorry."

Ben exhaled a breath he had been holding since he asked the question. "I understand. I wouldn't want you to get in trouble. I just didn't have anywhere else to turn. Thank you for calling me back, anyway."

"Don't hang up yet," she said in a hurry. "I said I can't tell you anything she put on her application or that I gathered during the employment process. I didn't say there was nothing I could tell you. Everyone knows I am a horrible gossip, and I had several long conversations with Abigail—a delightful girl, that one—so who is to say anything if my loose lips let out some little tidbit of information I received in one of those conversations?"

Ben's smile felt like it would crack his face. Claire Roberts was exactly the opposite of a gossip. She held personal information so closely she would take hundreds of secrets to her death bed, even if the person about whom the information referred didn't see it as confidential.

"That would be wonderful," he said. He could picture her firm nod, that bun of gray hair shaking as she did it.

"Good. She was a close-mouthed girl when it came to personal information. She would tell animated stories of her childhood and experiences she had, but she would never mention brothers, sisters, or any family member, really. Only once did she seem to slip, referring to some sort of estate—though it was clear it was not as grand as the Huntsman Estate—in Jackson, Wyoming. It seemed that it might be her ancestral home, old and with a history of several generations of her family. Maybe that's enough to get you started."

"That's fantastic," Ben said. "Thank you, Mrs. Roberts. I think that just may be the information I'm looking for."

"You're welcome, dear. I don't know how easy it will be to find. Most estates that have been in families for a long time have names unrelated to the family. It was very fashionable a hundred years ago to affix grand names to family mansions, like Thomas Jefferson's Monticello or George Washington's Mount Vernon and the like. With the internet, it could be enough, though."

"I think it will be. Thank you so much, Mrs. Roberts. You don't know how much this means to me."

"I think maybe I do," she said. "Don't forget that I basically raised you, Master Benjamin, nursed you when you were sick and even swatted your little bottom on several occasions. It's clear that you love the girl, clear to me, anyway. No one will ever find out from me, mind you, but I know you well enough to be sure. Go get her. The best of luck to you."

Ben felt his face heating. Why wouldn't she have seen how much Abbie meant to him? He almost asked if she knew how Abigail felt about him, but decided against it. It might insult her. "Thank you again. I have some work to do. Please keep this number and call me anytime. I miss the chats we used to have."

"I do, too. We will talk again. Take good care of yourself, Master Benjamin. Without me, I fear for your wellbeing."

He laughed at that, a genuine laugh that caused a feeling of comfort to radiate through him. "I'll do my best. I would ask you to tell everyone hello for me, but it's probably better that no one knows we talked."

"Correct. You always were a clever boy. Goodbye, Master Benjamin, until the next time we talk."

"Goodbye, Mrs. Roberts. Thank you again."

He hung up and put the phone on his night stand. He had a good feeling about his chances in tracking down Abbie now. All he needed to do was some research and then he could actually go and see her. That part scared him silly, but he had to know how she felt. He had to know.

With a little work on the internet, Ben found what he was looking for. It was a fairly large, historic estate situated just outside of Jackson. It was informally called the Henderson estate, but most references used the name Aqua Terra.

Ben's hands shook on the keyboard as he found

more and more information about the estate. It was built around a hundred years ago and was the current home of a number of the Henderson clan. The few pictures he found showed it to be exactly as he would have thought. It had ponds and little creeks everywhere, along with a fair-sized lake on the property. It was idyllic and seemed to match Abbie's personality just right. He wondered at her working as a maid with such a fair-sized estate.

There was nothing left to do but to go there. If Abbie hadn't gone back, her family should be able to tell him where she was. If they would.

He talked it over with JJ and Mabel, and they both encouraged him to go.

"We'll be fine," they said. "It has been nice having a little break from doing everything with the restaurant, but we're refreshed now and can handle things. Don't you worry about us."

"I feel like I'm abandoning you," Ben said. "After how you took me in and helped me out, I feel bad about it."

"Oh, nonsense," Mabel said. "We helped each other. Now, though, you need to go and try to figure out what is going on with Abigail. That is much too important to leave hanging. Go, with our blessing and encouragement. If you tried to stay here now, I'd shoo you out with a broom. Go. Go get the girl."

Ben laughed. "I'll go, but I'm not sure if I'll get the girl. She may hate me and not even speak to me. I'm just going to try to find out exactly what is going on."

"She doesn't hate you, Benjamin," the old woman said, patting his arm. "Trust me, she doesn't hate you. Talk to her, tell her how you feel. It will all work out right."

With hasty goodbyes, Ben got in his car and started the eight-hour drive to Jackson, Wyoming. He wouldn't get there until sometime in the middle of the night. He would get a room and go to the estate in the morning. He didn't want to show up tired from a long drive. He wanted everything going in his favor when he saw Abbie again. He felt he would need it.

Despite the late hour and the long drive, he couldn't sleep when he got a hotel room. He opened his laptop and looked at pictures of Aqua Terra again, wishing he still had pictures of Abbie. Before he knew it, he was typing up thoughts about her.

Maybe he should rehearse what he was going to say, just as a safety net. The thought of choking on his words terrified him. He would only have one chance at this. Ben had never been much of a poet, but he could write what he felt and then maybe memorize it.

He tapped away at the keys:

"I love to look at you. I could do that for hours. I wish you were not so incredibly cute, and I wish that every line and curve of you was not so fascinating. I wish that any and all parts of your body, your face, every last thing down to each hair, did not pull me toward you, causing me to wish only to touch you, to feel you, take your scent in with each breath. Simply put, I am lost to all when in your presence. Damn you and cruel fate that forced us to meet."

No, that sounded too negative. He tried again.

"The light in your eyes shines brighter than the sun to me. With it, I can see the future. Our future."

Uh, no. too corny. He'd turn her off for sure with a line like that.

"The world lost its light when I lost you, and there

is no room in my broken heart for anything else."

Nope, too needy. Ben slammed his laptop closed. He couldn't say any of these things to her. Hell, he couldn't even write them into a letter and give them to her. The thought of just talking to her was hard enough for him to imagine.

He finally got a few hours of sleep after lying on the bed and looking at the ceiling for what seemed like hours. When his alarm rang, he was up like a shot and getting ready. It was finally time.

Ben had never felt like this before. He had been nervous, sure. Every time he had ever been called to his mother's office, no matter his age, it had made him nervous. But right now, at this instant, he wasn't sure he would survive. His heart pounded so hard he could hear it. No, he felt it in his ears.

He lifted his hand in front of him. It was shaking. Why? Why was his body betraying him like this? It's not like he hadn't met the woman before. It was Abbie, the woman who had agreed to be his wife, the one he had been so comfortable with. Before she left. There simply wasn't a reason he should be feeling so weak and so vulnerable, right? Even if she could, with a word, make his life seem like it was not worth living.

No, he would not think about that. She loved him. He knew it. Unless she didn't anymore. She had left him, not telling him why or what was going on.

Yet here he was.

He waited in the entryway of the Aqua Terra estate, not being allowed further into the house. Normally, he would have thought about how rude it was, that he wasn't even shown into a sitting room where he could wait, but then again, he was probably lucky he was not turned away entirely. He would wait—patiently—realizing he was lucky he was even allowed to wait and see if Abbie would talk to him.

Footsteps echoed in the hallway above. Ben turned to see Abigail making her way down the stairs gracefully. He was totally unprepared for his body's reaction.

At the sight of her, he felt his eyes grow heavy with moisture. He wouldn't cry. He would not. His knees decided to do their part as well. He almost collapsed when they tried to buckle. His heart, beating fast before, jumped up its rhythm until it felt like it would explode. A dry, altogether unpleasant taste entered his mouth, much like the taste that signaled that he would soon throw up. As he looked at her, he wondered if he would be able to speak at all.

"What do you want, Benjamin?" she asked him frostily, and he thought his heart would break right then, killing him.

34

"*I*...uh..." he started. He took a deep breath, his heart a jackhammer in his ears. "I miss you." His eyes widened as much as hers narrowed at him. "I mean, you picked up and left and didn't even explain to me why. I think I deserve at least that much."

"You think that, do you?" she said, almost spitting. "I think that I deserve the truth. You see how everyone thinks they deserve something?"

"Abbie," he said, wincing at his pleading tone, "I don't understand. If I did something wrong, will you at least tell me what it was? How can I fix it if I don't even know what I did wrong?"

Those blue eyes of hers turned even harder. He thought he saw a storm in them, waves crashing, lightning flashing. He had the urge to back up a step, but he planted his feet more firmly and waited for the maelstrom to wash over him.

"You know full well what you did, Benjamin

Mason!" Her voice, even raised, was melodious and musical, though it cut him like the sharpest knife. "I fell for you. Quickly, stupidly, but I fell. You took advantage of that to use me for your own purposes. That's something I can never forgive."

"Use…use you? Abbie, what are you talking about? I never used you for anything. I—"

"Didn't use me? I know what you did. Arianna told me all about what she overheard you tell Lucas. 'I'll just marry Abbie. That will ruin my mother's plans. She's only a maid, but she'll do.' Tell me you didn't say that."

Ben's face went ashen. "I did." He looked into her eyes as he said it, and he saw the anger and the hurt building there. He continued before she could speak. "Did she tell you the rest of it?"

That drew her up short. The confusion in her eyes seemed to break the angry surge that had been there. She pinched her lips and considered for just a moment. "What do you mean, the rest of it?"

"The part after what you just repeated. The part about how I laughed at what I had just said and told Lucas what I really felt."

"No." She was curious, which was good. It seemed to cool her anger a little. "Why don't you tell me about it?" That last was delivered in a voice that could have been an executioner's.

He pulled out his cell phone and handed it to her.

"What?" she said. "What's this for?"

"Call Lucas. You won't believe me, but maybe you'll believe him if you call him now."

That took her aback. She bit her lower lip and then noticed what she was doing and stopped. She reached for the phone twice—pulling her hand back after extending her arm halfway—before finally taking it. She went to dial it.

"It's locked," she said, holding it out to him.

"4-2-2-2-4-3," he said, making no move to reach for it.

She entered the lock code. "That's a strange combination."

"It's '4-Abbie.'"

Ben thought he saw her flush, though it was hard to tell because her cheeks had been slightly red from her anger earlier. She put the phone on speaker.

"Hey, man," Lucas's voice said over the phone. "What's up? Are you still moping around like you're gonna die?"

It was Ben's turn to flush. He could feel the heat rising from his neck to his forehead. He wanted to speak, but he remained silent. Abbie looked at him as if asking if he wanted to answer, but when he didn't, she nodded slightly.

"Hi, Lucas, It's Abigail."

Ben thought he heard muffled curses through the phone. "Oh, hi, Abigail. You have Ben's phone."

"Yes, he's right here. I need to ask you something, and I need you to tell me the truth."

"Okay," Lucas said. "Go ahead."

"Do you remember when Ben told you he was going to marry me? The very first time he mentioned it, when he came up with the idea, before he asked me?"

There was a slight pause, but then he answered. "Yes."

"What did he say?" Abbie asked.

"He told me he wanted to marry you."

"I want his exact words, Lucas."

"Exact words? How can I—"

"Lucas," Abbie said firmly. "It's very important that you be completely truthful with me. Tell me everything."

"Lucas," Ben put in, earning him a sharp look from Abigail. "Tell her everything. Every word. I know you remember it. You have shoved it in my face enough times."

Lucas sighed. "He said he was going to marry you, laughing like he was joking. He said that would put a crimp in his mother's plans to marry him off to Penelope. He said, and I quote, 'She's just a maid, but she'll do.' He—"

"That's fine, Lucas. Thank you." Abigail looked at Ben, holding the phone up as if it was evidence. She went to end the call.

"Wait," Lucas said, "I'm not finished. He said that stuff, sure, but don't take it out of context. Please listen to the rest of it."

Abbie's hand dropped to her side. She rolled her eyes and sighed. "Okay, go ahead," she said.

"Thank you," Lucas said. "Like I told you, he said that stuff. Immediately after he said that bit about being 'just a maid,' though, he laughed. Then—"

"He *laughed?*" Abigail asked. "Lucas, you're not helping."

"Abigail, please," the voice coming from the phone said. "Will you please stop interrupting me and just let me finish?"

"Sorry," she said, though Ben thought she sounded more irritated than sorry. "Go on."

"He laughed. You have to understand we had just had a conversation about this very subject—rich people seeing those with less money as lower forms of life—a few days earlier. A conversation in which I ribbed him because sometimes he acted like a snob, though not nearly as often as often as his mother would like. Anyway, he laughed and then said, 'Yeah, right, as if the word *just* could ever be used with Abbie. The only sentence I can think of with an honest use of the word is this one: "Abbie is just perfect."' I rolled my eyes at that."

Abbie's face lost some of its color.

Lucas continued. "Then he went on in sickening detail about how absolutely perfect you are. How your eyes suck him in and make him feel like he's floating on clouds, how your smile makes him want to sweep you into his arms and kiss those sensuous lips of yours, blah blah blah. I won't bore you with the details."

"Bore me," Abbie said, her eyes alight now with interest.

"Seriously?"

"Seriously."

"Fine," Lucas said. "I'll tell you what I remember. There was a lot of it, though, and his poetry was lost on me. I'm not in love with you, after all." Ben thought he saw a small smile form on her lips.

"He talked about how when he's with you, the world seems a nice place, not at all like when you're not around. When you're not near, he thinks of you constantly. He said he thought he fell in love with you the first time he met you, and it only got stronger every time he saw you, every time he talked to you. He said—do I really have to go on, Abigail? It's kind of making me nauseous."

Abbie's face looked rigid, like she was schooling it so no emotion showed. There seemed to be a smile trying to shine through, though.

"I guess that's enough for now," she said, in much too sterile a tone. "Thank you, Lucas. I appreciate your honesty."

"Yeah, sure," Lucas said. "No problem. Umm, Ben, are we cool?"

"We're cool, Lucas," Ben said. "Thanks."

"Okay, great. Well, I'll talk to you later. Bye."

Abbie looked at Ben, that carefully neutral expression still on her face. She held his phone up for him to take it.

He tried to force a smile, but was sure it was a sickly thing. His stomach felt as if it had twisted into a knot. He wasn't sure where they were at this point. He stepped forward and reached for the phone. As he wrapped his hand around it, Abigail grabbed his hand and pulled him toward her. Her arms went around him and she enfolded him in a hug.

35

Abigail had her answer. Her doubt melted away like snow in the noonday sun, leaving only relief in its place. He did care about her, really cared about her. It wasn't some ploy, and he wasn't controlled by Margaret Huntsman.

"I'm so sorry if I did something wrong," he said to her. "If I did, I don't know what it was. Do you understand what the deal was with that conversation?"

"Yes," she said, "I understand. There were just so many things going on all at one time, and your mother and the maids were telling me things. I just didn't know what to believe. It did seem like you didn't care for me."

"I do, Abbie, I really do. I know sometimes I seemed to be a different person. I don't know why that happens. I should probably see a psychiatrist or something. There are times when it doesn't seem like

I'm even in control of my own mind. I can't really explain it." He stopped and his eyes narrowed. "Now that I think of it, I haven't felt like that since I left home."

"You left home?"

"Yeah, I kind of confronted my mother about the Penelope thing. It made me mad that she might have fired you. I couldn't get a straight answer from her or anyone about what happened. And she took my phone and canceled my service—it was one of the business accounts, and she told the phone company I was fired. I lost all my contacts so I couldn't call and—"

"She did fire me!" Abbie said. "I was escorted off the property and when I called you, your phone was out of service. I didn't know if you arranged it and hated me, or what."

"I'm so sorry, Abbie. I should have thought of a way to track you down before now. I should have—"

Abbie kissed him mid-sentence. The warmth she remembered and had thought about so much over that last several weeks, the comfort, spread over her body and she sighed. It felt like her muscles had turned to taffy and she sank into his embrace. They held each other for a long time, all tension leaving her, being replaced with a peace she hadn't felt for months.

She leaned her head back and looked at him. Maybe not all her doubt was gone. What if he was still playing an act and he was carrying out his mother's will? What could she do if that was the case? She decided to go with her feelings.

"Ben, is your mother…special in any way?"

Ben blinked at the sudden change of subject.

"Special? You mean other than that she's incredibly successful and can manipulate people expertly?"

"Yes, other than that. What I mean is, has she ever shown that she has special abilities or anything like that?"

"Abbie," Ben said, "I really have no idea what you're talking about. Can you please just cut to the point? All you're doing is making me more and more confused." He stroked her hair and his eyes became unfocused for a moment as he leaned in to kiss her again. She put her hand up to stop his lips.

Abigail took a deep breath, let it out, and spoke. "Ben, your mother is a witch."

He laughed at her. "Oh, Abbie, leave it to you to soften your words. I believe the word is 'bitch.' But yes, I am fully aware of that."

"No, no," Abbie said. "You're getting it all wrong. What I mean is that your mother is actually a witch. She can use magic, cast spells."

Ben's laugh slowed to a chuckle, but his eyes didn't show that he felt any humor. "What do you mean? What kind of joke is this, Abbie? My mother, casting spells, using magic like in the movies?"

Abigail saw that he wouldn't believe her if she explained it to him. Despite that, though, she let out a relieved breath. Unless he was acting—and if so he was a very good actor—the fact that he found it so hard to believe proved that he was not in league with his mother. She did the only thing that would convince him without having to explain things for the next hour. She cast her magic toward him, stopping up his mouth while at the same time lifting him off his feet to dangle in the air while calling moisture out of the air into a ball of water hovering above her open palm.

"Ben," she said calmly, looking into his wide eyes, "I'm a witch, too."

His eyes grew even wider, and he mumbled something around the plug of solid water she had placed in his mouth. She had only done that to stop him from interrupting her. She removed it.

He was breathing hard as he tried again. "You're...you're a witch?"

"Afraid so," she said as she lowered him to the ground and released the magic. She dispelled the water ball into the air as water vapor. "I figured it would be easier to show you than to try to explain it to you. Are you all right?"

Ben was bent over, hands on his knees, breathing hard as if he had just run a race. Abigail thought that if he didn't get his breaths under control, he might hyperventilate.

"Breathe slowly, Ben." Abbie came up to him and rubbed his neck gently. She was glad he didn't flinch or shy away from her when she did so. He was freaked out about the magic, but he wasn't afraid of her. She loved him all the more for it.

It was a few minutes until he was calm. She continued to rub his neck and shoulders, making soothing noises.

"I'm okay now," he said. He looked into her eyes and she felt a jolt, as she always did when he looked so deeply into them. "Will you explain this to me? I don't know what to think of it. I'd like to understand."

"Yes," she said as she smiled at him. "I will explain everything. Let's go into one of the sitting rooms and sit down. This will take a while."

*****

They settled into a comfortable little room with a fireplace, two sofas, and three big, stuffed leather chairs. Abigail sat down on one sofa and motioned for Ben to sit on the other, across a polished cherrywood table from her.

"Do you want some tea or anything else to drink?" she asked, still looking into his eyes as if to find out what he was thinking.

"I would say to give me something stronger—much stronger—but I think tea will do. I think I want my mind clear for this."

Abbie poked her head out the door and said something to a person Ben couldn't see. Not a servant, surely. For some reason, even though the house they were in was large and it seemed her family was fairly well off, he just couldn't picture Abbie the maid bossing around servants. The thought caused a pang of regret. He was judging based on those old prejudices again.

"You have to understand, Ben," she said as she seated herself again, "that most of what you have ever heard about witches is not true."

"Which parts? Like the parts about them eating children?" He tried to make it a joke but winced when he heard how it came out. "I'm sorry, Abbie. I think I'm still in shock. Why don't I just shut up and let you talk?"

She flashed the smile that made his heart pound in his chest—it was nice to see it still did that even with what he had just heard—and reached across the table to take his hand.

"No, the part about eating children is real."

She couldn't maintain her straight face, though, and gave it away with her snicker. "Seriously, though, there have always been people who could harness the power the elements provide. Some can use the magical energy from the earth itself, some from fire, some air, and some," she pointed to herself, "the power inherent in water.

"We are exactly the same as onlies…as other humans." She paused as if what she said caused her to remember something. "Except that we can wield these magical forces. We live, we breathe, we eat and drink, we die, just like everyone else. It's not like we're another species or anything, though there are prejudices, of course." She paused again, her mouth twisting as if she had tasted something rotten.

"I'm really sorry, Ben, but it's really hard for me to talk about the differences between us. I have…baggage, I guess you'd call it. Let me start by talking about something else. I promise to try to make sense of it all, but I want to start with the most important part."

She was still holding his hand, and he felt hers tremble. He looked more deeply into her eyes and saw something there, something he'd never seen. Was it fear?

"Abbie, you know you can tell me anything, right? I mean, how much more of a shock can it be than what you have just told me?"

She flicked her eyes downward, as if studying their clasped hands. She squeezed his.

"Don't be so sure it can't be," she finally said. "Promise me you will let me finish, that you will stay here and listen to me until I have told you all I need to tell you."

"Abbie, you don't have to—"

"Promise me, Ben. Promise."

He sighed. "I promise to let you finish." He realized his hand was trembling now, too. Was she going to tell him something worse than being a witch? Did they do sacrifices or something? Was he safe? He thrust the thought away. He trusted Abbie. She would tell him what he needed to know. Thoughts of the old TV show *Bewitched* flashed through his head, and he smiled at the thought.

"What did you just think of?" she asked, her eyes narrowing in suspicion. "What's funny?"

He told her, and she smiled weakly back at him. She was obviously too nervous for humor to work in calming her mood.

Abigail took a deep breath and then let it out slowly. She opened her mouth to speak when someone knocked softly at the door.

"Come in, Zoe," Abbie said.

The door opened and a woman came in holding a tray with an antique teapot, two cups on saucers, sugar, honey, and some wedges of lemon. She put the tray down on the table and then straightened.

Ben couldn't help to notice how attractive she was. She was short, maybe just above five feet, and she was slender but shapely. It was the twinkle in her brown eyes that gripped him, though. She flicked her dark hair, lighter highlights cascading around her heart-shaped face and the mouth that wore a smile that was nearly a smirk. She eyed him up and down.

"Hi," she said, turning to Ben. "I'm Zoe. I'm Abbie's obnoxious best friend." She winked at Ben and then met eyes with Abbie and raised her eyebrows in a way that made Ben feel like he had just been approved.

She swiveled her eyes back to him and put her hand out. Ben took it and shook it. She had a firm grip.

"It's a pleasure to meet you," he said.

"What is Abs doing to you?" Zoe asked. "You're shaking like a leaf."

"I…she…" Ben stammered, but Abigail came to his rescue.

"I just told him I'm a witch," she said.

"Ahh, I see. Well, not to make you more nervous, but I am, too. It's nice to meet you, Ben. Maybe I'll see you later at the animal sacrifice ritual." She drew her eyebrows down and focused on his eyes.

Abigail smacked her friend's shoulder. "Zo, play nice." Turning to Ben, she continued, "Don't listen to her, Ben. She's a joker. I should have known better than to have you meet her without a lawyer."

"I'm just having a little fun," Zoe said to him. "I'm not serious. Or am I?" she widened her eyes in a comical fashion and stared at him.

"Enough," Abbie said. "Shoo, begone. We'll call for you when we need comedy relief. Go."

Zoe laughed and tossed her hair again. "Okay, but I'll be right outside, probably listening at the door." With one more look at Ben, and a wink, she glided toward the door and out of the room, her hips moving in a graceful and exaggerated manner.

Abigail shrugged at Ben as the door closed. "Best friends from childhood. What you gonna do?"

"She's…" Ben started.

"I know. She has that effect on everyone. Men and women."

They settled back into their respective seats, Abigail pouring the tea for both of them. "It's a mint tea. I hope that's okay."

"It's fine," Ben said as he added a little honey to his. "Okay, I'm ready to listen. Fire away."

The look on her face when he said that last part was confusing. It almost looked like she was reliving a painful memory. It was very nearly a flinch as if he had thrown something at her. He was going to ask about it, but she started speaking.

"My mother was the leader of our coven. That's how we are organized, in covens, groups that originally started as families and that have grown to include others. In most cases. There are still some covens that are only one family, but they are rarer than they used to be, from what I understand.

"I'm getting off track. So, Mother was a powerful witch—strong use of the magic runs in our family— and everyone loved her. She was beautiful, powerful, smart, and everyone I had ever seen interact with her thought the world of her."

"You are your mother's daughter." Ben realized he was sitting there holding his tea cup halfway to his mouth. He took a sip and set it on the saucer on the table in front of him.

"She was murdered six years ago," Abbie continued, her eyes becoming liquid but her voice not faltering.

Before Ben could speak, she continued. "She was performing one of our rituals, for the Spring Rain festival—a simple thing to align our coven with the energy of the local bodies of water, not any kind of sacrifice or anything—along with a friend of hers. Emma Williams. She was attacked in force while she did it, ambushed by fire witches and warlocks, as well as onlies...humans without magical abilities with guns. She fought as best she could, she and Emma, too, but they overwhelmed her. As one of her last acts in this life, she sent me her memories of the battle, a way of explaining what happened to her.

"She actually sent that memory to my brother and sister as well, but they got only scattered pieces of it. Whether it was because they were not as receptive to the water magic or their powers were not developed quite enough yet, no one knows. Only I got the entire scene. I have relived it over and over again, many times throughout the years since."

Abbie stopped for a moment and breathed deeply, dipping her head so Ben couldn't see her eyes.

"Oh, Abbie," he said, "I'm so sorry. I lost my father, too, but not like that. It must have been horrible to get that memory sent to you." He didn't mention that he couldn't understand how such a thing could be done. They could talk about that later.

"That's the thing, Ben." Abbie lifted her head, sniffled, and wiped at her wet cheeks. "We have more in common than you know.

"In the vision of my mother's death, I saw the witch who orchestrated the ambush, the one who led those who murdered my mother. She launched the final volley of magic that overwhelmed my mother and killed her. I saw the woman's face clearly, but it was unfamiliar to me. I hadn't ever met her. Until I started working at the estate."

"What?" Ben said. "You saw the woman again at the estate? A murderer?"

"Yes."

Ben sat there, staring, his mouth open. It took a

few seconds to recover and ask the obvious question. "You're not saying…" He paused for a moment. "Abbie, who was it?"

"Margaret Huntsman," she said.

36

"Margaret...my mother?" Ben said.

"We'll get to that in a moment," Abbie answered. "It was Margaret Huntsman. Let's leave it at that for now. Seeing her face again was enough for me, but not enough for the leading Council of the coven. They wanted more proof before any action was taken. My mission at the estate was to get that proof."

"Wait," Ben said. "Wait a minute. Are you saying that you were working there as a spy, some kind of undercover thing?"

"Yes." She wouldn't meet his gaze but shifted her eyes around the room as if uncomfortable looking at him.

"To prove that my mother killed your mother."

"To prove that Margaret killed my mother, yes." She looked at him, though it seemed to pain her to do so. "I have a talent, a rare talent. I am able to detect magical residues, the leavings of energy when magic is used on someone or something. I used that talent to find something with a strong magical residue on it, something that had been subjected to Margaret Hunstman's magic. Margaret Huntsman's fire magic."

Ben's head was still spinning. He could hardly keep up. Looking at her, he wondered where this was all going. "Something she used her magic on?"

"Well," Abbie said, "someone."

"And?"

"You. It's you, Ben. Margaret has used magic on you. Quite a bit. I don't know why, but you reek of it. I never noticed because in order to detect magic, I have to focus on using my power, something I never did with you. It's not like hearing, where any sound that comes around will make it to your ears. It's more like seeing, where you have to open your eyes to get an image."

"This magic," he said, "that you say is all over me. You say it's my mother's?"

"Margaret's. It has to be. I detected no other magic on anyone in the house besides her. Other than the residues, I mean. She's the only one who herself is magical. At least, she's the only one I've come into contact with who has the use of magic. My ability does not let me identify particular people from the residue, but one of the witches here can. I would like her to read the residue on you, if you are willing."

"Abbie, this is a lot to take in. You're a witch, my mother's a witch, my mother killed your mother, it's kind of a lot, you know."

"I do know, Ben," Abbie said. "I do. Please, just trust me for a few minutes more. Just a little while longer. It will all make sense, I promise."

Ben raked his fingers through his hair. He did trust

her, but all this witchcraft stuff. And murder. He didn't know what to do. "A few minutes more, Abbie," he said. "If it doesn't start making sense, I'm going to need some time alone to sort through everything."

"Agreed." Abbie turned toward the door. "Isabella?"

A wiry woman, probably in her late thirties or early forties, came into the room. Her thin face held an expression of resolution, but still seemed friendly.

"Hi, Ben. I'm Isabella. I'm just going to take a reading of the magic on you, if you don't mind. You won't feel anything, and you don't have to do anything. Is that okay?"

"Uh, sure."

She closed her eyes and moved her hands slowly in front of her as if she was feeling his aura or something. It only took fifteen or twenty seconds and she opened her eyes again.

"It matches. The witch who cast the magic on him is the same one who killed Olivia. The residues are identical."

Abigail sighed. Whether it was in relief or agreement with the result, Ben didn't know. "Thank you Isabella."

"Oh, and Abbie," the woman said, "that other item you gave me, the ring, it also had the same residue on it, but from much earlier. I'd say it's been about eleven or twelve years, I'd guess, since the last time magic was used on it, but it has layers from at least twice that long ago.

"Thank you," Abbie said, taking the ring the other woman held out for her. Ben was surprised to see that it was the engagement ring he had given her.

"Abbie? Is that my grandmother's ring?" Ben said, but couldn't even put into words what he wanted to say.

"Yes. I asked Isabella to check the residue on it."

"I've had that ring for about ten years," he said. "It was my grandmother's, and when she died my dad took it and kept it in his pocket at all times. When he himself died, it came to me. It's been in a special box I had made for it, sitting on my nightstand."

Abbie shook her head sadly. "Okay, Ben, here is the whole story. Margaret Huntsman is a fire witch. She orchestrated the ambush of my mother and Emma. She herself landed the killing blow. She has been casting spells on you for some reason, maybe to try to control you in some way. Her magic is on you in thick layers, and must have been placed there over a long period of time. What Isabella just said about the ring confirmed what I thought was true. Your father did not die of a heart attack, stroke, or some disease. Margaret Huntsman killed him."

Ben stood up and started to speak, but she raised her voice over him.

"And Margaret Huntsman is not your mother, Ben. She is not your mother."

The angry words he was ready to say froze in his mouth. He stood there, trying to catch his breath. The room seemed to be moving around him. He sat down hard on the couch.

Abbie sat across from him, looking into his eyes, waiting to see what he would do. He took two more long breaths.

"What do you mean she's not my mother? How could you possibly know that?"

Abbie got up and moved around the table to sit

beside him. "We have researchers, Ben. They are very good. Margaret did a fairly thorough job of destroying all evidence of your real mother, but she didn't get it all. There was a photograph of your birth certificate that she didn't know existed. It has your mother's name on it. Grace Mason."

"Grace?" Ben whispered reverently.

"We have pieced things together. Margaret, a friend of the family, killed your mother, then inveigled her way into your father's affections. When he had given her what she wanted—power and wealth—she killed him too so she could be in control. She has killed quite a few people, actually, including several other witches in the last year or two. We're still not sure what her master plan is, but it obviously involves removing anyone who could hinder it."

"Including you?" Ben asked.

"Yes, including me. If she had found out who I was, she would have killed me, too. She may have done it just because I caused problems with you and your engagement."

Ben knew he still wasn't thinking clearly. Organizing his thoughts felt like swimming in molasses. "Are you...are you sure about all this, Abbie? I mean, those are some pretty serious accusations."

"Ben, you know in your heart that I'm telling the truth. But yes, we have evidence. I'll show it all to you, if you need it."

"I...might. Not right now, though. Right now, what I need to do is go home and confront my mother about this, ask her to explain."

"Ben," Abbie said, grabbing his arm, "don't you understand? You can't just go and confront her and ask her about things like this. She killed your mother, your father, my mother, she won't hesitate to kill you. It's too dangerous. Maybe, with some time to think about it, you can get the information from her own mouth, but you'll have to be clever about it. You do not want that woman to suspect you know the truth. She doesn't like loose ends."

A feeling started in Ben's belly. It was just a sort of buzzing at first, a rumbling. It grew to a type of vibration and then to a little ball of heat. As it did, his mind cleared, bit by bit. And the heat grew until it felt like a softball of molten lava in his middle. It didn't stop there. It continued to build, to get hotter and bigger, and soon his whole chest felt like it was on fire. He was angry, but it was a different kind of rage than any he had ever felt.

"Abbie," he said calmly as he took her hand from his arm and kissed it lightly. "I am going to see her now. If all this is true, if she tries to kill me, too, she better be very fast, because I plan on being ready for her. My father's collection of handguns is still in the room where he kept them when he was alive. I know how to use them."

Abbie looked as if she would object, but then a look of resignation came over her face, as if she realized she could not stop him. "I don't suppose you'll wait until tomorrow morning? If we leave now," she looked at her watch, "we won't be there until late tonight."

"No, not tomorrow. Tonight. Right now. I don't...wait a minute. Did you just say 'we'?"

"I did. If you're going to go and put yourself in danger, you're not doing it without me. Isn't that what a good wife does?"

Ben laughed in spite of the situation. "I guess so. I wouldn't know. It might be useful to have a witch with me in case everything turns out to be true. Not that I doubt you precisely, but…"

"I understand, Ben. Just so you know, though, I don't think I'm a match for her in magical ability. I think she's more powerful than me, and I *know* she's more experienced in using the magic as a weapon. I might not be much protection, when it comes down to it."

"It won't come to that. You'll see." Ben kissed her hand again and then released it. "Let's get going."

37

~~~~~

The car ride to the Huntsman Estate was over four hours long, though to Abigail it felt much longer.

"Are you sure you want to do this, Ben?" she finally asked more than an hour into the drive. "Maybe we should think about it again and decide on a more…conservative approach."

Ben shifted his eyes to her for a few seconds and then back to the road. To her and back to the road. "Abbie, you almost sound like you're scared."

Abbie held the little angel figurine tight in her hand and rubbed its smooth surface with her thumb. "Scared? Maybe. I like to think of it as cautious, though. I told you the things Margaret has done. Those are just the things we know. I suspect there are many other things we don't know. You know better than anyone how ambitious she is. Our lives are insignificant to her."

"That I can agree with," he said. "I'm just not sure

about the other stuff. Your information could be false, or misunderstood—"

Abbie tried to object, but he held up his hand to stop her and continued. "I know, you believe it is all true, but as mad as I am, as much anger as I have boiling inside me trying to get out, I have to make sure. I have to talk to her now, try to read her when I confront her with it."

"Let's just assume for a second that you believe everything I've said," Abbie said. "Don't you understand the danger you'll be in by confronting her? There is a long history of accidents happening to those around Margaret Huntsman. Arranging one for you won't be a problem for her."

"I'll have my father's gun. And you to watch my back. We'll be fine."

"A gun is a poor weapon when faced with a skilled witch." She needed to find a way to talk him out of this. She had a very bad feeling about what they were doing.

"Abbie, you don't have to come with me. I can drop you off somewhere before I go to the estate. It's fine. I am going there, right now, to talk to Margaret. Nothing you can say or do will stop me, unless you plan to use magic to hold me or something. I would hope you would never do that. I don't know that I could ever trust you again if you did."

He had her there. She had been thinking of how she could use her magic to stop him without actually assaulting him with it. It was clear now that she couldn't do that. She recognized that set in his jaw; he would not give in. She sighed.

"Fine, I'll stop trying to talk you out of it." She switched the angel into her other hand and felt the warmth it had absorbed from her handling.

"Thank you," he said with a forced smile. He was nervous, too, but he was trying to hide it from her. "Abbie, what is that you have in your hand?"

"Oh, this," she held up the little pale blue angel and chuckled weakly. "It's something I carved for my mother when I was a girl. It's an angel, carved by my water magic out of a piece of aquamarine. It's sort of a worry stone for me. I hold it and rub it and it calms me down, makes me feel connected to my mother."

"Can I hold it?"

"Of course." She handed it to him.

Ben flicked his eyes to it and then back to the road. He rubbed it lightly with his thumb as he had seen her do and a smile came to his face. "I see what you mean," he said as he handed it back to her. "It is soothing to rub it like that."

"My mother carried it with her always," Abbie said. "She had it in her pocket when she was killed. It was the only thing left of her, covered in ash and soot and lying on the ground. Isabella gave it to me after she tested the residue of the magic used on it."

"Margaret's?" Ben asked.

"Yes."

"Oh, Abbie, I'm so sorry. I wish I had known. I wish I could have done something."

"I know." She took his hand in hers and squeezed it. "There was nothing you could do. There may be nothing you can do now. She is a very powerful witch."

"Something has to be done, Abbie. I have to try, at least.

"Um, Abbie," he scratched his head. "Something confuses me."

"What is it?" she said.

"Why did you use your real name when you got the job at the estate? I'm glad you did, because it was how I found where you lived, but what if my mother recognized your name, your mother's name?"

Her face got hot. "I know, it's stupid to go undercover and use your own name. I just couldn't bring myself to go by another name. I figured with all the Hendersons there are in the state—"

"You're right about that," he said. "Over five hundred of them listed."

She raised an eyebrow, but then shook her head and continued. "Anyway, with all those, it's a fairly common name. I didn't figure Margaret would notice. I also counted on Mrs. Roberts being the only one who would see my application. It just didn't seem like a big risk. It worked out. Margaret didn't work out recognize me."

"Yeah, I guess you're right," he said. "It just seemed strange to me."

They were silent for a few minutes, each with their own thoughts.

"What is your plan?" she asked. "You surely have some kind of plan, right?"

"Sort of. I'll park outside the grounds. No use in causing a ruckus by appearing when I've been gone for so long. We'll walk to the house. My mother will be in her favorite sitting room. She always is this time of night, if she's not away on business. I'll ask her about my real mother and about my father. I'll judge her reaction and go from there. Simple."

Abbie hoped the woman was out of town on business so they could take a longer, more measured approach. "And the gun?"

"Oh, yeah, first stop when we get in the house is the room with my dad's gun collection. There are two or three that fit the bill perfectly. I'll grab a couple and then go talk to Margaret."

Abbie noticed that he had already seemed to accept that she wasn't his real mother, referring to her as "Margaret." That was good. She wasn't sure how much of the rest of it he believed. If he confronted Margaret Huntsman, he would have to admit belief in a great many things. Hopefully that admission wouldn't be the last thing he did in this world.

They arrived at the property boundaries at just after 10:00 PM.

"Are you ready?" Ben asked her.

"As ready as I can be, I think." She found herself furiously rubbing her angel figurine and forced herself to stop. She wanted to ask him to reconsider one more time but had promised him she wouldn't.

*****

They easily made their way to the house. Surprisingly, the estate's security wasn't that extensive. Ben had not really thought about it before, but it seemed barely adequate for an estate that size. He guessed that if all this was true, Margaret was confident in her own abilities to protect herself and didn't want others monitoring what happened at the estate, including some of her activities she might want to keep private.

As he opened one of the side entry doors—he still had his keys, after all—and allowed Abbie to go in, he thought again about what he was doing. He had played the entire thing off as if he was in complete control of the situation, but fear lurked in his middle. His mouth seemed dry, though his palms were starting to sweat. If all Abbie said was true, he could be killed tonight. Worse, she could be harmed. He'd never forgive himself for that. He almost wished she would ask him if he was sure about what they were doing one more time. He just might let her talk him out of it.

She wouldn't ask, though. She promised not to. She would loyally stand by him. The least he could do was pretend to be calm.

"It's this way," he said, motioning down the hall toward the room with his father's collection. It was all he could do to keep his voice steady as he spoke the three words.

A few rooms down, he stopped in front of the door to his father's collection room. Taking out his keys, he put the correct one into the lock and turned it. He took a breath, used the knob, and pushed the door open.

Ben entered the room first to flip the light on and turned to see Abbie crossing the threshold. Once he had closed the door, he surveyed the chamber he had not been in since the day he had been there with Abbie. She looked toward the black powder rifle they had discussed but then shifted her eyes away from it.

It was a largish room, probably twenty feet by twenty-five. A couch and two comfortable chairs sat in front of the empty fireplace, a long low table between them and smaller tables next to each chair. The walls, lined with photographs and paintings of natural settings, many of his father's beloved Yellowstone, seemed to close in on him. In glass cases and in a few carefully curated collections were handguns and rifles, ranging from antique black powder weapons to more modern firearms. Scattered throughout were edged weapons, too, knives, even a few swords.

Ben surveyed the cases, all the things his father had loved and collected. He sighed. He missed his father. So much.

The rage he had felt earlier began to stoke anew as he thought about his father and what Abbie said had happened to him. How different would Ben's life had been if his father was still with him, or even better, if both his father and mother were?

Ben set his jaw and retrieved the two handguns he had come for. He had already decided which he would use. He was familiar with all of them, having spent hours in this room talking with his father over his collection. He had fired every one of these guns, multiple times, and knew them well.

The two he reverently removed from their cases were a Beretta 92 and a Walther P99. He only glanced at Abbie as he did so, registering that she was watching him carefully, as if she was evaluating his resolve.

"Do you want to use one?" he asked her.

"No," she said. "I've never fired a gun and wouldn't even know what to do, let alone be able to hit anything. If it comes down to a situation where one might be needed, my magic will serve me better."

Ben nodded and opened another cabinet with ammunition.

As he worked, Ben saw Abbie fidgeting with her little angel figurine and smiled at her. She returned the smile, stroking the curve of the angel's wings with her thumb.

After loading the ammunition into the clips for the guns he had taken, he put extras in his pockets and slipped one of the guns into the waist of his pants and the other into a shoulder holster under his jacket.

Mentally inventorying his weapons, he confirmed he was prepared. Or as prepared as he would likely ever be.

"Are you ready?" he asked Abbie.

"Yes."

"Then let's get this over with." Patting his waist to make sure the gun was secure, and smoothing his jacket over both of them, he took her hand and squeezed it, then released it as he reached for the doorknob.

Ben was hoping he wouldn't be seen by anyone. He wanted to confront Margaret with no one else around.

His luck was in, it seemed, because he didn't see a soul as he and Abbie moved through the empty hallways like wraiths. Ben had to fight the urge to slink, as if he was trying to sneak into his own house. Abbie seemed calm and comfortable, walking with a normal gait, no indication at all they might be facing danger within the next few minutes.

The two reached the ground-level sitting room Margaret favored. As Ben reached for the doorknob, he heard muffled voices through the door. His hand froze and he looked over at Abbie.

She shrugged.

Ben pointed to a location just down the hall and walked five steps to get there. Abbie followed him.

"I don't know how many people are in there," he whispered. "I don't want to confront her with a bunch of witnesses. What if she has reasonable explanations? It'll make me look like an idiot."

Abbie frowned at him. Maybe she took offense to him even suggesting that everything she told him might be false. The expression disappeared quickly, though. She was smart; she understood what he meant.

"Hold on," she said. Looking toward the door, she waved one of her hands in a gesture almost like she was waving something away from her. "There are only two people in there."

"How do you—"

"I'm a water witch. People are made mostly of water. I can get a rough sense of where people are and how many. Trust me. Only two."

"It must be Helen. She's Margaret's oldest and best friend. They are inseparable. Or it could be Frank. He's one of her main assistants. Whoever it is, maybe I can just ask them to leave. I don't think we'll have a better opportunity than this."

Abbie didn't say anything.

"Okay," he continued, deciding. "Let's do it now."

He led her back to the door and knocked solidly on it. The voices stopped.

"Come in," Margaret's strong voice said.

Taking a deep breath and reaching up to squeeze Abbie's shoulder, Ben turned the knob and pushed the door open.

38

~~~

Abbie had been in the room before, the time she went searching for magical residue. It was smaller than most of the rooms in the house. She could have crossed the room in five or six steps and covered the distance of the other wall in maybe a pace or two more than that. As with many of the rooms, there were several bookshelves with books, assorted pieces of pottery, and other pieces of art. This particular room had furniture all of dark wood, mostly highly polished cherrywood.

The large fireplace—all the fireplaces in the manor house seemed to be very large, big enough for a person to walk into without ducking too much—held several fiery logs. The heat of it washed over Abbie from where she stood at the door. A fair-sized desk sat just off center of the floor, and three ladderback chairs were arranged in front of it. Behind the desk, sitting in a leather executive chair, was Margaret

Huntsman.

She looked as she always did. Her severe face was pinched in displeasure at the interruption, especially when she saw who had knocked. As her dark eyes shifted from glaring at Ben to her, they seemed to grow harder. She was not happy to see Abigail. Not at all.

The other person in the room was Helen Shapiro. Abbie had seen the woman a few times, but not from this close. She was taller than Abbie had realized, and much more muscular. The woman was intimidating. Her eyes were like a hawk's, but her face held a slight smile, an almost hungry look that told Abbie that the woman was anticipating a fine conflict, maybe the resolution of an ongoing one.

"Benjamin," Margaret said.

Ben didn't address her as either as his mother or by name, but simply started speaking. "I need to ask you about some things. Alone."

She raised her chin and tilted her eyes down so it seemed like she was looking down at him even though he was standing and she sitting. "Anything you want to say to me can be said in front of Helen. I hold no secrets from her."

"It's family business," Ben said. "Personal."

Margaret looked toward Abigail as if to question her presence. "Helen is like family to me. Out with it. I have things to do."

Ben sighed. Abbie knew he was getting frustrated. She was, too. She calmed herself and then willed calming thoughts toward him, as if she could telepathically lend him her peace.

"Fine," he finally said. "Are you my real mother?"

Abbie's mouth dropped open before she could

stop it, but she recovered quickly and smoothed her face so it held a neutral expression. Margaret's eyes tightened, but she didn't register the shock she must be feeling. Helen's eyes grew wide and she shifted her stance as if she was getting ready for battle.

Abbie wakened the magic in her and prepared to defend herself and Ben.

"Why would you ask such a thing?" Margaret said. Her quick glance at Abigail revealed that she thought she knew why.

"Answer me," Ben said.

"I have raised you since the death of your father, and before. I am your mother."

"Are you my biological mother?" Ben asked again.

Abbie felt magic building in the other woman. Helen crouched down slightly as if she was ready to spring.

"She's using her magic," Abbie whispered to him. She was already weaving an invisible shield of water around herself and Ben. Invisible water shields weren't as strong as thick, visible ones, but she didn't want to tip the other witch off to her powers just yet. It was unlikely Margaret had the talent to detect magic users, since she hadn't detected her when they had met before.

Ben drew the gun from his waistband and pointed it at Margaret. "Did you kill my mother?" he asked. "Did you kill my father?"

"Benjamin," Margaret said, not even flinching at the gun pointed at her. "You have made your final mistake. I have tried so hard, so hard, to bring you around. I realized you would never truly agree with me or be part of some of my…weightier projects, but I had hoped you would be controlled enough to be allowed to live. It seems that you will be the victim of an accident. Such a pity."

As the final word was still in the air, Margaret looked to Helen and nodded.

The other woman burst into flame.

It was so abrupt, so unexpected, that Abbie could do nothing but stare in astonishment. Ben's gaze was locked on the flame, too, the gun seemingly forgotten in his hand.

Then the living flame smiled a fiery smile and began to walk toward them. Ben blinked and shook his head. He fired four shots directly at the head of the human-shaped flame. The bullets flared into little meteors as they came close and then winked out. The creature continued her progress toward them unharmed, as if she had all the time in the world.

There were a few legends—most of them so wildly unrealistic as to be completely unbelievable—about elemental shifters who could turn into creatures of pure elemental magic, but Abbie had never believed them. They were fairy tales to tell young witches and warlocks to entertain them or to teach them lessons. They couldn't be real. Could they? Obviously, the vision of living flame in her mother's death memory was accurate, not some psychosomatic fabrication. This woman, this Helen, was as responsible for her mother's death as Margaret.

Abbie could wait no longer. She strengthened her shield, allowing it to become visible—Margaret's eyes did widen at that—and Abbie called into being a lance of solidified water and projected it toward Helen. It caught the flame creature unaware and threw her back against the far wall of the room with a shriek. Whether it was from pain or frustration, Abbie couldn't tell, but it gained her a few seconds before the shifter could re-enter the fray.

"Now," Margaret hissed, punctuating her word with fireballs thrown at Abbie, "I finally understand. You will die, too, water caster!"

The fireballs were powerful, but the shield Abbie had put up absorbed them. For now.

Ben swiveled his gun toward Margaret. Abbie saw on his face that he was warring with himself. He knew she wasn't his mother, but he had a lifetime of conditioning to battle against.

Within seconds, he had made his decision. He fired several times until the gun in his hand clicked impotently when he pulled the trigger. Throwing it to the ground, he drew the other gun from the shoulder holster and fired at Margaret until that gun, also, was empty. Only then did he pause to see the effects of his attack.

There were none.

Apparently, Margaret had put up a shield as well, one that protected her from the bullets. As with the earlier projectiles fired at Helen, every one flared and then disappeared before they could strike Margaret.

The entire exchange took mere seconds, time Abbie used to strengthen her shield and begin a more powerful attack spell. Helen had recovered and rushed toward them, this time angling to attack Abbie instead of Ben. She had been judged the more dangerous of the two.

"Ben," Abbie said through her labored breaths, "get out of here. Run. I'll hold them off."

Ben turned to her, but his eyes were wide and glazed. He was in shock not only from firing at the woman he had always thought was his mother, but because the bullets had no effect. Knowing what that meant must have stunned him.

Helen left the floor, diving at Abigail, as she completed the spell she had meant for Margaret. With no other alternative, she loosed it on the fire shifter.

A massive force of hardened water erupted from Abigail's outstretched hands, catching Helen Shapiro in midair. She spun away like a leaf in a hurricane, flipping head over feet. Halfway to the wall of the room, she reverted to human form, the flame not able to survive the concentrated water power.

She struck the far wall flat, her feet toward the ground and her head right side up. Abbie didn't hear the sound of the impact, but she could imagine it. The entire wall shook and the nearest window blew out in a shower of glass. As Helen bounced to the ground and then lay still, Abbie had no doubt the woman was dead. A bloody crater in the wall's wood paneling was the only indication she needed.

Her foe defeated, Abbie turned her attention to Margaret Huntsman. She had been casting a powerful spell also and was just about to release it. Not at her, though.

At Ben.

Abigail drew as much of her power as she could. The attack on Helen had exhausted her. She knew, even as she poured as much of her vital energy as she could into the shield around Ben, that it wouldn't be enough. Margaret knew she would be weakened. Maybe she even purposely sacrificed her friend in a strategic move to win the battle. The fire witch could kill Ben and then turn her attention to Abigail.

They would both be weakened, but Margaret Huntsman was at least an eighth level witch according to all the information the water witches in her coven could gather. She wouldn't know Abigail's strength, but since there were so few ninth or tenth levels, she could safely assume that in a weakened state, she could still overpower Abigail. She was right. Abigail was barely at the seventh level of power, and that was when she was fresh.

Still, Abbie had no thought for herself. If there was any way she could protect Ben, she had to do so. She drew more deeply into her power than she had ever done before, scratching for every little scrap of it to shield him. All the moisture in the air was brought in and utilized. She wished there was a lake close by to lend her its power. If she failed and Ben died, she didn't really care if she lived or died, anyway. She would deal with that later. Right now, Ben was all.

Margaret let loose with a blast of focused energy more powerful than Abigail had ever experienced. She saw it as a wall of flame, but she felt the power of the thing, much stronger than mundane fire. It made every cell in her body vibrate. At her strongest, she didn't think she could deflect that much power with her shield. But she had to try.

She watched in horror as the flame swept her shield away as if it did not even exist. Her heart dropped when she realized that Ben would be burned to ash in moments. Time slowed, each second an eternity. It was like dreams she had where the entire world was in slow motion.

She blinked away the ash and dust from her eyes. She widened her eyes and her mouth dropped open.

Ben was glowing. Not from the wall of fire coming at him, but from within. She watched as he...oscillated. A thin layer of something flickered around him, changing almost too fast to track. A bit of what looked like flame, a layer of the dust from the surrounding air, a swirling like a wind made visible, and splashes of water. The water she saw more easily, not just water but water magic. What was going on?

In two blinks, the layers she had seen coalesced into some type of barrier made of pure white light. She didn't even have time to speak, couldn't raise a finger to help. As if she would know what to do or be able to help in any way.

When Margaret's attack reached the light surrounding Ben, the breath caught in Abigail's throat. She wanted to look away, but she could not.

The wall of fire struck the barrier and was absorbed. It disappeared into it, like a stream of water into a sponge. Abbie's heart started beating again. Rapidly.

Then the power came back out of the barrier, reflected back toward its caster.

Margaret Huntsman's eyes grew to twice their normal size and the smirk she had been wearing disappeared to a thin line. She was as surprised as Abbie. Ben's face held a look of fear mixed with surprise and wonder.

The magic, even more powerful than it had been before, was still flame, but it had other elements mixed in with it. The color had changed, almost disappeared, but if the original attack was the most powerful thing Abbie had ever felt, this surely must be the most powerful thing ever to exist. It hurt to be near it, made her body ache like she would be torn apart.

It all happened so fast that no one could react. The power slammed into Margaret and threw her back so quickly she was barely visible.

Abbie blinked and when she was able to focus on the woman once more, her hand went to her mouth and she let out a small gasp. Margaret Huntsman, head of Huntsman Enterprises, level eight fire witch, murderer and schemer, was actually embedded in the wall, a series of shelves broken from her impact, books and broken items still sliding off to crash on the floor. Her clothes had been burned off and her skin was blackened, bubbled and cracked from the flames. That shouldn't be possible for a fire witch. Her head had flattened into a splattered mush as it was forced against the strong outer wall. She was obviously dead.

All around, the room was burning. Abbie reached for her power to create another water shield, but she was far too weak. The thought of dying now in the fire resulting from the battle made her want to giggle insanely, but she was too tired even for that. At least she would die with Ben.

Ben.

She looked over to see him. He was unharmed but his eyes were glassy as if he was in shock. She wondered if whatever magic had saved him would keep him from dying in the more mundane fire they were facing now.

The question died in her thoughts when it started raining. Hard.

No, not rain, but the fire sprinklers embedded in the ceiling. Abigail breathed for the first time in what seemed like hours and let the cooling water wash over her. They may just survive after all.

Ben's eyes locked onto hers and she saw them become lucid. "We better get out of here," he said.

"I'd rather no one ever know we were here."

She nodded her agreement and took his offered hand. The remaining windows in the room had been blown out in that final blast, so they stepped out through one of the full-length holes that used to hold glass. A few dozen feet into the surrounding trees and they were off toward their car.

As they ran toward their waiting vehicle, Abbie's mind whirled. They had survived. And they had killed Margaret Huntsman. Her mother was avenged and future deaths would be prevented. She looked over at Ben, looking the same as he had always looked, but a bit more bedraggled. What had he done? Or what had been done to him?

Something in her mind wondered if it was safe to be with him, but she cast the thought out immediately. No matter what that power was, he was still Ben. She trusted him with her life. They'd get to the bottom of this thing. Once they escaped.

39

They drove straight through back to Abigail's house. Ben glanced over at Abbie. She looked exhausted, but he didn't think she was hurt. They were wet, smelled like smoke, and there were singe marks in a few places on their clothing, so they couldn't stop and change without arousing suspicion. Neither of them thought they were seen by anyone at the estate itself. She was asleep in moments and remained so until they pulled up to Aqua Terra.

"Abigail!" A tall, solid-looking older man said as he caught sight of the two of them entering the house. "What happened? Are you all right?" His eyes flicked to Ben and then back to Abbie. "You must be Ben. I'm glad to finally meet you." He held out his hand and Ben shook it.

It was a firm handshake, and Abigail's father had the same calming effect as his daughter, maybe more so. Ben felt some of his stress melt away when the man looked at him.

"Papa, we have a lot to tell you, but first we need to get into some dry clothes. Do you think Ben could use some of yours?"

"Of course, of course. Yes, get cleaned up and dry and we can talk in my study. I'll wait there for you. Is there anything else you need from me until then?"

"Just this," Abigail said as she hugged him tightly and kissed his cheek. "Sorry for the mess. I just kind of needed that."

Abbie's Father smiled at his daughter. "No worries. I can get some clean clothes on now, too. You're covered in ash."

Within half an hour, Abigail led Ben to her father's study. When they entered, he was surprised to find several other people in the room.

"I thought it would be a good idea to have the Council hear this," Landon said. "If I was wrong, we can just talk with the three of us."

Abbie looked to Ben, and he gave her a nod. "No, it's fine. It involves everyone here. Would it be too much to ask to have Isabella join us? Is she here?"

"She is," Charlotte said. "She's been doing research here. I'll have her notified." One of the other witches went to retrieve the researcher.

Ben shifted his feet under the table. He looked to Abigail, but she seemed to be deep in thought, her eyes focused on nothing. He caught the eyes of a few of the five people at the table and he tried to smile at them, but after the events of the night, the wild swings of emotion, he was too exhausted to manage it.

"While we are waiting for Isabella, why don't we introduce ourselves?" an older pale yellow-haired woman in a smart business suit said. "Please forgive us our rudeness. We are all a bit out of sorts at the moment in anticipation of your news. I am Charlotte Whinson." He nodded to her as they shook hands.

"Ava Martin," another woman, said. Her wide smile made her cheeks color. She was small and thick bodied with blue eyes and bobbed blonde hair.

"Hi, Ben. I'm Sophia Hill, and this is my husband Julian," a tall, thin woman said, gesturing to a man who looked like he could have been her brother, maybe a twin. Ben shook hands with both of them.

"And we've met," Landon said, putting his hand on Ben's shoulder. "Everyone, this is Ben Mason."

Isabella came through the door, Abbie's friend Zoe right on her heels. Isabella waved to Ben and Zoe winked at him. "I hope it's okay that I asked Zoe to come. She has information that may be important."

"That is fine," Charlotte said, "Okay. We are all here. Now please tell us what happened, Abigail."

Abbie looked at Ben and took a deep breath. He smiled at her and nodded.

"Margaret Huntsman is dead," she said. "As of about"—Abbie looked at her phone—"five hours ago."

Several of those present sighed.

Abbie continued. "Isabella has confirmed that Margaret was the one who killed my mother, proven by the unique signature of her magic, which she tested on Ben himself." She motioned toward him. "She had been casting spells on him, increasing the frequency and duration lately. I'm not sure why."

Zoe cleared her throat. "I've been thinking about that and I have a theory. I believe Margaret Huntsman may have had a talent for forcing people to do her will. A sort of magical compulsion. That would explain why she would be casting spells on him and why, as he became more difficult to control, she would do so more often."

"That doesn't make any sense," Abigail said. "Why—"

"I think that's what happened," Ben said. "There are too many holes in my memory, too many times when Lucas, or even you, Abbie, saw me acting irrationally, incoherently, or just plain out of character. I do believe she was trying to use some kind of mind control on me. If that's even possible. I felt, at different times, headaches, pressure in my brain, thoughts that weren't my own intruding."

"It is not an unknown talent," Landon Henderson said. "It is possible, but to have to increase the power over such a long period of time, that is puzzling."

"Unless he began to develop a resistance to the magic," Zoe said. "There are cases in which a warlock or witch who has not yet come into their power suddenly shows a resistance to magic used on them or around them. Is Ben a warlock, then?"

"No," Ben said quickly. "I am not a warlock."

Abigail looked at him thoughtfully, as if going over something in her head.

"Abbie?" Ben said.

Abigail took his hand and squeezed it. "Let me finish the events of tonight and then maybe things will be clearer.

"I told Ben about Margaret, how she was a fire witch and how she has murdered several people that we know of, probably more. I explained to him what Zoe and Isabella found about his past. Margaret killed his mother and took her place and then, when she was satisfied with the financial holdings of Ben's father, killed him, too. Ben went to confront Margaret tonight, and I went with him.

"When we got there, Margaret's friend Helen Shapiro was with her. Ben asked Margaret about his mother and things happened quickly after that. Ben had two handguns, but as you know, those are not much use against a witch who knows you have them. But something completely unexpected happened.

"Helen turned into a creature of living flame. A fire shifter."

Gasps and exclamations erupted in the room.

"Calm down," Charlotte said. "Let us at least try to act like we're the leaders of the coven." The others looked at their hands in embarrassment.

Abbie continued. "I always believed legends of elemental shifters were just that, legends, but I saw her change. I was able to defeat her with Trasin's wave, but at the cost of not being able to shield Ben against Margaret's powerful flame attack. I thought he would be killed, but there was another surprise.

"As I watched, helpless, a glow around him changed from water magic to fire magic, to air, to earth, and then finally to pure, white light. When Margaret's magic struck his shield, it was absorbed, magnified, and cast back at the woman. It blew the room apart, burned her clothes and much of her skin off her, and crushed her body against the wall. Everything close to Ben turned to ash."

Ben looked around the room. The expressions on the faces around him ranged from surprise to curiosity to certainty, these last accompanied by nods.

"It should be impossible for a fire witch to be burned that badly," Isabella said.

"That's what I thought, too," Abbie said.

"What did you find out about his parents?" Charlotte asked.

"Just what Abbie said," Zoe answered.

"That's not good enough. We need to find out his lineage. Does he have elemental magic in his blood? Is he, perhaps, in a family that has had a series of skips?" Charlotte turned to Ben, "Have you ever shown any magical abilities? Ever? Any type at all?"

"No, of course not. I'm just a regular guy. An…only."

Charlotte frowned at Abigail over that, for some reason, but didn't say anything about it.

"There are two important things here," Landon said. "One is that elemental shifters are real. The other is that—whether it is related or not—Ben has a talent for withstanding very powerful magic. And turning it back on the user. We will have to learn more about both of these. With your permission on the second one, of course." He nodded toward Ben, and Ben returned the gesture.

"There is one other thing," Ava Martin added. "It is possible that both Abigail and Ben could be charged with the murder of Margaret Huntsman."

"No," Abbie said. "No one saw us. The fire looked like some kind of explosion, and the estate's fire sprinkler system activated and put the fire out, so at least the rest of the house was safe. We walked out the window, which had been blown out, went through the trees, and left in Ben's car which was parked a half a mile away. Everything between Ben and Margaret looked to have been destroyed by the heat. I don't think there were even shells from the guns left."

"Ben, you will have to go there soon, as soon as it would be practical that you would hear about it," Charlotte said.

Ben's phone rang. It caught him by surprise because very few people had his new number. He pulled it out of his pocket and subtly looked at the screen. It was Lucas.

"Oh, I better take this. Excuse me." He thought for a moment and then changed his mind. "Actually, maybe it's better that I put it on speaker."

Lucas's voice came over the speaker. "Dude, your house just exploded!"

"What? What are you talking about Lucas? Take a breath and calm down."

"It's on the news. There was some kind of explosion at the estate. I don't know how bad it is or if anyone was hurt, but some of the neighbors more than a mile away felt the jolt, like it was an earthquake. There were reports of the sound of several smaller explosions and then one big one."

"Oh my God," Ben said. "I'll head over there right now. I'm four hours or so away, near Jackson, but I'll get started now. Keep me posted if you hear anything else. And thanks, Lucas. I hope no one was hurt."

"Will do, buddy. I'm glad you weren't there when it happened."

"Yeah, me too." Ben hung up the phone and looked around. "Well, I better get going. If it's going to look realistic, I better hurry over there. Wish me luck. Maybe we can talk about this other stuff at another time. It was nice meeting all of you, even if the circumstances weren't ideal."

Abbie started to get up but Ben put his hand out.

"Ben, I want to go with you," she said.

"No. You know you can't. It would be too suspicious. We can't give them anything out of the ordinary to make them think twice about me."

"He's right, Abbie," her father said. "He'll be fine. Trust in him."

Ben smiled. Well, at least he had won her father over. And all it took was defying death and killing the woman he thought was his mother.

"I'm going to walk you out, at least," Abigail said, resignation in her voice. Turning toward the others, she said, "I'll be back in a few minutes to answer any questions." She saw Zoe wink at her as she left the room behind Ben. Incorrigible, that one.

A few steps down the hallway, Ben turned toward Abigail. "Abbie, so much has happened today that I really haven't been able to talk to you about us. My life has been hell the last several months without you. I don't ever want to go through that again. You know I love you, and I want to spend the rest of my life with you. Have your feelings changed for me?"

Abigail stared at him for a moment, but didn't say a word. Then, when he was about to ask again, she put her arms around him and kissed him so thoroughly, he lost all track of time. He didn't remember when he enfolded her in his own arms, but he knew that she felt right there. Her body fit within his embrace so perfectly. Her lips were intoxicating, the perfect mix of tender and firm. Even the taste of her and the texture of her tongue on his sent a shiver up his spine.

They kissed for a long time. He had thought before that it was heaven when he kissed her at the waterfall in Yellowstone, and again the few times he had the circumstances to do so, but if that was

310

heaven, then this was somewhere outside of the universe. It could have been what they had been through, or it could have been that he knew now that they would be together. When they finally broke free and she stepped back, he could hardly catch his breath.

"W—" was all he had time to get out before she stepped back in and kissed him again for good measure. This one didn't last nearly as long. That was probably a good thing because he wasn't sure his heart could handle the rush. He might have to work up to it. He would gladly practice any time she let him.

"You were saying?" she cooed.

"I do really have to go, huh? Damn."

"Ben, take care of what needs to be taken care of, but come back to me as soon as you can. I can't wait to pick up where we left off." She trailed her finger across his chin and tapped his lips. "Can't. Wait."

"I can't, either," he said, more than a little breathily. "So, I can safely assume that you still care for me?"

She reached around his neck and pulled his head down to hers and kissed him again. "I love you, silly. Of course I do. I have for ages. Now go before my willpower is not strong enough for me to let you go."

He understood exactly what she was talking about. "Okay. I'll be back soon." He headed straight for his car, got in, and drove back the way he had just come.

40

~~~~~

*B*en returned to Aqua Terra four days later. Remembering to get her number before he left, he and Abbie had been in contact by phone and text any time he wasn't busy with lawyers, police, relatives, and friends. As soon as he stepped from his car in the large circular driveway, Abbie ran from the house and nearly bowled him over with her embrace.

He leaned down and kissed her, savoring the feeling of her, the taste of her mouth on his, and her scent.

"Mmmm," he said when they came up for air. "I missed you."

"And I missed you, Master Mason." She bit at his lower lip as she said it.

"Ahem," a deep voice said from the doorway. "Would you like something to drink, Ben? It's sort of a long drive."

"Yes, thank you, Landon. That would be perfect."

He swept his arm down and scooped Abigail up, kissing her as he walked.

"You don't need to carry me over the threshold just yet," she said. "Soon, I hope. But not yet."

"I want to practice,' Ben said, nuzzling at her neck. "I don't want to mess it up when the time comes."

They went inside and sat in the sitting room. Landon Henderson had some tea brought and they discussed the state of things.

"They're not looking at me as a suspect," Ben said. "In fact, they're considering it an accident. There's not even a case open. I've been talking to the lawyers and after all the paperwork is done and filed, I'll own all my family's holdings, including the controlling share of Huntsman Consolidated. Margaret had the will written up with me as the heir because it would have been too suspicious to name someone else. She probably figured she would outlive me, anyway."

"That's...great," Abbie said, though her tone didn't match her words.

"It *is* great, Abbie. The first thing I did was make it clear that there never was and never will be anything between me and Penelope. As soon as you marry me, it will all be ours."

"Ben," Abbie said. "I won't be upset if you have your lawyers write up some kind of complex prenuptials. I'll understand."

Ben stared at her, then at Landon—who shrugged—and then back at Abbie. He took her hands in his and looked into her eyes.

"Abbie, you just don't understand, do you? None of that stuff means anything to me. If you want, I'll give it all away to charity. You're the only thing I want. I already chose you over money, and I would do so again. Every time. I don't want to hear anything about prenups. We're going to be together forever, so what use will those be?"

Ben didn't remember much in the minutes after he said that because Abbie pushed him back and kissed him so thoroughly he forgot his own name.

When she released him, Ben saw Landon sitting there, staring at his tea cup.

"Sorry," Ben said.

"Don't apologize," Landon told him. "I understand completely." Turning to Abbie, he continued, "But you, young lady, need to comport yourself in a more polite manner." He winked at her and she smiled back at him.

"I'll do my best, but it has been days since I've seen him."

"Yes, yes. Ben, I was asked by the Council if you would be willing to meet with them. Abbie told us you would be back around this time and they are all here at the estate."

"Sure," Ben said. "I'll tell them what's going on and we can finish our conversation from last time."

"Good," Landon stood up. "Please follow me."

The same women and men were sitting around the table in the meeting room. Witches and warlocks, Ben guessed he should say. It was going to take some getting used to, marrying into a family like Abbie's.

"That's great news," Charlotte said after Ben told them about the state of his inheritance. "I'm glad you weren't implicated. It is not much of a consolation after what Margaret did to your family, but it's something."

"Yes, it is," Ben said. "Thank you."

"We have been doing some research and have

some theories on how you were able to withstand Margaret's powers," Charlotte continued. "We believe that it is possible that you have the blood of witches and warlocks in your family.

"When a member of a magical family does not manifest the talent for using magic, we nickname them a 'skip.' It is conceivable that your family had several skips in a row, enough that no knowledge of your magical background survived.

"In situations such as that, a witch or warlock will begin to demonstrate their powers around the time of puberty, or just before, if they ever do indeed come into their power. They will suddenly be able to do things, to manipulate the element to which they are attuned, and they soon find others who can teach them.

"For you, though, there was no such manifestation. Your power, whatever it is, activated on its own in response to a dangerous situation or maybe in response to interaction with Abbie and her magic. I know a witch from a water coven in Idaho who has the ability to read not only magical ability, but the element to which the person's power is attuned. I would like her to read you, to test your abilities and give us more information on exactly what your powers are. Would you agree to this?"

"Sure," Ben said. "I'm as curious as you are, but I don't think I'm any kind of warlock. I've never shown any kind of power over any element or any other magical ability."

"Be that as it may," Charlotte answered, "the testing will give us more information. I'll call my friend and have her here within the next couple of days. Thank you, Ben. Sometimes little mysteries end up being very important when it comes to magic."

"I'll definitely do what I can to help," Ben said. He looked to Abigail and then around the table at the others. Finally, he asked, "Did you ever figure out what Margaret's plans were? I mean, why was she killing other witches? It doesn't make sense to me."

Sophia Hill spoke up. "We are still not sure. We do know that in some of her attacks, she tried to make it look as if other elemental magic users, air or earth, were causing the deaths. We can't figure out what benefit that would have for her, though. It almost looks like she was just trying to start a war for no reason at all."

"It's the only thing that fits," Landon Henderson said. "All those they killed were in some way working to unite different covens or different elemental groups. We may never know. At least her plans for fomenting war are over now. Maybe we can settle back into—"

A loud knock at the door interrupted what Abbie's father was saying.

"Yes," Charlotte called out.

A young man poked his head in the room. He was breathless and a sheen of perspiration covered his forehead. "I'm sorry to interrupt, but someone is here wanting to see Uncle Landon. He says he's a friend, that something has happened you need to know about. His name is Michael Morgan."

Landon rose from his seat. "Michael? Where is he, Jack?

"He's right here behind me."

"Let him in," Charlotte said.

"Michael," Landon said. "I wasn't expecting you. Is there something wrong? Can I help you in some way?"

"Yes, Landon," he said, "I hope so. We have a crisis in my coven, and in a few other air covens I know of. Deaths. Deaths caused by magic users, mostly fire witches. We have kept it internal, but yesterday, the leader of my coven was murdered. You and I have talked about your wife and the way that she was killed, and I convinced the Council to allow me to seek aid from your coven, and to offer ours to you."

"Yesterday, you say?" Landon asked. "What time? Where?"

"It was evening, just as it was getting dark," he said. "In the hills just southeast of here. She and two others were ambushed. It seemed very close to the way you described what happened with Olivia."

Landon pondered for a moment. "It couldn't have been Margaret this time." He turned and looked at the rest of those gathered. "I don't think we have resolved the problem after all. Please Michael, sit. Have some tea and tell us everything. We have a lot to tell you as well."

THANK YOU!

Thank you for reading Water & Flame, the first book in the Witches of the Elements series. **Please consider taking a moment to post a review** where you purchased the book. Reviews are important in helping other readers find exciting books and help authors to continue to write them, as well as providing valuable feedback for the author. Your honest review would be very much appreciated.

If you would like to get information on upcoming books, such as book 2 of the ?Witches of the Elements series (Wind & Wave), please visit my web site at **pepadilla.com** and join my mailing list.

I also appreciate any comments I receive, so please feel free stop by my web site and comment on the site itself or to send me an e-mail at **pep@pepadilla.com**.

Other books by P.E. Padilla

Adventures in Gythe:

Vibrations: Harmonic Magic Book 1

Harmonics: Harmonic Magic Book 2

Resonance: Harmonic Magic Book 3 (to be released in 2017)

Tales of Gythe: Gray Man Rising

The Unlikely Hero Series
(under pen name Eric Padilla)

Unfurled: Heroing is a Tough Gig

Boxed Set (with other authors)

Gypsies After Dark

About the Authors

Aside from working a regular job, raising a daughter, and wrangling a dog that outweighs her, **Alejandra Vega** is also a superheroine. Don't ask her about it because she'll deny it. Press the issue and she may have to kill you. Nevertheless, despite her busy schedule, she still found time to co-write her debut novel in the Witches of the Elements series, Water & Flame. Look for her wherever people are in danger from supervillains.

A chemical engineer by degree, air quality engineer by vocation, certified dreamer by predilection, and writer by sheer persistence, **P.E. Padilla** learned long ago that crunching numbers and designing solutions was not enough to satisfy his creative urges. Weaned on classic science fiction and fantasy stories from authors as diverse as Heinlein, Tolkien, and Jordan, and affected by his love of role playing games such as Dungeons and Dragons (analog) and Final Fantasy (digital), he sometimes has trouble distinguishing reality from fantasy. While not ideal for a person who needs to function in modern society, it's the perfect state of mind for a writer. He also writes young adult fantasy/action & adventure under the pen name Eric Padilla, and lives in Southern California, though he would like to be where there are more trees.

Made in the USA
San Bernardino, CA
13 April 2017